DESCENDANT OF SIN

The Descendant Series - Book 3

M. SINCLAIR

Editorial Team
Editor: Refined Voice Editing & Proofreading
Cover Artwork: Pixie Covers
Formatted By: Kassie Morse

CONTENTS

DESCRIPTION

Did my mages, my demi-gods, and I *need* to hold a
Halloween party? No, of course not. Was I going to anyway?
You better freakin' believe it. I didn't even feel bad! We
needed a break! Even if it was for a day, a healthy work and
life balance was essential... even if it was holding a bloody
Halloween party and the work was determining who was
sucking magic out of people like goddamn juice boxes.

Except my relaxed plans don't go exactly as I thought...
Instead, I am left with a shredded costume, a surge of memories that I could have lived without, and two new friendships
that I couldn't have seen coming. That didn't even count the
dangerously hot connection that was growing between my
men and I.

What I did learn after a trip to the Demonic realm? We had to
go to the God realm. We didn't have an option anymore.

Note from Author: The Descendant series will feature characters from both the Reborn series and Tears of the Siren series. It will not be necessary to read either of those to understand the plot, however they do intertwine in a way that enhances the universe. Don't worry, no spoilers are present!

Join Nova on her 9 book series adventure! This Fantasy slow/medium burn RH contains several dark themes that readers should be aware of: swearing (I know, surprising, right?), gore, violence, assault, PTSD, and sexual themes suitable for +18. Additionally, this book does have mature m/m themes that develop over time.

PROLOGUE

River

I'd been staring at Nova all night.

I couldn't help it, even if I wanted to. *I didn't, for the record. I never wanted to stop looking at her.* Here I had thought that Everett had been the one acting like a total creep, tracing her features after she fell asleep each night. Memorizing every element of Nova's normally impassioned face.

No, clearly this obsessive tendency was not just an issue for him, because whatever madness was plaguing my teammate was hitting me like a fucking freight train, solid and hard into my chest. Thoughts that I had absolutely never considered before were occupying space in my head, and as a chronic overthinker, I could feel them expanding and growing on their own as the seconds ticked by. I was positive my head would explode any moment now.

I had never believed that I would be this guy. I had never put stock in this bullshit about finding 'the one.' Especially for our team. Hell, I think I'd even been in denial of having anything more than an insane chemical attraction to Nova up until the other day. All in a futile effort of self-preservation.

But the moment that she'd surrendered her body to me?

The second she took a goddamn sledgehammer to the shell around my heart? Well, I think I realized in that second just how thoroughly fucked I was.

Nova would be smart to run, and I would be smart to encourage her before she took the rest of my sanity. Not that I would let her go. I didn't think that was an option anymore. If she ran I would find her. The monster inside of me had claimed Nova, and trying to fight that pull was a fruitless effort. She was mine and would be until I said differently. I couldn't let her go, and I was wrapped so tightly around her finger that I was surprised she could move.

No woman should ever lightly give the type of permission that Nova had offered me. She had let me use her. She had given me, without me even admitting it, exactly what I had needed. She'd let me hurt her to soothe my own pain. I was so screwed up, and all I could focus on was being buried alive in everything that was Nova.

She didn't realize that when she had given up control, she had slapped a shackle right onto me, making me more her prisoner than she was mine. I was completely hers.

My head fell back against the headboard as I muttered a curse, feeling stupid as hell. Had it only been last winter that I'd been naive enough to make fun of Commander Edwin and his team for how they had acted about Vegas? I think my exact words were 'they've lost it' to Everett. To be fair, at the time it had seemed like a valid analysis. I hadn't met Nova, and I sure as fuck had never felt anything they'd expressed feeling.

The two of us, along with Commander Cannon, had been assigned to watch their house while Commanders Edwin and Byron's teams went through the Red Masques trials following the Horde and Dark Fae war. I hadn't minded the assignment, and it had given us a good change of environment as we talked about this exact mission and the plans moving forward for it. I nearly smiled at that thought. If I'd known then what it was going to be like having someone that was as important to me as Vegas was to them, I probably would have been more understanding and cautious.

You know, cautious about maintaining my fucking sanity. I was starting to think that we were a little more like those loonies than I would care to admit. I couldn't blame them, though, for how insane they acted. Not anymore. Not when we were possibly even worse than them.

I was jealous, in a way. They knew Vegas was theirs. It was clear from the time I'd met the ten of them that they each had a secure place in her life. Nova? I had no idea how she felt about any of us. Alright, that wasn't completely true, but I was terrified she would wake up one day and realize we weren't worth it.

Did I have attachment issues? No doubt. So yeah, as I said, I didn't blame them, because once Nova agreed to be ours forever? I was probably going to tie her to me so she couldn't leave. I wasn't speaking metaphorically. I very literally meant I was going to chain her pretty ass to me so that wherever she went, I would be forced to go as well. She wasn't going to ever be rid of me, and I had no way to make that sound less fucking crazy.

I remembered one of the mornings we'd shown up at Edwin's house, and Kodiak, once of Vegas's mates, had been acting insanely overprotective. More than usual, even. I had been extremely confused. More so when Edwin had told us that Vegas was pregnant, something that had thrown me for a complete loop, because at that time I could not fucking imagine being a father. I had no urge to ever bring a child into this fucked-up world.

Now, though? Well, now I understood more. I swallowed,

thinking about Nova and our future, *if there was a future*. No. There was going to be a fucking future, I would make sure of it. Sure, everything was unknown and we had no idea what the next few months would bring, but that didn't bother me... too much.

Alright, it bothered me a fuck ton, and maybe that was why I felt so much more urgency to secure our place in her life. In her future. A future like that? With her and the only family, my brothers, I'd ever had? Well, I think I could imagine having a family. A real one. With kids and shit.

One part of me, one that had no excuse to be so prominent, wanted her to be tied to us in any way possible so she couldn't leave us. Like when she ran away. My chest clenched at the idea of waking up and finding her gone from our life completely. I would never let that happen again. I had promised that to myself long before I realized just how fucked I was when it came to the thunderbolt of passion sleeping next to me.

The other part of me wanted to be able to prove to her, especially after seeing that stupid fucking tape, that I could be better than that. I knew she would never ask me to change. Nova wasn't like that. She found imperfections more beautiful than perfections, which was a bit twisted, but I loved that about her.

I think the idea of one of us not being authentic to ourselves was more upsetting to her than the crazy shit that we did. Seriously, I felt like the woman would get mad at me for not exacting revenge on someone if I wanted to. She was just fucking perfect like that. Still, I wanted to be more for her. I wanted to show her I was worthy of the respect and trust she showed me. Hell, even the forgiveness she offered whenever I fucked up.

I'd been such an asshole to her. She should have made me

beg for way longer. I had deserved far more than that. I'd been so fucking terrified of how she would react after seeing that tape. I had reacted poorly, an understatement for sure, and I had taken out my fear on her. I shook my head and looked back down at Nova.

She stretched like a house cat, a small peaceful smile on her lips as my hand tightened on her soft, silky, naked form. Right now she was wedged between Everett and I, sleeping peacefully. I was glad I'd kept on my boxers, honestly, because it would be far too easy to just slide into her right now. Her wet heat had my dick twitching as if he was trying to fucking reach her. Goddamn ridiculous. Still, I wanted to bury myself inside of her and wrap her multi-colored hair around my hand as I fucked her until morning, exhausting both of us so that I was forced to sleep.

But - I didn't want to wake her up. See? Wasn't that some shit? That was just one example of how someone important in your life can change shit. You start thinking about them and their needs instead of what you want. And trust me, I fucking wanted her badly. For so long it had just been myself, and then it had been just me and my brothers, so this was new. This was unknown territory, and I knew I was fucking stumbling through it like an idiot.

In an attempt to distract myself, I ran my large fingers through her silky locks. I swear to the Maker, her hair was getting longer every time I turned around. Right now, the ombre effect of navy through the blue spectrum looked ethereal underneath the moonlight-lit bedroom. I was glad she was sleeping, because I knew she'd been exhausted.

Yet I had the urge to kiss her awake so I could see her bright eyes, see the icy color that swirled into a dark navy. When they weren't on me, I felt anxious, like she wasn't real. The lightning in her gaze fucking fueled me. I was becoming dependent on her, and I had no idea whether she realized it or not. This was really bad. All of this was fucking bad.

But I didn't plan to put a stop to any of it. If I was going to burn, then I would. Happily, and knowing exactly how I felt about her.

Right now, I wanted to wrap my arms fully around her and beg her to love me. To not give up on me. I was so pathetic. This wasn't even funny anymore. This was what happened when you gave an orphaned kid that had grown up without any love someone that cared about them. Not even loved. Just simply cared. It was enough to bring me to my knees, and all she'd done was forgive me and understand me better than anyone else had. Yeah, as I stated before... *fuck.*

Nova looked so different than she had when I'd first met her. Don't get me wrong, she was, and would always be, stunning. But I could see the difference, and it was almost like she'd been set free, making me feel like we'd at least done some good amongst the bad of interrupting her peaceful life. I could see the confidence and freedom in the way she expressed her magic and in the tattoos that ran along her golden skin, visible proof of the entity that lived within her.

Running my fingers along her skin, I traced the tattoos that ran along her golden body, the scales of the Egyptian death god right between her perky breasts. I swallowed, trying to not get harder than I already was, and fighting the urge to roll her over so I could kiss down her delicious body. The next time I had her I wanted to take my time, at least at first, so that I could bite and kiss every single part of her.

I let my eyes flicker down to the small strand of coptic words that surrounded the scale, drawing my attention to her tiny delicate waist. It was the newest addition and had come after the scales and the massive intricate piece of Egyptian artwork on her small bicep. It included a twisted crocodile that appeared to be crawling from behind her arm, upstream to a jackal that sat baring its teeth at a long, thin-necked cat sitting on top of a massive scarab. Honestly, in full effect the little witch was a bit surreal to look at.

I smoothed my fingers over her soft, small neck, my magic having healed her golden skin from the bites and bruises I'd left on her. Wasn't that some fucking irony? I wanted my marks on her, but my magic had almost immediately healed them after I'd fucked her senseless.

I cursed softly, thinking about the dazed, almost euphoric look in her eyes after I'd screwed her into the wall of my bedroom in the Horde. I had the image of her at that moment burned in my mind, lips parted and pupils blown out as she had gone limp, breathing nearly as hard as myself. I think the reality of how much she had enjoyed my rough treatment had hit me in that moment.

In that second, the thing that lived inside of me, something that was far darker than anything she should ever come in contact with, became ridiculously pleased and extremely territorial. I considered Ramsey somewhat of a friend now, yet when he had interrupted us, I'd considered snapping his neck as my initial reaction.

Yeah, healthy, I know.

In a way, none of this was completely surprising to me. There had always been a part of me that was far darker and more damaged than it should have been. You couldn't see it from the outside. I didn't have scars like Rowan, and I had never formed that haunted weight that Cassian carried on his shoulders. Yet buried underneath all of my 'normality' was something that had been fostered and forcibly formed as a child.

Something that had grown every time I'd been hit.

Beaten unconscious.

Forced to fight another child and ignore my instincts to heal them.

Throughout the experience, my magic had separated into two beings that were in constant conflict with one another. My greatest fear? The darker one would win dominance and everything would go to shit.

It didn't help that everything about Nova encouraged that darker part of me. She teased it out without meaning to, and she had no idea how much danger she was in just being around me. Sure, all of my teammates were dangerous, but I knew most of them would rather hurt themselves than Nova.

I had no idea where the line was for me, and I didn't trust myself to draw it. I couldn't imagine truly hurting Nova enough that the light of pleasure left her gaze, but how far would she let me take it? I trusted her to tell me when to stop, but *fuck.* I was here overthinking everything that could go wrong.

I needed a goddamn safe word with the woman. But not just for sex, like for fucking life, and more for me than her. I was a goddamn mess.

I rubbed a hand over my face as the word *sadist* rang in my head. I refused to believe that I'd fully hit that definition, because I didn't exactly take pleasure in hurting Nova. It was confusing because I enjoyed taking my pain out on her, but only if she was enjoying it… I could never lose her, and if hurting her would make me lose her then it wasn't an option.

Actually, the only option I had in this was allowing her to take somewhat of the lead in what she would let me do and not. I groaned, trying to shake the image of turning her entire pert ass bright red and fucking her so deep that she was crying as she climaxed on my cock.

I wanted to apply pressure until her airway was slightly constricted and I could feel her life pulse beneath my palm as she released a whine of pleasure because of how deep inside of her I was. Fuck. Do you know what it's like to have someone dependent on you for their next goddamn breath?

The high of Nova trusting me like that with her body was absolutely incomparable to any physical pleasure I could receive. I could imagine all of it, and that was making it just that much harder to not try it out right now. There was so much I wanted to try and do to her, and my fear was that I would take it too far. I was scared I would hurt her, in every way possible. Fuck. I didn't want that, and I was hoping that was what mattered because this balance was confusing the fuck out of me.

I looked down at her peaceful face and ran a thumb along her bottom lip as she nuzzled slightly against my hand, making me smile. No, I never wanted to lose Nova's trust. That would be worse than any pain I'd gone through yet, and that was saying something.

I knew I needed to tell her about the tape to ensure I would never hurt her again. I would need to explain myself and the horror I'd been put through… but she would be the first person to hear the entire story. The concept scared the hell out of me. I needed time. Opening up and expressing that side of me could let something out that even my own team wasn't ready for. My teammates had ignored it for so long I wasn't positive they even thought about it anymore. Not like I did.

But that's how we had always functioned. Most of us came from fucked-up pasts, so we didn't even attempt to psychoanalyze one another. The Red Masques had even ignored it, and it's not like Byron or Edwin could say they didn't know about it. They'd been around me when I'd killed before.

Hell, I had nearly killed that asshole, now very-dead

fiancé of Nova's the first day I'd met him, but I'd controlled myself within an inch of turning his insides into a cocktail of melted organs and blood. Barely. I think everyone assumed that the darkness would either make itself known or I would learn to control it over time.

I didn't want to let it out, that would be the start of something irreversible.

Well, that was a damn lie, actually. I craved the release of that side of me like I craved Nova: with an intensity that I would have never expected. I stiffened slightly as she turned, her bare back against my chest and her ass wedged up against my cock. I swear to the goddamn Maker she did this shit on purpose.

I had recognized a storm inside of Nova the first day I met her, but I had never expected to release this torturously teasing and sexy, coy side of her, either. I wrapped my arms around her small feminine waist as my nose trailed her delicate neck. Despite being small and lean, the woman had curves that were slowly fucking destroying me. I swallowed, trying to not think again on how tightly I had gripped her elegant neck and bit her bottom lip, making her climax on my cock.

I was a fucking monster.

Who wanted to hurt the woman they were in love with? My thoughts froze on that.

Love? Fuck. Did I love Nova? I wasn't exactly positive I knew how that felt. Love. I loved everything about her. I loved how brilliant she was. How much of a fierce little warrior she was. How compassionate and loving she could be towards those that she deemed worthy. I was a lucky bastard to be part of that group. Lucky that she continued to forgive me when I kept fucking up.

I didn't deserve Nova, but I was going to keep her.

I'd been so stupid the other day. You see, I'd been so shocked that she'd gotten turned on by my rough treatment that I'd said some stupid shit about her not knowing what she wanted. Why? Because I was scared.

The same reason I had flipped out when I'd found her crying over those stupid fucking tapes. The reason I'd gotten mad when she had acted in such a reckless fucking manner again and again. I was always so goddamn scared. I'd grown up with nothing, so now that I'd found something that I wanted to keep, I would be damned if I lost it. *Lost her.* I didn't want her to be tainted by my past, and I sure as hell didn't want her getting hurt because of us being in her life. Yet I couldn't lock her up even if I thought it best... that wouldn't make me any better than her fucking father.

A woman like Nova wasn't kept.

She may let you believe you're in charge or that you won her. And you may own her completely for periods of time, or when she's clutching so tightly around your cock you're about to pass out, but make no mistake... she was always in charge. We could spout as much shit about her being 'ours' as we wanted, but we all knew that we were *hers*. I would drop the Red Masques and anything else to follow her.

Her strength inspired me in ways I hadn't even realized I'd needed. In the face of everything these past two months, Nova hadn't shown the fear you would have expected from someone in her situation. In fact, she had adapted far better than I ever could. I envied that ability.

The woman was a lethal predator, bright in color and stunning, but she had sunk her fangs into me and I was marked. There was no getting away from her. She'd probably have to kill me, and even then I would try to find a way back.

I groaned and put my head down. The internal dialogue in my head was so unhealthy and complicated.

I wanted to delve into this woman and learn every fucking thing about her. I needed to know. My magic felt the same, and it loved that we'd marked her so that we could heal her, the two elements of my magic only agreeing that we liked it when she needed us. Needed us to heal her.

I knew it was wrong that I liked seeing her eyes flutter shut in pain and pleasure. Wrong that I loved the bruises and bites I'd marred her skin with. Wrong that I loved how tightly she gripped my cock and how her nails clawed into my skin, marking me savagely. Yet, for as wrong as it was, a peaceful fucking expression had filled her face post-climax as the stone wall crumbled behind her. Like somehow I had brought her a sense of satisfaction and relief.

Or maybe I was just trying to justify my actions.

I'd even considered, maybe hoped, that the moment would have been forgotten when we returned back to Earth realm. Yet we'd come home yesterday, and she was still surprising me around every bend. Even tonight, right before bed, she had not only fallen asleep easily between Everett and I, naked and vulnerable, but then when I'd slid my hand between her breasts and around her throat, she seemed to relax further into me. As if I hadn't fucked her savagely in the Horde and took out my deeply repressed emotional bullshit on her and her tight little pussy.

I had no idea what the hell was going on here, but this was by far the happiest I'd ever been in my entire life. And that was the problem. *I was disgusted with my own happiness.*

I'd never realized how deep my self-hatred went until now, bringing up issues that I had long buried but now wouldn't go away. I couldn't talk to my brothers about it either, even if I wanted to, because hell, most of them were pissed at me about the comment I'd made about 'not living here' in reference to the Horde.

I hadn't meant it like that… I mean, not really. Sure, I'd been pissed, but I'd never been able to ignore misplaced statements of fact, and I'd thrown the correction out there before I'd thought it through. Then Everett had threatened to bury me alive, so I had gotten the general message of just how bad all of it had sounded.

But that was behind us, and I knew my brothers wouldn't stay mad for long. Well, I fucking hoped they wouldn't - we didn't have time for that. I could feel a much larger issue heading our way, which was why I wasn't sleeping like Nova and Everett. Around three hours ago, an odd premonition had washed over me and completely removed any chance of sleep.

I felt like we were going to lose Nova.

It was a strong and real fear, and the closer we got to the God realm, the more intense it became. I knew we had to go eventually, not just because of our situation but because Nova wasn't a normal demi-goddess, so it was essential to figure out what made her different in order to make sure we could protect her. I just hoped my worries weren't real.

Yet sometimes the look in Ramsey's eyes when he stared at Nova made me feel like we were all digging our own graves with this shit. As he kept saying, we were involved with a woman that was far above any of us, and yet none of us, including him, were heeding the warning.

Everett's voice startled me as it rang out, making me turn my head to where he was offering me a dry look. "Get some sleep, River, your overthinking is bothering me. I would die before I let someone take her from us."

The bastard always did know what I was thinking. He said it so casually, but I understood what he meant and I hoped he was right. I'm not sure what I would do if someone tried to take her from us.

NOVA

O ctober 31st. *Halloween.* A day that would live in the halls of infamy in my life's history because it personified the concept of a 'boring day.' Well, I should say it usually did, because I was determined to make this year different than normal.

My father, who was unsurprisingly absent after we uncovered his serial killer den, usually hosted this obnoxious ball for our coven. In truth, the day used to be very important to our coven, and there had been an entire ceremony that worked to cleanse and protect our homes for the upcoming year. Around my fifteenth birthday, my father had nixed the ceremony for a reason he never explained and switched to a ball instead. So every year since then, I would dress up as the same thing… *go ahead, guess!* Please. You won't be shocked.

I dressed up as a fucking witch.

I know, it was extremely creative, and my father found it just so 'charming and amusing.' I found it… what's the word? Oh yes, lame as fuck. Yes, that would be the right descriptor. No matter though! I was going to fix that this year while proving my popularity to Rowan because the bastard still totally thought I was lame. I just couldn't let that stand.

So yes, these were two very important aspects in my long-term goal of *figuring out who the hell was draining everyone's magic and why*. I know proving my popularity and changing my Halloween habits didn't seem important, but trust me, it was. It was essential to my sanity. After all, you have to treat yourself. I took the lessons learned from *Parks and Rec* very seriously, thank you very much! I was actually currently working on getting some of my guys to watch reruns of it and *The Office* on Netflix, but we'd yet to see whether it would work or not.

We were taking a break from our mission, and to say that it was needed was a goddamn understatement. Plus, we were waiting on our contact to respond back to us in order to proceed forward in our mission of kick-assery.

"We are not holding a party, Nova," Fox growled. The sexy sound rolled over my skin as I bounced on my toes slightly while grabbing water from the fridge. I had just finished a fantastic workout after school, and the idea had hit me out of nowhere. A party! It would be festive and fun! I mean, sure I only had one day to plan with Halloween being tomorrow, but now seemed as good a time as any for a party.

My limbs were actually surprisingly a bit sore from my workout, but I could happily state I'd worked myself to near exhaustion. I'd noticed that I had not only gained a more diverse array of magic recently, but with that came with a strength and agility I hadn't had before. Not that I wasn't athletic as a witch, but this was far more extreme. It was frustrating because exhausting myself sometimes felt impossible. Hopefully, my workout today would help me sleep deeper tonight. I seemed to be having more difficulty with that since our return from our trip to the Horde. My sleep had been very light, and I'd been plagued with dreams all last night and woken up exhausted.

So I'd been attempting to wear myself down until I had to sleep. On the plus side, working out meant I could prance around in spandex, which I loved. It made all of my boys frustrated, turned on, and growly, which meant there was a higher chance of them attacking me. Fox was a fantastic example of that, actually.

Currently, I could feel his dark fathomless eyes crawling over my body that was only covered in shorts and a sports bra. I turned, and he flicked his eyes upward while running an umber hand through his black inky hair that had vibrant emerald ends, trying to look as if he hadn't been staring at my ass.

Today his lean, muscular, tall frame was covered in an oversized shirt with some German rock band's name, and his dark jeans and Vans had nearly matched my own outfit today at school. It was some cute shit. The man's shirt and hoodie collection was one that I dreamed of, and I used it often, sometimes not even telling him before I walked downstairs ready for the day.

The silver flecks in the blood mage's eyes were nearly absent right now, making him feel nearly predatory because of their obsidian depths. It didn't help that his raw, chaotic magic already had mine tied up. Well, I suppose that implies he had control over her, but it was more like my magic was trying to get entangled with his. Freakin' hussy.

You think I'm joking, but somehow we'd gone from my magic staring at them in a forlorn way, waving to them all Scarlett O'Hara romantic, to… well, whatever the hell this was. She was bent over his lap with her hands tied behind her, completely naked. It was some kinky shit. I loved it.

"We are," I noted with a smirk, "and you are going to

have so much fun. I will even wear a sexy costume so you have something to stare at."

Fox let out a low rumble. "You aren't helping your case, Nova." *So possessive.*

Walking up to where he was seated at the kitchen island, I moved to stand between his legs and ran a hand down his chest. "What would help my case?" He caught my hand right before it reached his belt buckle. He narrowed his eyes at me, making me grin even further.

My Fox was quite the contradiction. He was a lot unhinged and very sarcastic. He also had terrible OCD that he wouldn't admit to, and he was rather closed off… until he wasn't. Then you had all of his emotions, and you either rolled with it or you drowned. He was like a terrifying flood that swept up everything in his path, including any sense of self-preservation that was keeping you from falling for the dangerous man.

I was a fan of the *not drowning* option when it came to the flood of his emotion, so I rolled with his crazy, and it really wasn't very difficult if we were being honest. He was very lovable. Love? No, I'm sorry brain, you must have confused me with my kinky-ass magic. Or my brain didn't and I was in denial. That was completely possible.

"What are you trying to convince him of?" Cassian's voice didn't even surprise me as his lips trailed across my shoulder and I shivered, Fox's hands gripping my waist. I had no idea how his twin had gotten behind me without me noticing, but he and Everett did that shit a lot. I think they were hoping to scare me, but all it did was turn me on.

What? The intensity was hot. You're telling me that a sexy man randomly appearing behind you wouldn't turn you on? Okay. I guess it could be a bit terrifying, that's fair.

"That we should hold a Halloween party," I purred, drop-

4

ping my head back to look up into the twin's gaze. His rough, large hands were gripping my hips from behind, but honestly he was totally grabbing more of my ass than anything and I could feel how hard he was against me. Cassian always seemed to be on the threshold of ripping my clothes off, so I was hoping I could break him. Soon. His gaze heated, as if he knew what I was thinking about.

Okay, so the only risk to breaking Cassian was that I wasn't 100% positive on what I'd be unleashing. I mean... I totally knew he was kinky as fuck. I just had a sixth sense for these things, and the man looked at me like he had a list of dirty shit he wanted to try out. I loved it, but I needed to know, like a compulsion, how deep that ran. Like, I wanted him to show me how kinky he could get... *yeah, alright,* I might be the one with the problem here.

Both of them had those stunning fathomless eyes with dark lashes and richly-colored skin, but Cass's hair was tinted with silver, and more silver glinted off of the piercings and rings he showcased, including the one on his lip. Oh, and let's not forget about the one on the tip of his cock. I couldn't forget that one even if I tried.

My center clenched as I thought about how good it would feel to be bent over and... I needed to get my head on straight or I would lose this 'convincing the guys to throw a Halloween party' game. As if he knew, he flashed me a full smile, his magic surrounding me in a cool, soft kiss. My magic loved Cass. Really, really loved Cass. She was a clingy ho.

"I don't know, brother." Cass tipped my chin back, running a finger down my neck. "I think that could be fun." His movement was possessive, and I could feel his muscular chest under his tight, dark shirt, and I would bet you a million dollars he was wearing dark boots and jeans. I didn't need to look down to know that. I was a bit obsessed with my men and knew more about them than I would willingly admit. I shivered, my core tightening as my breathing hitched.

"Have you lost your mind?" His twin growled as Cassian's eyes lit up with humor despite his calm and measured reaction.

"If everyone is there from school," Cass rumbled, "then we can show them exactly who Nova belongs to."

My eyes widened. *Ah, fuck.* Maybe this was a bad idea. Wasn't I supposed to be dating Ramsey, technically?

"Alright, you might not have lost it," Fox offered, his eyes drawing up my body to where my nipples had tightened against my sports bra. "In fact, I think she may like that idea, brother."

"No!" I shook my head as my skin rose in shivers. "That's not the point of this…"

"What *is* the point, Nova?" Cassian purred, his hands running up my ribs right below my breasts. His magic was rolling against my skin, distracting me as I tried to focus on what I needed to say. A difficult task, because I felt like there was something seriously dangerous, nearly volcanic, building with Cass. You'd think that the pending explosion would worry me, but it did the opposite. If anything it made me want to encourage him. I wanted to see him lose control. Badly.

"I want to dress up." I let out a breathy gasp as Fox gripped my hips and trailed his lips up my bare stomach, his tongue flicking out to taste my skin. I had the urge to have him bite me, leaving marks across the surface of my skin wherever he wanted.

"You could just dress up for us," Fox offered, grinning. "Or dress down."

"You guys," I mumbled and Cassian nipped my neck, causing me to moan, "have to stop."

"I think I may be losing my mind," Fox mumbled. "You look so fucking sexy in these shorts…"

"Who is losing their mind?" River, the sexy bastard, broke the tension while strolling in and freezing as all three of us snapped our heads toward him. My ears turned pink as I tried to slip away from the twins' toxic sexy touch, causing Fox to chuckle as Cassian growled quietly, nipping at my ear and refusing to let me go. I couldn't stop the moan that escaped, but to be fair I was too busy looking over River to try.

River. River. River. *My sprinkles.*

"Hey, sprinkles," I goaded with a grin as his eyes darkened. What, did he think I'd forgotten?

My eyes trailed slowly over his massive muscular body, his shoulders at least double my width and his height nearly 6'5". My tongue darted out as I tried to not get distracted by how delicious he was. What was I going to do with the man? Well, fuck him, for sure. I had no idea I liked a little pain with my pleasure, but let me tell you… I totally did. My magic offered me a thumbs up and I sighed happily, glad I had so many men to help me explore what I did and didn't like. So far I'd liked literally everything.

My sexy lumberjack was wearing a dark tank top with jeans and boots and was currently tugging on a flannel. His dark hair was damp from his shower, and I noticed the sides looked a bit longer than normal, the rune behind his ear still very vibrant. I didn't even realize he was standing right in front of me until I was running my hand through his hair. How did someone that big move so quietly?

"You need a haircut," I mumbled as his truly hazel eyes danced with amusement. He nipped my nose, bending down, chuckling softly at my attempt to sound like I wasn't gawking at him. What? The man had fucked the hell out of me this past weekend, how was I supposed to *not* get turned on by him?

"You can cut it, if you want?" he offered.

"You would trust me to cut your hair?" I arched a brow, surprised by that.

"Should he not?" Fox goaded.

"I think Nova is probably good at cutting hair," Cassian offered honestly. I offered him a full smile because that was sweet. He was so damn supportive.

"Thanks," I tossed him a smile as Fox scowled at his brother. I focused back on sprinkles, letting them continue their glaring contest, and looked at the man that had kicked my butt in training today.

River was a fantastic workout partner, but I was a bit miffed that he'd showered without me. The least he owed me was a sexy shower after he smacked my ass several times without me striking him with lightning or some shit. I wasn't joking about that - when we were down in the gym and I was stretching, he hit my ass really hard. The issue was that instead of complaining, I may have let out a small needy sound that had him nearly fucking me right there and then. We called quits on our gym time sometime shortly after that.

My magic looked up from where she was between Fox and Cassian's magic, her eyes narrowing in challenge at River's calm, measured power. But we both knew what was underneath that now.

The man was complicated as hell.

For example, this morning he'd gone and picked up donuts for me without even asking if I had wanted them. It was cute, and of course I had wanted them. He was on my good side, and for the most part I had forgiven him for the other night, but I would kick his ass if he pulled that shit again. I also knew that while he had said he wouldn't close me out, it was going to take some serious time and trust for River to open up. No problem there, all I had was time! Especially while avoiding my important godly work.

Honestly, not that I would ever admit it because this is corny as fuck, but... even if I was busy, I would make time for River. Always. Plus, I knew that once I convinced him to let down his walls, they would collapse on me like a fucking avalanche. I would willingly let him bury me, though; that didn't bother me in the least. Especially if it would make him feel better.

"Can we go back to the awesome Halloween party we are hosting?" I chirped while looking between the three of them. "I already sent out texts to all the humans, not the witches, *obviously*, for tomorrow around nine. This house will be filled with drunk humans! Come on! Doesn't that sound wonderful?"

River blinked at me. "That was probably the least appealing way you could have put all of that."

I smirked, exclaiming, "That isn't a 'no,' though. Thanks, sprinkles!" I darted out of the kitchen before they could argue with me. He let out a low rumble that had me smiling, knowing it wasn't going to take much to get him worked up anymore. Cassian wasn't very far off-base, though, with his idea about showing the students who belonged to whom.

As in, these boys belong to me. I'd been getting very annoyed lately because some of the female population thought that the other guys were fair game because I'd told everyone I was dating Ramsey.

Ramsey. Now he was complex. So many little twists and turns, all surrounded by a cinder block wall that he stood behind. It was a good thing I had dynamite.

What? I liked the guy and he kissed like a god… *ha! Get it?*

Speaking of the devil, I rounded up towards the stairs and came face-to-chest with a very large, muscular body. My eyes shot up as I offered a flirty smile to one of my demi-gods. The bossy, overbearing bastard offered me a once-over as a low rumble broke from his throat, his metallic gold eyes darkening into amber.

Both he and Nour, his twin, brought every twin fantasy to life. Not that the fantasy hadn't been there before, but now I had two fucking sets of twins. *I was a lucky woman.* Not that Nour was mine… but anyway. Talk about sexy. They were both very large, like River-sized, and had muscular, perfect builds that I wanted to sink my nails into. I had yet to get Ramsey to kiss me again like he did when we were heading to the Horde, but I was a very determined individual.

"Nova," he rumbled in his accented voice, stepping down so that he was in my space, his dark, wavy hair looking messy and perfect to run my hands through. Why was it that the men always got thick, almost eyeliner-like lashes and wavy, beautiful hair? It was wholly unfair.

"Sunshine," I corrected as he chuckled, the sound soft and low. His god-like magic wrapped around me and I swayed slightly, enamored by him. What? I had a total crush on the guy, and until a few days ago I thought he sort of hated me.

"Do you dress like that on purpose?" He arched a dark brow, trailing his fingers along my bare waist. I looked down at my spandex shorts, sports bra, and gym shoes.

"Like what?" I offered an innocent expression. "Do I look bad?"

His eyes narrowed and my smile widened as I stepped back. "No really, Ramsey. I'll even give you a turn. You'll tell me the truth, right?"

I knew I looked good, for the record. I turned as if to show off my outfit and didn't even get half a rotation before the man had caught me up against his chest, his arm a cord around my center as I looked up and behind me slightly. Instead of offering anything, he nipped my ear, his hard length pressed against my ass.

His voice was like rocks as I shivered. "I think you know exactly how you look, sunshine. You better be careful, though. A man only has so much restraint."

I nibbled my lip while trying to not laugh. "But you're a god."

His eyes sparked with amusement as he leaned down and pressed a kiss to the corner of my lips, making everything melt inside of me. Then he was gone, walking away towards the kitchen. Frustrating bastard. I narrowed my eyes at his retreating form, already crafting his demise. His very sexy demise.

The man was like an emotional fortress, and while we'd kissed, in some ways I felt like we were still as far away as when we'd first met. I knew nothing about him, and it was going to be like forcing myself to push through a blizzard to get through to him. A battle I wasn't positive I was completely prepared for. Then again, maybe all it would take was telling him how I felt. Which I wasn't even 100% decided on, besides the obvious - that he was sexy as sin and I had a stupid crush on him.

I walked up the stairs of our large gothic estate while I let my mind wander. My hand trailed the wooden beam as I began thinking about all the cool decor we could put up for the party. I bet Everett could help me. He liked scary shit. I reached the landing of the second floor and stepped into my room, the door shutting behind me.

What? Sure I liked them, but a bit of privacy was nice. I

groaned with a stretch and kicked off my gym shoes, rolling off my spandex and sports bra. I let the bathtub fill with steamy water but rinsed off in the shower first to get any sweat off me. When I sank down into the bubble- and hot water-filled cast iron tub, I let out a moan, my head falling back.

"I am jealous of that tub," August's voice sounded in the space, making me jump. My eyes opened to find him lounging on the vanity stool, facing me. I scowled, trying to hide my surprise and my ridiculously turned-on reaction to him being so close to me while I was naked.

"Auggy," I inhaled sharply, "give me some damn warning."

"But then I would have missed the strip show." He offered a cheeky grin, causing me to blush, which he narrowed in on like a fucking hawk. I knew Auggy was hiding a side to him that wasn't all sunny and handsome. I wasn't positive it was even dark or scary; in fact, I got the distinct impression it was rather haunted.

I offered a fake scowl as I felt a shiver roll over me. "All you have to do is ask."

The alchemy mage was absolutely unique. All of my men were, but August always struck me as truly one of a kind. Usually light-hearted and filled with cheeky comments, being around Auggy was like basking in sunshine. He even smelled like summer and sunshine, which completely contradicted his shadows that were a black, smoky texture. Hell, even right now they were running along the floor and circling the edge of the tub, tempting me to touch them. Somehow, I knew the tone of this room would alter drastically if I did.

It was very tempting.

I was smart enough to know that Auggy's magic wasn't a sunny thing, nor was it something to fuck around with. He kept such a tight hold on it that I was sincerely worried he would snap one day. I'd only seen him lose it once, and that was when Everett let me fall from the staircase. He'd been livid that day.

So who the hell knows who would survive that shit if he broke. Well, besides me, of course, because I'm immortal and shit. That was okay though, I would protect my other men and then the nine of us would figure out what the hell to do next. We were a resilient bunch, so I knew we could make it through anything.

Auggy leaned forward, his dark, almost raven-colored hair hanging silk-straight to his shoulders, showing off his perfectly structured face. His dark, smooth skin was contrasted by his perfect white smile as he teased me. "Don't scowl, sunflower. I'm only joking."

I offered him a lazy smile, dropping the scowl. "I'm not put out, but I am in a grumpy mood. My muscles are sore as hell. River put me through loops today. If only I had someone to give me a massage…" He chuckled at my prompt, his truly stunning deep-blue eyes growing more gold as the natural streaks expanded. It made me ponder how the hell they turned to black when he was upset or angry. I felt like covering a color like that was damn near impossible.

The bastard ignored my 'massage' comment and tilted his head. "Why are you working out?" To be fair, it was a good question. I had slowly upped my workout frequency to nearly every single day since coming back from the Horde.

"To keep my girlish figure," I rolled my head on the tub ledge, hoping he would let it drop. I had no urge to talk about my nightmares and the desperate need to exhaust myself so I could sleep better. Unfortunately, August was smart and he narrowed his eyes at me, shaking his head.

Before he could say anything, Rowan busted in and

scared the living shit out of me. What the hell? Was this 'hang out in the bathtub with Nova' time? Least they could do was get naked as well. It was just rude not to.

"Wildcat," Rowan's smooth sexy voice almost sounded pleading, "could you possibly come help me? It's Everett." *Oh Lord.*

I searched his golden-boy face, which was accented with panic, as he ran a hand through his soft blonde hair and bright, almost sky-blue eyes. What ruined this boy next door look? The extensive tattoos, for sure. You know… like the one he gave me. Except his stark ink crawled up his arms and neck and down to his fingers, making him impossibly sexier. Those rough fingers always felt amazing on my skin and were currently covered in thick black rings that were the same shade as his eyebrow piercing today. The man personified every bad boy biker wet dream I'd ever had. *And he was mine.*

What? He'd marked my skin… with a tattoo. If he got to keep me, then I got to keep him. I was finding that my magic and I were possessive bitches. I wish I could tell you I felt guilty. I didn't.

My eyes flickered down to his semi-hard cock, visible through his jeans, as he made a low noise, drawing my attention back up. Auggy chuckled as I inhaled, thinking about being in Norway and how I'd had Rowan's hard length between my lips right after the two of them had finally kissed and made up.

Ha! Literally!

There was something very unique and intense developing between the three of us, and it was like getting caught up in the tsunami of Rowan's emotions and the possible tornado that August's powers could cause at any moment. This could end in chaos and destruction. Or in fucking. Most likely, hopefully, both.

"What?" I asked, curious again because I'd forgotten the entire reason he was here.

"Everett. Problem. Now," he explained, looking urgent. *Ah fuck.* I cursed and stood, wrapping a towel around myself as both of them let out groans. Good. They should suffer, I had been ready to relax.

I snapped, using my natural witch magic to gather a pair of leggings and some other clothing items for myself. Honestly, I had no idea if that element of my magic was *actual* witch magic. It worked like it… so I guess it was the same? No one had accused me of being anything different, ever. Well, before all this nonsense started.

"Give me a minute," I shooed the two of them from my room and got dressed, pulling my multi-colored hair into a tight braid. I could only imagine what Everett was getting us into now. My lips pressed into a small secretive smile because his crazy was addictive and absolutely yummy.

I was out the bedroom door and down the steps. Rowan loved trouble, so if he was worked up, it probably wasn't a good situation. My magic pulsed through the house, and I muttered a curse as I walked through the front door, pushing past River and Ramsey to find three police cars and a handful of officers surrounding our house with guns drawn.

Everett looked back at me and offered me his trademark insane smile.

Fucking wonderful.

NOVA

I made my way down the sidewalk barefoot. The sky rolled
overhead as thunder rumbled, causing some of the officers to look up, no doubt worried about the change in
weather. I could feel my magic crashing into Everett's as our
life force bond pulsed. I literally saw the tension in his shoulders, despite being well-hidden, relax at seeing me. I couldn't
deny I felt better around him as well.

I felt stronger around all of them, but Everett and I had
a… special bond. As in, we weren't positive if he could live
without me because our life forces had melded together. Well,
his had melded to mine. So to say Ever and I had become co-
dependent was the fucking understatement of the century.

The sexy, somewhat clingy bastard offered me a mint-
green gaze that darkened with heat as he pulled me into his
grasp. If I was within the same vicinity as Ever, I was
usually somehow touching him. I would find it annoying if I
didn't love it so much. If I didn't love *him* so much. The
bastard had sunk his crazy hooks into me and I was addicted
to him. To him, his magic, and hell, even his cock. I loved
his brand of crazy. I couldn't get enough of these men, and I

had no doubt it was going to probably get me killed somehow.

"Miss," an officer demanded my attention as Everett let out a territorial sound at his attempted interaction with me. I knew the guns the men held didn't phase my necromancer at all. Probably because he was batshit crazy.

His lean, muscular body, far larger than my own, was hard against me as I turned to face them. Immediately he had his arms around me, his lips on my neck as I tried to focus on the humans. It was difficult, though, because Ever's messy dark hair kept brushing against my neck, making me shiver and pulling me into the hurricane that was this insane man. He turned me on way too much. It should have been illegal.

Maybe I could have him arrested. My smile slipped, knowing he would just kill the entire force in a second. Okay, that was also sort of hot. Man, I was in deep with these guys.

"What's going on, officers?" I asked curiously as Everett smoothed a finger down my arm, his touch near electric.

"We have a warrant to search this house. There have been several accusations that he is behind the disappearances of some students," one stated gruffly as Ever chuckled. Maker.

So what I'm hearing is that my dad was making bullshit accusations. I'm sorry… but last time I checked I wasn't a murderous serial killer like he was. Well, not the serial killer part. Probably. Wait, did it count if I was killing the 'bad' guys? You know what, I didn't have time to get into the ethical dilemma in my head of 'good' versus 'bad,' plus I wasn't positive I wanted answers to the questions in my head.

"What students?" I arched a brow, feeling a bit over this conversation already. I couldn't even be fully mad at the dumbasses because I was positive my father funded every single piece of equipment and clothing they had on.

They offered me a torn piece of paper, looking like it had

17

been crumbled, as I sighed looking over it. I recognized the faces that looked back at me because I'd seen them recently.

Dead.

In my father's serial killer den. I really didn't think it was my job to inform the families though. Right? I looked up at Everett, who was offering me an affectionate look. "Were you giving them a hard time?"

Why did he have to be so cute right now? I was trying to be upset about all of this nonsense, and he was smiling at me like I had just made his day by showing my face.

His eyes danced with amusement. "I told them to fuck off. They've yet to show me the important piece of human paperwork they are supposed to have."

The warrant, he meant the warrant.

I shouldn't have looked up at the sexy man, though. I tried to not get distracted by his model-like looks, even in a simple black shirt and worn jeans. I just wanted to strip them off his hot body while licking and kissing every divet of his abs… gods, I needed to stop.

"Can I see the warrant?" I turned back to the humans so we could get this over with. They exchanged looks, seemingly uncomfortable at my demand. Let me guess, they didn't have it? Surprise, surprise.

"Leave," I stated softly as thunder cracked the sky and Ever's smile grew wicked against my neck.

"Miss, we don't want to have to force the issue--"

Thunder struck down on one of their squad cars and all of them froze. Then rain fell from the skies as they opened up and instantly soaked the humans. I let the missing person report fall onto the sidewalk as the cops, except for the one I'd been talking to, raced to their cars to avoid the odd turn of weather.

I continued to stare at the man in charge, his face growing

pink before he stalked away and they took off. No doubt they would be back with some other way to hassle us, because my father thought that games like this would wear me down. Honestly, it just decreased his life expectancy. The rain stopped, but it didn't really matter since neither of us were wet. Well, not from rain. That was one benefit of being able to control storms.

"Baby," Everett nipped my neck, "that was so fucking sexy."

I turned into his arms, pretending to not know what he meant. "What was sexy?"

"Scaring them." He flashed a dangerous smile and dipped his lips down to mine. I let out a soft moan as he lifted me under the thighs so that I was wrapped around him, his familiar hard length pressed against my center. I pulled back a bit, out of breath from the chaotic storm that was Ever and his madness.

"Fuck," he groaned, putting his head against my chest. "I love you so much."

I offered him a teasing smile, not speaking, as he looked up. His eyes narrowed as I tried to not laugh at his expression. "Nova."

"What?" I asked innocently.

"Tell me what I want to hear."

"What do you want to hear? I have a lot of interesting things to say," I teased as I ran my hands through his sexy messy hair.

"Nova," he growled.

I laughed and kissed him, his hands biting into my ass as I pulled away. "I love you, Ever."

"Everett," Ramsey's voice sounded, interrupting us, "can we not do this outside where people can see you guys? More specifically, her?"

As if my necromancer hadn't considered that, he looked around, rumbling dangerously before walking me towards the house. I smiled at Ramsey, messing up his hair in passing as he narrowed his pretty eyes at me. Ever dropped me onto the couch before lifting me onto his lap and settling, all in about three seconds. The man worked very quickly. Just another thing I found sexy about him.

"What the fuck was that?" Ramsey demanded softly, his eyes filled with worry.

"My father is a twat," I offered.

Nour, the handsome bastard, strolled in at that moment, unintentionally interrupting us. Much like his brother, his smooth, umber skin and dark hair looked almost impossibly perfect, but his silver eyes took the cake.

I wouldn't admit it, but the carefree demi-god was totally one of my best friends. I had been a bit mad when he had just left this past summer without reason. I tried to not think about the total crush I'd been nursing the entire summer, either.

It hadn't really been the seashell collection that had upset me… still, I had no idea how Nour felt about me, and things were still a bit weird between us as we tried to find our footing in this new situation. I swallowed, trying to not think about how sad I'd been when I'd woken up to him gone from my father's small witch community. I didn't have time to overthink that. I figured I would deal with it when I absolutely had to or attacked him because our attraction became too much for me.

Right now there were more important things to worry about. I could see the stress that his future-seeing bullshit magic was causing him, and I was starting to understand why Ramsey had the better end of the deal. I wanted to take a nighttime walk with Nour like we used to, but I was nervous that things weren't the same as before. Those moments had been everything to me - he didn't understand half of it.

I stood on the edge of the forest line, my eyes watching my father's room warily for signs of him waking up. Luckily, he seemed fast asleep, but I was distracted enough by it that when a hand pressed to my lower back I jumped, trying to muffle a squeak in my fingers across my lips.

I turned sharply to look up into a pair of silver eyes that were lit with humor. I offered a smile, trying to not notice how good he looked in just a shirt and jeans instead of those stupid polos all the men around here wore. Quietly, we started down the forest path in our normal comfortable silence. It had always been like this between us, even on our first walk when we had both seemed to have the same thought and unintentionally met up while walking.

"What was on your mind today?" he asked quietly as I snapped my head, frowning, always surprised when he noticed stuff like that. I swallowed, noticing there was a slight darkness to his gaze, and I felt a bit cold despite the warm early August air. Something was wrong with me, wrong with us, and I wondered how to ask him without sounding a bit crazy. So I decided to be honest.

"When are you headed back to New Orleans?" I asked softly, my eyes darting to the path in front of us.

He made a small worried sound. "Probably sooner rather than later, moonbeam."

I nodded and looked up at him, wanting to say so much more but keeping it to myself. "Are you excited to go back?" Because I wasn't. At all.

"No," he stated softly, running a hand through his hair.

I nodded and sighed. "I'm going to miss this, our walks."

His fingers found my wrist to pull me to a stop as I looked

up at him, always surprised by our height difference.
"What?"

Nour's jaw clicked, and I could see something churning
through his thoughts, but instead of saying anything, he
pulled me into a hug. I usually tried to not touch him too
much because I didn't trust it, but this time I melted into him,
letting my head rest against his pectoral.

I had no idea how long we stayed there, with me in his
arms, but when the light began to rise he walked me home.
I'd said goodbye to him, feeling like there was so much
more to be said. About what he felt. About what I felt.
About us and everything that we had shared these past
three months. But after a kiss to my cheek, soft but some-
what intimate, he was gone, leaving me feeling sick to my
stomach.

When I woke up that next morning he had been gone, and
I would be lying if I didn't admit to it breaking my heart just
a smidge.

"Don't yell at her," Everett snarled defensively at
Ramsey's question as if I'd never responded in the first place.

"I wasn't," Ramsey looked at him incredulously, making
me smile. I ran my hand through Ever's hair as he leaned into
my touch, not ashamed in the least to show public affection.

"It's fine," I waved my other hand dismissively. "But
don't mind the police, they are just under my father's finger.
They can't do shit except show up and annoy us." Ramsey
offered me a nod, looking content and relieved with my
answer, before dropping into a chair and looking up at his
brother. Aw. I think Ramsey had been worried. That was a bit
cute, to be honest.

Taking a bit of a risk, I reached over to the demi-god's
hand and squeezed it lightly while giving him a small smile.
His eyes snapped to the movement before heating. I redi-

rected my attention to Nour so that he didn't notice the bright blush on my face.

Nour had just returned from the store and was placing the bags down so he could rummage through them. He offered me a bag of M&Ms as well as a small little pocket calendar. He didn't say anything, just tossed me a small, sweet smile before taking what appeared to be groceries into the kitchen.

My eyes followed his ass because it looked so fantastic in his jeans. It was unfair for the god twins to be so muscular and built, with athletic fine asses as well. I mean, I already had to deal with Fox and Cassian being sexy-as-sin bad boys, how was I supposed to handle another set? I just couldn't.

I totally could.

"What is that?" Ramsey asked curiously, and I clutched my calendar to my chest playfully, narrowing my eyes up at him.

"It's a secret gift," I teased as his eyes narrowed right back. I didn't buy it. I could see amusement sparkling within them.

He grunted, shaking his head and standing up to no doubt find his brother. *Serves him right for being a broody, handsome ass that refused to kiss me*. I relaxed into Everett and opened the calendar. Immediately I smiled, because every single photo was of a tropical location. I knew he'd gotten it for the pictures rather than the calendar aspect, and my face softened because that shit was cute.

My toes curled inside my fuzzy socks, and I sort of wished I'd dressed a bit sexier than leggings and an oversized hoodie. I hadn't known he was going to be all cute and shit. Made me want to attack him.

"You like him," Everett stated softly as I blushed, tucking the calendar on my lap before opening up the candy. I knew I would have to answer him because if the bastard was anything, he was persistent. I had been worried that after we slept together he might get weird about the other guys, but clearly I was dead wrong. I mean, hell, I had no idea why I'd even thought that.

In fact, I would accuse Ever of pushing us all together. I suppose that was why he was in charge of their - well, now mine as well - team. I was a Red Masques *person*, I'd decided. If Vegas was in it, I would be also. It seemed cool, and as I had stated to Rowan, I was very cool.

"It doesn't really matter," I mumbled, offering him a handful as he instead took from my stash.

"It does if your emotions are involved," he stated honestly, his eyes turning into clear mint leaves.

"You can't say shit like that!" I exclaimed, horrified.

"That your emotions matter?" He chuckled at my response.

"Yes, it's all cute and shit," I scowled. "Makes me feel like a mushy pile of love. I have to be a badass, Everett, or else I am going to start to consider you a bad influence."

"I think I can be both," he whispered, tugging on my bottom lip with his rough thumb as I shivered. Okay, that was fair. I had no doubt the man could multitask when he needed to.

"Wildcat," Rowan called out as I winked at Everett and hopped up. Before sliding into the kitchen, I wrapped my arms around Nour's center tightly, whispering *thank you*. I walked around him, finding that his silver eyes twinkled slightly, and while his ears were pink at the top, he had a content look on his face.

"What's kicking?" I sat down on Fox's knee as Cassian's gaze flickered to my ass and back with a dangerous smile. See? I'm telling you, the man had plans for when he got me under him… or on top of him. Honestly, I was down for anything.

"Are you serious about this party?" River asked, his smooth voice making me look up at him.

"Am I ever not serious?" I deadpanned.

Cassian broke out into a chuckle as I smiled and continued, "Yes, I am very, very serious. I need this before we go do more intense shit. Work-life balance is essential."

"Saving people's magic isn't really work…" Fox drawled.

I snapped my head back at him. "Then I suppose infiltrating a witch community to stop a magic serial killer isn't work either, huh?"

His lip twitched and he nipped my shoulder. "Labor of love."

My cheeks flushed, but Rowan was talking before I could comment on the 'love' concept. His voice was amused when he asked, "What if no one shows up to your party, wildcat?"

I arched a brow. "Well then, Rowan, you can totally say I'm officially not popular."

"Deal," he cemented, folding his muscular arms.

"But," I drawled, walking over to the fridge, "I've already gotten over 50 responses that were 'absolutely thrilled' to have been invited…"

"Fuck," Rowan muttered.

"Baby," Everett groaned somewhat dramatically, "you're puting stupid humans, specifically men, right in my path. What if I accidentally kill one? They are so fucking fragile. I just want to make it clear that I'm not liable for any snapped necks."

I blinked. "Why the fuck would you snap someone's neck?"

August chuckled as Ever tilted his head. "Well, if they looked at you, that would be a just cause."

"I can get behind that," River offered, winking at me as I mumbled under my breath. Crazy bastards.

"I believe in you," I waved off, trying to move past murder. "Now who is coming shopping with me? We need costumes, decor, and a ton of other--"

"Not it," Fox stated immediately. My eyes widened as I put a hand to my chest, pretending to look wounded.

"You don't want to spend time with me, Fox?" I sounded despondent. Honestly, my acting was becoming more impressive as the days passed. I needed to learn how to fake cry. Then if I get put in jail a third time, I'll really get out right away. I almost smirked thinking about how I had a criminal record. *That was fucking awesome.*

Fox rumbled, "Yes, that's it."

My lip dipped intentionally. "Oh, okay."

"Gorgeous," Fox narrowed his eyes.

Nour shook his head, trying to not laugh, as I looked off to the kitchen window and let out a tired sigh. "No, I get it…"

"Fuck it," Fox stood up and I heard him grab the car keys a moment later, the front door slamming open.

"I'll go," Nour offered with a bright smile before leaving the room. Auggy and Rowan followed, engaged in a quiet conversation that was totally suspicious.

"Oh man." I looked at Cassian, Everett, Ramsey, and River all together in the same room. I shook my head, backing towards the front foyer. I would not think about a fivesome. I would not think about… I totally was thinking about that fivesome.

Could we have a ninesome? That was an orgy, I suppose. I could roll with that. My magic looked up from where she was randomly poking Ramsey's magic with an eager expression.

"What?" Ramsey asked in his demanding way.

I smirked as Cassian narrowed his eyes at me. I knew they could tell I was about to pull some shit. "I don't know. I mean, just sort of wishing I was staying home now with the four of you…"

My foot was out the door and I narrowly avoided Ever's reach as he swore. I slammed the car door shut as he scowled from the porch. *What?* I knew he would have tried to keep me there, which is exactly why I said it. I liked getting him all worked up. Now when I got back, he would be all upset and needing to take his frustration out on me.

"Are you guys excited?" I asked in a chipper mood.

Their mumbled responses made me grin. *I loved this.*

⸻

I loved shopping. Now, I'd been serious about not caring about my father's money or the luxury it provided me, but there was an actual thrill that came with shopping. Fashion was probably as close as I got to having an artistic ability, and my old closet had been filled to the brim with clothes I was very 'meh' about.

I promised myself the minute I had time I would go on a shopping spree. I smiled thinking about all of the spring clothing lines that would be coming out from designers soon. I absolutely was obsessed with Burberry and Gucci, but unfortunately they would need to wait until I was done saving the world and shit.

We were currently at Party City, and I had to admit today's shopping spree was even more fun because of my guys. As I sorted through long rows of costumes, the options endless because we'd driven to one of the largest stores in Seattle, the guys argued about what to dress up as.

At first, they hadn't planned on dressing up until I

explained they had to or else they would look weird. Since that didn't convince them, I then said if they didn't wear one neither would I and instead I'd wear a bikini. I think that was what pushed them. I smirked at the idea I had running in my head about what they could be. Honestly, I was sort of hoping they'd love it instead of hate it.

"Why are you smiling so much?" Fox accused, his hands gripping my waist as I pulled out a cute zombie doll dress, wondering if I could have two costumes instead of just one. That was reasonable, right? Didn't women some-times have two wedding dresses? I totally deserved two dresses.

"Because I have a good idea of what you all should be, but you may hate it." I explained simply, putting the dress back.

"I want to know your idea," Auggy offered from across the aisle, his eyes sincere despite the teasing smile on his lips.

"I do also, actually," Nour offered from my other side, my head tilting back as my face flushed, causing him to grin. He might go along with it, actually. I tried to shake the emotion running through me at his closeness.

It was like a slow-burning wildfire with him. Your emotions grew for him so slowly and so naturally that you didn't realize how screwed you were until he had you completely lit up in flames. I knew the fix to put those flames out, but I had a feeling he would be surprised if I demanded that he kiss me. Also, it was possible that it would only fan the flames...

"Fine," I inhaled and smiled," I think that all of you should keep it simple. Wear all black, and then each of you wear a different mask with some type of scary monster on it."

"Okaaaay..." Rowan drawled.

My smile grew, goading. "Then instead of Nova's mages

you become Nova's monsters! Don't you love that? Plus, it's far more inclusive for Nour and Ramsey."

Nour chuckled as Fox shook his head, making me blush as I realized I had literally just admitted to including Nour and Ramsey in my affections. August started spouting another idea, saving me from my slight embarrassment as I continued to scan through the options.

I wasn't worried, they would totally come back to my idea. I had no doubt. My smile grew as Rowan called the other guys, and I could hear Ever and Cass say to go with my idea. See?

The discussion faded into the background slightly as I wandered down the aisle, knowing this would take them a bit. Plus, I didn't want them to see my costume before tonight or else it may 'disappear.' I went down the section I knew to be based on the catalogue and found it almost immediately, thrilled that I'd looked up options in the car. I suppose this one was badass enough that I didn't even need a second costume.

My fingers played over the black lace-covered outfit that was supposedly for a 'gothic vampire.' It was ridiculously hot. The lace started at the strapless sweetheart neckline of the structured, black bodysuit, which would hug my torso but leave my back covered in nothing but lace. The lace continued past the bodysuit, which stopped just below my ass, to cover my legs with its sheer sexiness. Essentially, the costume covered the important parts but left everything else exposed. I planned on adding some gold jewelry and boots, turning me into a pirate.

That was right, I was going to be Captain Nova, but I had to find a big hat for that. I turned down another aisle as I looked at the large clock on the wall -- time seemed to be passing quickly today. My cart back by the guys was filled with decor, but I was glad I had magic to help me decorate or else I would be cutting this real short.

Well, I suppose I also had a not-so-small army of... monsters. Ha! I still loved that.

I turned one last corner, seeing the hats in the distance, and nearly slammed right into another woman. I let out a small sound as I braced myself, grabbing onto her arm as she let out a small squeak as well. I immediately stepped back and laughed. "I am so sorry." I didn't feel awkward very often, but I totally felt awkward right now.

"Oh you're fine." She waved her hand, smiling brightly, her tan complexion literally fucking sparkling. And underneath these lights? That shit was impressive. For the record, I was not into girls. Not my cup of tea, as they say.

But with that being said, I could only describe this woman as stunning. Different than how Gray or Vegas were beautiful, but still pretty damn perfect. Man. Thank god I was confident because if not, being around these women would be intimidating as hell.

The woman in front of me was about the same height and size as myself, but she had a tousled braid with chocolate brown and gold waves that had come loose around her tan face. Her thick lashes surrounded eyes that were brown but speckled with gold, and her small button nose made her look like a doll. The woman was literally adorable.

She was dressed in a massive oversized jacket, one I assumed belonged to a guy. I would know, because my quick departure from the house had left me chilly, so I'd stolen Nour's comfortable dark leather jacket. It was actually a bit comical, because the two of us were surprisingly alike right now. Although she was more sunny-ish. Then again, the moon had always been my favorite, so I would take it willingly.

See? I had already started to determine the roles we would play in our best friendship that she had no idea would be occurring. Was it obvious yet that I very much wanted a best friend?

A man's voice called out and I couldn't hear her name, but it caused a small laugh to come from her as she literally tugged my hand down two more turns so that we were further away. She offered me a smile. "Sorry, trying to give someone the slip so I could find something for them as a surprise."

"A guy?" I guessed.

"My mate," she sighed happily and then looked at me with curiosity. "Do you have a mate? I have quite a few."

Was that her scent? Now that I recognized it, I realized that she was very clearly a shifter. I couldn't tell you what type for the life of me, though. Then again, I wasn't around a lot of shifters or other magical beings since I'd been so sheltered. Good thing that shit was over. I probably should have found it odd that a random woman had dragged me down two aisles, but *meh.* It was sort of nice to have someone who was so friendly to me outside of the guys. I also appreciated that she herself seemed a bit awkward. I mean, she'd just asked me if I had mates, so she was either aware I wasn't human or just didn't give a shit.

"Sorta," I grinned, loving how honest she was. "They are mages though."

And demi-gods… wait, what? Where did that come from? Weird.

"Mine are dragons," she offered and then smiled. "They get very worked up when they can't see me."

"Wait, like dragon shifters?" I raised my brows.

"Yep." She nodded before looking at me. "What are you? Also, did you dye your hair like that? I would love to color

31

my hair like that. But I would probably do pink again. I don't think blue would look as good on me."

My smile grew because I know I said Vegas was my best friend, but I was allowed to have two, right? Gray was a bit intimidating to be my best friend, but she was in the running as well. What? I didn't have a lot of badass females around me, and I was always looking for people to join my squad.

Yes. Yes, I did use that word. Deal with it. But really, it could be epic. I mean, shit, we could easily get an entire army going with them, all of their guys, and mine. We would be so badass.

"I'm a demi-goddess," I offered as her eyes widened.

Her eyes moved over my shoulder as her smile broke into a huge, affectionate grin. "Oh! They found me. Well, it was wonderful to meet you. What's your name?"

"Nova," I offered.

"Maya." She put out her hand and I met it.

"Firefly," a low voice had me raising my brows because the concern was palpable.

"Please don't run off like that, Maya. That scares the shit out of me," another offered as they rounded and she smiled up at them with affection. Both men were handsome, but I had no idea how they were friends, since they were night and day.

One had a very expensive suit on, and the other had tattoos and indigo-tipped hair. One thing I could say about my guys, including the demi-gods, was that they had a very 'bad boy' look to them. No one, literally no one, would ever believe they were a suited-up clean-cut guy like the second man. I mean, don't get me wrong, they could wear a suit and look hot as hell, but they were still very much the type your mother would warn you about.

I loved that way too much.

"I didn't run off," she smiled. "This is my friend Nova."

Both men looked at me, offering polite smiles before going back to fussing. I nearly rolled my eyes as a hard arm wrapped around my center and pulled me back. The suit-wearing one looked up, and I am nearly positive that it was because another guy had just entered into the equation.

Mind you, it was *my* guy, specifically... *Nour?* I watched how tense his jaw was as he looked down at me, seemingly very protective all of the sudden. Then again, hadn't he always been? If I remembered correctly, there had been a lot of times this past summer where he had sort of lost his cool around human men. I had pretended to not notice at the time... but now I definitely was noticing and loving it.

This was going to end in a dick measuring contest if the others got here. Which was ridiculous and not needed, considering the two of them were clearly a bit focused on Maya. Obsessively.

"Maya," I chirped, "can I give you my number? I would love to hang out, but I have three more psychos roaming around this store, and well, you know..."

She offered me a smile. "You mean because they get all growly? Do yours do that also, or is that a dragon thing?"

She handed me her cell phone and I typed in my number before giving it back and muttering, "I think that's just a crazy dude thing."

"That means both of you are crazy," she offered, amused, while looking down at her phone as one of them growled, proving her point. I sighed as Fox's energy wrapped around me, having found us, but then the tension broke.

"Ledger?" Fox chuckled suddenly. "What's up, man?"

"Fox? Hey man," Ledger replied with a grin, meeting his hand. "I would have come over and said hi if I'd known you guys were here. Is Cass around?"

"Nah." Fox shook his head. "He's home. We were just taking Nova shopping for a Halloween party we are holding tomorrow."

"Oh?" I arched my brow at the blood mage. "Are *we* holding the party now? If I remember correctly, you didn't want to hold one." He deserved that completely, and when his smirk grew dangerously I knew I would probably get it later for that comment.

"Can we hold a Halloween party?" Maya asked curiously.

I held in the urge to tell her to hold it whether they wanted to or not, *but* I was adult enough to know not everyone had the same relationship as I did. Didn't make mine right or wrong. Plus, it was clear as day that they were crazy about her. On the other hand… she should totally fucking hold a Halloween party.

"Sure," the suit guy offered, his energy a bit intense even for me. "With our family." Also, was it just me, or did this guy seem like one of those crime bosses? Like he didn't look particularly scary, but I had a feeling he was, just not in the same way my boys were. It was the insanity. The insanity was missing. He was far more calculating and neat. Well, that was no fun. I looked up at my four boys thoughtfully. Yeah. I sort of liked my men a bit crazy and my new family a bit messy. The chaos fueled me. Literally.

"Marco," she scowled.

"Alright," Ledger tried to clearly redirect. "Let's head out, shall we?"

Maya burst from Marco's arms and hugged me. "It was so great to meet you. I will use my cell phone to call you. It does that, right Ledger?"

Ledger offered her a soft smile. "Sure does, Firefly."

See? There was something I was clearly missing between

them. She seemed to not understand how Earth worked very well.

"I'll do that then," she nodded. I didn't even get a chance to say anything before they were walking away, both practically hovering over her. I smiled because it was pretty damn cute.

"They're cute," I pointed out.

Fox growled and I poked his chest. "I meant as a couple."

"Good," he mumbled, his voice softly dangerous. "I like Ledger. Don't want to have to kill him."

I looked up at Nour and he offered me a smile, my back resting comfortably against his chest. "What about you? Worried I'm going to run off with dragons?" Fox had already walked away, leaving just the two of us. Rowan and August were talking quietly. I was fully convinced they were plotting something. I hoped it was sexy.

His eyes heated as he spoke quietly. "You make it sound like running off is an option, moonbeam."

Then the bastard was gone, leaving my face pink and my breathing a bit halted. Well, what the heck did that mean? You know what? No. I wasn't going to think that over. I couldn't. I shook my head and went back to the costumes, finding the boys in deep conversation. Fox hung up the phone and offered me a cheeky smile.

"What?" I frowned.

"Let's finish up costume hunting because we need to go home to make ours. Well, Cassian is making them," he explained as I realized I'd yet to get my hat. I was going to need that, but I didn't want them seeing it. I would have to find an excuse to go use the washroom or something.

"What are you guys dressing up as?" I frowned.

"Come on sunflower." August grabbed my hand. "Let's find you your costume. Just trust us." Clearly he was distracted as hell, because I was holding it and he didn't seem to be seeing anything but his thoughts. It worried me. August and Rowan being serious usually spelled trouble, and unfortunately not the fun kind.

Also, why did I not trust the boys about this costume thing they were 'making?'

About an hour later, I stood shocked. I could never say that they weren't creative. I had to give it to them. They had taken my idea and… well, I'm not sure what the hell they did.

Cassian had crafted thin metallic half-face masks that were actually horrifying. They were monsters, but it was off-putting. The deep ingrained etchings were nearly as bad as the closed mouths with fangs. There was a wolf one. A lion one. A few fucking creatures I had no idea what they were. I ran my fingers over them and looked up at Cassian.

"These are scary as fuck," I mumbled.

His chest rumbled against my back as his hand circled my neck, causing me to shiver. "Don't be scared, baby girl. I won't let the monsters hurt you." *Cocky bastard.*

I growled, "I wasn't worried about that."

He hummed and nipped my shoulder. "Oh yeah, of course."

I turned and pointed a finger into his chest. "You haven't even seen my costume yet." August had been so distracted that I'd been able to hide it in the mess of decor after grabbing a hat. I'd been about to ask him what was going on, but I didn't feel like it had been a good time since the cashier was gawking at the amount of money I was spending there. Oh, also because I was holding hands with August and Fox had kissed me, which had no doubt freaked the poor kid out. Well, at least he would have a good story for later.

"Is it scary?" He offered a smile.

"Scarier than you," I teased as his eyes lit up and he

backed me up against the wall, his head dipping down to skim my lips.

"You haven't ever met the monster inside of me, Nova," he rumbled as something flashed in his gaze that made me think he wasn't just teasing.

"Maybe I want to meet him," I admitted as a low rumble broke from his chest. He gripped my waist in a hard hold that had me gasping.

"Be careful what you wish for," he mumbled, his teeth tugging on my bottom lip before he was back to stacking up the masks, leaving me wet and standing with wide eyes. Fuck, come on man. I clearly needed to up my game if I was going to get Cassian to break.

I smirked. Yeah, the outfit for tomorrow night should totally do the job.

AUGUST

Nova's long legs were relaxed over me as she moved her fingers in a delicate pattern in the air, all of us watching post-dinner as the entire house came alive with festive decor without us having to touch a single thing. Honestly, it was very impressive.

Festive autumnal leaves and gourds were paired with a ton of skulls and candles that had the house appearing as you would expect it to at its old age. The news was on in the background, but my fingers were moving over her skin in a distracted pattern. Her soft flesh was addictive to touch, and I knew if I started to kiss and taste her, I would never stop.

Rowan sat next to me, his eyes half closed in exhaustion, and I frowned, realizing he looked drained. Then again, so did half of us. Both he and I had been up for most of the night with Fox going through some of her father's documents in an effort to figure out if he had any more serial killer dens or where we could possibly look for him. I knew Nova was annoyed and very much over the man, but I didn't trust him to not come back and try to hurt her. So I would keep looking until I saw him die in front of me, hopefully by my own magic.

I was worried, though, that this pace and travel schedule would wear us down to the point where we let something slide. I shook my head, hoping like hell that it wasn't my control on my magic that would slip, because that… that would be awful.

Today had been particularly bad, and Rowan had been worried my magic was going to lash out. It had gotten so bad that I had considered locking myself in my room. Nova's magic was interacting with mine and drawing it out more forcefully than usual, and I knew she had no idea. She wasn't doing it on purpose. If she knew what she was tempting, she would probably run in the absolute opposite direction.

I was glad we were holding this party, and despite us giving her shit, I understood why she felt the need to. It really wasn't about the event as much as it was about needing some stress relief. Something else to focus on.

Whether or not we wanted to dwell on it, all of us were young. Nova, who had gone from being sheltered to being the center of this complicated and stressful new world, deserved this. I had no idea how she was dealing with all of this so effortlessly.

I was a bit jealous of her ability to handle and control herself. I had always struggled with that more than I cared to admit. I think I was also a goddamn masochist since I was falling for a woman that was the embodiment of chaos, the thing that I avoided at all costs.

Then again, I couldn't control these feelings if I wanted to. It did make me want to give in. Let loose the control. The unknown of what would happen was what kept me from doing so. Even if she accepted that dark side of me, I couldn't accept the very real possibility that I could hurt her.

Our contact was going to be calling soon, and I knew I would have to use my magic more and more the deeper we embedded ourselves into this issue. The God realm respected raw strength, and it may become a matter of life or death when it came to using my magic. I knew the choice that I would make if anything threatened my family or Nova, so it was a no-brainer. I was just putting it off.

But yeah, I expected King Desmond to call soon because he wasn't the type to ignore shit when it came to other realms. Then again, I'd heard rumors that there was some crazy shit going on in Arizona, so I supposed we would see. I was thankful for the time we had before we found out more information about the power drain issue, because it would no doubt push us in the one direction we had all been avoiding.

The God realm.

I wasn't looking forward to visiting the God realm - or the Demonic realm, for that matter - but I was far more excited than when we'd gone back to the Horde. Hell, our team specifically took as many jobs as possible to get the hell away from that place. I'd had the most relaxed childhood out of my brothers, but the notion of that relaxed tendency was what led me to the biggest fuck-up of my life. I swallowed, trying to shake the thoughts from my head.

An odd buzzing in my magic had me drawing my eyes towards the windows. I could feel Nova staring at me, worried about how tense I was no doubt, and shit did that kind of perceptiveness make me want to let her in.

What would happen when she found out what I'd done? How could she ever trust someone that'd fucked up that much? I frowned, seeing an odd shadow in the treeline as Rowan tensed, the wards pulsing slightly.

Before any of them could comment on it, I stood up casually, not wanting to worry Nova, and stretched my arms above my head. I would bet you a million fucking dollars that this had been why my magic had been so tense today. I wished it would give me a clearer fucking message next time. Rowan offered me a dry look from where he had her pulled up against him, snuggling comfortably.

I walked towards the kitchen hoping that she wouldn't follow until I figured out who the hell was trying to get onto our property. Thunder cracked above me as I wrenched my hands through my hair, focusing on the shadow that stood on our property line, not attempting to hide themselves. Instead, they were patiently waiting, and in some ways that made me far more cautious.

It started to rain lightly as I narrowed my eyes at the woman standing right at the edge, looking tired and concerned. I strode forward and tilted my head, realizing that she looked somewhat familiar. I couldn't place how.

"What do you want?" I asked gruffly, feeling her witch magic even from the space between us.

She swallowed nervously, her eyes darting to the house behind me. "Is Nova there?"

"She's not available," I noted cautiously.

Her eyes searched mine, and I realized the nervous look was what I recognized. John. This was John's fucking mother. A rumble broke through my chest and she stepped back, looking scared. Honestly, that was probably smart of her.

"I need you to tell her something. Can you?" she asked meekly. "I can't stay. My husband will notice I'm gone. But I had to warn her. Nova's always been a good girl, far too good to be caught up in my husband's and Earnest's bullshit."

The word was harsh from her lips, unnatural. I wondered how mad she had to be to speak that way. I also noticed she didn't mention a word about her very dead son.

"Possibly," I conceded, wanting to know what she was going to say.

She stepped forward and spoke quietly. "Earnest is still missing, but I heard my husband on the phone tonight. He'd been gone until this morning, when he returned acting as though nothing had changed. On his phone conversation, I heard them planning to do something. I don't know what, but I heard Nova's name and they seemed pretty pleased, which means it can't be anything good. I just wanted to warn her to be careful when she leaves this property."

Her ramble had me nodding because I could see the honesty there, and truthfully her words didn't surprise me in the least. I'd already figured the witches would keep up with their usual bullshit and escalate it further.

"I will tell her," I stated, knowing that I would tell everyone despite not wanting to. I hated the man, but she had a seething hatred for him that I couldn't even describe. I had a feeling that eventually it would come to a boiling point.

As much as I wanted to kill him, I had a feeling Nova had very specific plans that she wanted to enact on him. If she ever confirmed that the details of those nightmares of her mother being tortured were accurate? Well, it would be so much worse. I couldn't fucking wait till Earnest got his, but I was worried what that revelation would do to my sunflower.

"Thank you," she stated softly as thunder cracked, followed by lightning. Then she was gone as I turned back towards the house, seeing Cassian standing on the back stone patio, his eyes filled with darkness at the conversation he no doubt heard.

"What do you think?" I asked as he took out a cigarette and lit one for me before lighting his own. I leaned against the stone pillar near the stairs as Cassian narrowed his eyes at the forest line, considering his answer. If there was one thing

I knew about Cassian, it was that he never said something he hadn't thought out. Well, usually. Nova seemed to cause a bit of a slip in his normal process.

"I think that she has no reason to lie," he admitted, looking annoyed. "Well, I suppose it could have served the purpose of freaking Nova out, but I doubt that's the case since they have done so much legitimately crazy shit already, I don't think they'd waste their time with scare tactics. I saw how her husband treated her at that stupid fucking welcome party. I think the woman hated her son and her own husband. I just don't think she knows it."

"Repressed bullshit," I muttered and then exhaled on the smoke. "Do you want to go tell them? I am going to sit out here for a bit."

"You good?" Cassian fixed me with a look as I grunted.

"Just one of those days," I muttered as he nodded sharply and turned to go inside after giving me a shoulder pat in support. I dropped to the stairs and stretched out, trying to clear my head.

Some days were better than others, and today while my magic had relaxed, I was trying to fend off repetitive thoughts that threatened to overwhelm me. I knew it wouldn't be good for anyone if I fully lost it.

Honestly, I had no idea how long I sat out there, becoming chilled as my eyes closed in relief as I felt the anxiety drain from me just enough. When I felt Nova's small hand on my arm, I tried to school my features. I knew it had to be at least ten o'clock, maybe even later. She should have been tucked comfortably in bed. But I also knew, based on the concern radiating from her, that this was my own damn fault.

I looked at her as I stood, stepping into her space as her head fell back, exposing her stunning face to me. I couldn't help but slide a hand around the back of her neck before pulling her against me.

"Are you alright, Auggy?" she asked softly.

My shadows instantly swarmed her as if her concern was like fucking catnip for them. They wrapped up her legs and pulled her further against me, causing her to shiver. Was it wrong that I wanted my shadows to absorb her? I wanted to wrap her up completely so that even when she found out what a monster I was, she wouldn't be able to get away.

"Yeah," I grunted after a moment, pulling back to look down at her. "Just a lot going on in my head. I needed a bit to sort through it."

"You've been out here for three hours." Her worry radiated authentically off her. Inhaling her electric storm scent, I tried to muster a smile or comforting set of words, but instead I just hugged her. I needed it, terribly. Hell, I was usually fucking great with shit like this… but then there were moments like this when I had trouble containing everything. Moments where the guys gave me some fucking space. I used to think that was what I needed. What I wanted.

Holding Nova, though, as she asked me if I was okay? Her soft arms wrapping around me and her scent filling my lungs? I was finding that this felt far better than any amount of alone time I'd ever experienced. Even before what had happened when I was younger, my family hadn't been the type to talk or focus on emotions. At least on this level. No, my parents were far more interested in getting high than talking with their kids. Guilt surged through me at that thought. I shouldn't have been thinking bad about them, not after what I'd done. They deserved more respect than that.

"Sorry, sunflower," I mumbled. "I just am in a weird place tonight."

"Do you want to come watch a movie with me?" she

suggested softly. "Everyone else has gone to bed." My chest squeezed because I knew the bastards had done that on purpose.

With an easy movement, I slipped my hands under her ass and lifted her as she let out a small squeak. Her legs tightened around me and she buried her head in my neck, seemingly content with me picking her up. As I moved through the doors into the house, I made sure to lock it. She was correct, most of them were sleeping. I could hear that Fox was up, but that was unsurprising. The man never slept when he had something on his mind.

Once in the living room, I sat us down on the couch, my eyes flicking to the TV behind her. A random Western was on. Nova moved off my lap, keeping her legs across me as she lounged back against the arm of the couch and looked at me with a bright smile.

"What do you want to watch?" she chimed, trying to lighten the mood. I didn't bring up what had happened with John's mother because I was positive Cassian had already informed her.

"I'm not very familiar with Earth realm movies," I admitted as she nodded and tugged a blanket over us.

"We could watch something on Disney Plus? Or this new series on Netflix. Apparently, it has crazy humans and tigers, sort of sounds right up my alley." She laughed softly, filling the space with the lightness that came natural to someone like her.

I tilted my head in thought. No, *lightness* wasn't exactly the right word. I didn't think there was anything light about Nova. She had a wicked glint in her eyes almost constantly, paired with a natural sensuality that spread out around her as if she was a black widow waiting for you to fall into her trap. Not that she wasn't a good person. I think Nova had a lot of good in her, but lightness? No. I think she was more like a dangerous predator. It made me want to lick and bite her entire body until I had memorized her more than I already had.

"And what is Disney Plus?" I arched a brow as she flipped through a few screens.

"I bought it for us recently," she offered with a devious smile. "It has a ton of princess movies, but I really only watch the older ones for nostalgia. I would never show those to my kids." Her ears turned pink at her ending remark, as if she hadn't meant to so naturally allude to her future children. It was adorable.

"Why not?" I asked curiously, the tension falling from my body at the normality of all of this. Then again, I suppose nothing was normal about Nova or my family, but at least we weren't mid-fight with someone or meeting another goddamn god. This was a rather relaxed and normal feeling.

Her eyes lit up as she turned to face me. "Okay, so, the old princess movies, like *Snow White*? Well, that shit is from the 1930s and has massive sexist undertones to it, so of course I would never want to expose my kids to that bullshit. The new ones though? Amazing! It's one of the many reasons I love *Frozen*. Elsa is a total badass, and the entire plot isn't solely focused on romance or her being 'saved.' I feel like kids should grow up with the notion that they don't have to stop being their kickass selves just because of love. Although, I still debate the notion on whether children should even be introduced to notions like 'falling in love' so young. I feel like they totally have better things to do."

I couldn't control the smile on my lips at her little rambling tangent. When she caught me staring at her, she blushed, her ears turning pink, making my grin widen. What? Nova was so confident, it was nice seeing this softer side of her. It made me feel more comfortable with my insecurity and how off I felt tonight. Something I'm sure she noticed, because I wasn't nearly as talkative as normal.

Brushing her dark hair over her small ear, I said "I like that. The part about being a badass along with falling in love." Alright, that hadn't been exactly what she said, but I liked that she was thinking about love when it was just the two of us. My chest squeezed tightly knowing exactly why that was. It wasn't complicated. Rather simple.

I had fallen in love with Nova.

It was clear and present in my head at almost all times. My feelings towards her weren't confusing. The hard part? Knowing how she felt. Trusting that she loved me enough to not go running for the fucking hills. I tried to control my reaction at that thought but pulled her closer. I could still see the nervousness in her eyes from the statement she had made alluding to the future.

Part of me wanted to tease her, but I didn't think that was a good idea tonight. Everything felt heavy and dark, and I didn't want to make her think that her thoughts were bad in any way. No, I wanted to encourage those and a million fucking others. My thoughts instantly went to her between Rowan and myself. I felt my cock twitch at the concept of her on her knees, looking up at us with those stunning eyes. *Such a submissive position had never looked so fucking powerful.*

"Do you want kids one day?" I asked for a way to break from the fantasies that plagued my head. Between her and Rowan, I felt like I was constantly uncomfortably hard, and it was a constant hum under my skin.

Her head tilted as she twisted her lips. "Yeah, I do. More so than ever, in some ways. I used to want to have kids to prove that I could pay attention to them and love them more than my father ever did... now, well, now it's far more than that. Although, I hope it won't be too hard to follow up a serial killer… What about you?"

My eyes flickered up from where they had been focused on her lips at the hesitation and worry I heard in her voice. I didn't like that she was afraid to ask me questions tonight. That didn't sit well with me at all.

I swallowed and tried to keep positive. "I would love a family one day."

Since I destroyed my own.

Intuitively, Nova searched my face. I knew she wanted to ask about my family. Hell, it had been on the tip of her tongue for some time now. Instead, after a soft look at something in my expression, she curled into my chest. I breathed out a slight sigh of relief because it was just a bit more time she'd given me.

Just a bit more time… until I ruined everything. Until she realized why I valued control so much. Fuck. I wouldn't lose her. I wouldn't let her leave, I knew that. I didn't know a lot, but I know that if Nova tried to run, I would follow her. Maker. I hoped that when she found out, she'd care about me enough to think I was worth sticking around for. *At least that was the idea.*

"Oh!" she chimed. "Have you seen *A Bug's Life*?"

"Please tell me it's not all about bugs," I teased.

She scowled. "No shit, Auggy. It's about ants! Isn't that fantastic?"

"Humans are so goddamn weird," I mumbled as she laughed, making me smile in return.

I had to admit, despite her pressing play, I couldn't tell you one singular thing that happened in that movie. My eyes were halfway closed through the first scene, her body tucked against mine and my nose buried in her sweet smelling hair that surrounded the two of us. This was better than any fucking movie. I felt my entire body relax.

On a good day, Nova made me feel fucking elated, like a cocaine high. On tougher days, I found that she was like a soothing balm. I easily fell asleep before I could even rationalize that I had. Rationalize that my nightmares wouldn't stop just because I wasn't sleeping alone.

Of course, my brain did not disappoint.

Thick, heavy smoke and dark shadows filled the space around me as I hacked up a goddamn lung, trying to push into the room ahead of me. I just had to get to the stairs. Shattered plates and glass crunched under my hands as I tried to push aside furniture. The rubble and debris was particularly heavy because of how zapped my magic was.

I had to keep pushing through. I couldn't give up, because the screams would forever echo in my head if I did. I did this. This was my fault. Tears leaked down my face, and my magic tightened around me in disagreement of moving toward danger. But I had caused this fire, so I had to help. I began shaking, and I cried out for my mom and dad when a hard arm yanked me back, making me nearly throw up.

I had been too late. I was tossed from the burning house as I landed with a painful cry on the grass, my breathing ragged. I snarled, looking up into a pair of green eyes, my fury rolling through me, misdirected at the person that had just saved me.

Of course, my temper had been exactly what had caused this. I watched as people rushed the house. I shot forward, wanting to help, but the kid stopped me again. I was only thirteen, but I knew I was powerful enough to be of some goddamn help.

My chest shattered and filled with dark, thick guilt as the scent of burning flesh filled my lungs. My magic locked me in place, and the kid who had saved me didn't offer consoling words, just an understanding look. I didn't think he understood though. He thought that I was sad my family was going to die or already had.

No. I was tormented with guilt… because I'd killed them.

"Auggy!" A delicate but concerned voice shook me from my nightmare, causing my heart to literally skip a beat as my eyes flung open. Fuck. The ceiling of our living room grounded me because of the familiarity of it, but not nearly as much as the lightning eyes and veil of multicolored hair that surrounded me as Nova sat next to where I'd fallen asleep, looking extremely concerned.

I inhaled sharply and realized that she had probably been witness to that entire nightmare and whatever the hell I would have said out loud. Her eyes watched me carefully, not in fear, but in concern. I noticed that she was shaking slightly. Hell. I was fucking shit up right and left.

I didn't think she was shaking just because of my nightmare, though. Her eyes were haunted with something darker than anything she could have conjured from this moment. If I had to guess? It was because Nova was dealing with her own nightmares. Her own fear of sleeping.

The dark circles under her eyes accented her pale skin, and I could almost see the disastrous cracked and shattered exposé of her mother's repeated torture and death she had no doubt been witness to. Her subconscious had protected her by making it a nightmare because I had no doubt the truth was so much fucking worse. No amount of working out to exhaustion would fix this. I would fucking know. Nightmares like ours didn't go away. They multiplied and grew until you didn't understand what was real and what was fake.

"Sorry I fell asleep," I muttered obviously. I could see the knowledge behind her eyes. Along with the questions. Fuck.

How much I wanted to confess my sins to her. I was selfish, though, and my self-preservation instincts were telling me to not fuck shit up even if it meant not telling her my truth.

I swallowed as the time around us seemed to slow down, my shadows crawling over her skin as she relaxed into me, moving to lay on top of me as she rested her chin on my chest, looking more serious than I was used to seeing her. Maybe serious wasn't the correct word. Somber? Haunted? Older? Whatever the fuck it was, I felt guilty for being part of the reason it existed. I knew it was impossible for her to be eternally happy, but it was my goal at the end of the day.

"Do you want to talk about it?" she hesitantly asked as my hand ran through her thick hair.

"No," I answered honestly, wishing I could offer her the full truth. Wishing I could offer her some of the sunshine she needed. I continued, my curiosity demanding it. "Do you want to talk about why you haven't been sleeping and have instead been working yourself exhausted?"

It had been an honest question, but she sighed in understanding. "No."

Yeah. We clearly had this emotional intimacy thing down pat.

After a silent moment, her frame shivered against mine as she crawled further against me, straddling me and burying her nose in my neck. Her words were soft and nervous as she spoke. "I think I'm scared that I am going to realize the nightmares are completely real, Auggy. That I am going to have to come to terms with... well, all of it. I don't know if I can handle knowing that every aspect of her torture, her extreme pain, was all real..." Her words were strangled as I tightened my grip on her.

I didn't press her but instead tried to share something. Anything. I knew that it had taken a lot for Nova to admit to a perceived weakness on her end. "Did you know that I met Everett when I was thirteen? He pulled me from my burning house the night I lost my family."

See? I could open up. *Maker.* We were both terrible at this. I wanted her to meet my gaze, but I understood why that made her nervous. I kissed her head softly and tensed slightly as she pulled back at my words. Fuck. I wanted to be so much stronger than this for her.

"What?" She looked alarmed.

I nodded, letting my gaze roam her lips for a moment. "I was fucking furious at him."

"But he saved you?" Nova's voice held something soft and understanding. I swallowed, leaning into her touch as I realized how good such a simple action felt. I think that people forget that guys like fucking hugs as well. I mean, I also liked fucking, but sometimes just the simple intimacy of a moment like this, especially to broken kids like the six of us, meant more to us than Nova would probably ever realize.

That was why we had been a lost cause when it came to her from the start. She had given us each something that we needed, and the attachment was instantaneous. The concept of understanding and acceptance was often underrated. But Nova's existence was like a center point in our galaxy we hadn't realized we were missing.

Now that we knew she existed, there was no going back. I knew I would be ruined for anyone else, ever. I had made peace with that.

"Only me," I confirmed. "My entire family died."
Because I killed them.

"Auggy," she whispered, her eyes prickling with tears as I watched them leak from her dark lashes with some small sick fascination. My thumb brushed them from her soft skin.

When was the last time I'd cried? I think it had been that night.

"Let's get some sleep, sunflower," I encouraged, and after a moment she nodded and tucked her head back into my neck. I wrapped her up and rolled us to the side so that I could practically cover her with my own body, wanting to shield her from everything. Even if that included myself.

I knew I'd have to explain more of what happened. But anything more would… well, would require the full story.

The full story of how I had been the one to kill my family.

NOVA

I had given my best effort to fall asleep, tucked against Auggy's hard, warm chest as I listened to his breathing and relaxed heartbeat. But it was a futile effort. My brain wasn't having it. I didn't want to move, either, in fear of waking him up, knowing that sleep was evading him as well. Most likely due to nightmares, if what I was gathering from the haunted tone in his voice was correct. Still, being here wide awake was giving me far too much time to think. Far too much time to consider what he had said.

Honestly? I was thrilled that he'd told me something. Anything. I'd taken a huge gamble admitting my fear because I hadn't even admitted the concept out loud to myself. Now that I had, it felt so much more real. Auggy's admission had distracted me from it momentarily, allowing me to breathe through the harsh possible reality, but now it was back. The question of the fucking year that I seemed to not be able to answer. Although, my search wasn't very well conducted, considering I wasn't positive I wanted to know.

So, were my nightmares embellishments of the truth, or were they authentic, gruesome memories?

I couldn't blame August for not completely opening up, despite knowing there was obviously much more to say between the two of us. Hell. I couldn't even face my own goddamn truth. How the fuck was I supposed to help him with his? My chest squeezed darkly as concern flashed through me. I wanted to be strong for these men, and Maker knows I usually was. However, the underlying questions plaguing my own mind regarding my past were becoming a distraction.

Sometime around 4 a.m. I made the decision to get up and proceed forward on a path that could potentially really fuck with my head. To be fair, it was hardly a decision since I knew it would have to be made.

I had been putting it off like a fucking pro, though. If there was an Olympic medal for *avoiding your childhood trauma like a boss,* I would have won gold across the board. It was a skill. A goddamn art. And yes… I was once again putting off my plans. I stared at the staircase, wondering if it would be better to just handle it tomorrow. *No.* I needed to at least ask.

As I stepped forward, I gripped the back of the couch, black spots dancing in my vision. My bones felt heavy, and I could feel gravity practically pressing me into the wooden floors. I knew it was only a matter of time until I did fall asleep, and I had no doubt that when I did it would be deep. I just hoped I passed out in the bed instead of at school or some shit. I groaned, knowing that would cause a fucking panic throughout the house.

I looked at August and watched as he rolled slightly, holding the pillow I'd put to replace myself in his reach. Cute. A soft affection filtered over my heart and I sighed like a lovestruck idiot… probably because I was.

I hadn't realized it was possible to feel this strongly about so many men. So many amazing men. I mean, could you blame me? I turned on my toes, humming slightly as I walked towards my destination.

When I stepped through the heavy doors of the ballroom, my eyes fell on a slightly open window, the soft rain bringing me towards the piano. I looked at the doors of the large office that had been turned into a spare bedroom for the twins and wondered if I should reconsider bothering them.

My fingers rested over the keys of the piano and I experimentally pressed down on one, a sharp, light noise echoing through the space. I began to hum under my breath as I tried to remember how Everett had moved his fingers so gracefully.

Before I knew it, I was playing a soft waltz, and my eyes closed, my body swaying with the tempo. Something about the soothing sound had me relaxing, and I barely paused as the doors of the suite opened, Ramsey's eyes meeting mine in surprise.

Well now they for sure know you are out here.

"Sunshine?" he asked, confused. I should have known that he would be up this early in the morning. He just seemed like the type.

"Morning," I whispered, tapering off my music as he reached the piano. His massive muscles were covered in a soft, gray t-shirt and dark sweatpants. He was so unfairly hot.

"How much did you sleep?" he demanded, standing in front of me. I stood and stepped into his chest, feeling tired and knowing what I was going to ask of him was probably going to be painful for both of us.

So I allowed myself to be a little bitch for a moment, wrapping my arms around his solid waist and resting my cheek against him. A low rumble broke from my throat as he wrapped a tight arm around my waist and the other on the back of my head, plastering me to him.

I let out a soft amused sound as classical music began to play, phantom indents on the keys whispering with the scent of his magic. Ramsey tilted my chin up and I offered him a soft look, not feeling very combative as I continued to avoid the true reason I was here.

"Do you know how to dance?" I asked curiously.

"I do." His voice was deep and rough. I let my magic intertwine with his as the music turned into something even slower and deeper, his eyes darkening.

I was aware this entire moment was odd. In a weird way, it was almost dream-like. Still, I couldn't help but feel warm as Ramsey slid his hand from the back of my head to my lower back and took my hand in his, my other resting on his chest so that we were in a waltzing position.

Before I had a moment to tease him about the fact that I hadn't actually agreed to dance yet, we were turning and moving gracefully across the floor. I felt my toes graze the floor, but Ramsey was essentially lifting me off the ground so that he was completely in control. His eyes were heated with something I wasn't fully looking into, and I couldn't help but grab his chest slightly tighter, loving how close the two of us were.

I let out a small giggle a moment later as he dipped me back slightly, his lip twitching. The first few streaks of sunlight at dawn were shining through the windows, and his eyes flashed with that metallic gold as the room lightened. The skies outside were oddly cloudless, and a soft breeze pushed the window open further, scenting the air with dew.

When the music finally slowed, neither of us said anything. Ramsey gently placed me on the marble floor. I didn't stop holding his gaze, though, my tongue darting out to wet my lips as he let out a small groan, his head dipping. Then he really surprised me.

The first time I'd kissed Ramsey, I'd goaded him, and our magic had clashed in a beautiful, chaotic storm. The second time had been a slight surprise after being fucked by River. So it shouldn't have surprised me that this time was much different than either of those two.

A small sound broke from my throat as his warm solid lips met mine. I found my hands intertwining in his hair as my tongue traced his lips, a growl echoing through the space. The tension was tight as a rubber band, but the moment was intimate and far more serious than I had intended.

I whimpered as he lifted me closer against his chest so that I could grip his hair tighter, and his other hand tilted my jaw, forcing me to give over to his demanding, rough kiss. I shivered, loving the dangerous magic rolling over my skin. Around me his magic grew heavy and dense, making it feel as though I was frozen and plastered, hanging onto him as an anchor.

Ramsey reminded me so much of a blizzard. Honestly, I may have just lost it enough to start relating those around me to storms… but the analogy stood. He was a blizzard. The journey was hard, and sometimes you wondered if there was anything ahead, but the prize? The warmth of a home, the center of his emotions, shone in a tempting fashion, willing me forward. I knew the man didn't trust easily. He didn't do anything with ease, but there was so much about him that I was curious about. I wanted to be the person he opened up to. I wanted to be the person that forced my way through the blizzard.

My eyes widened, pulling back. *Holy crap, I really liked Ramsey.*

"Nova," he whispered roughly as my heart beat rapidly out of control.

"Ramsey."

His large thumb ran over my lips. "You are so fucking beautiful, sunshine."

I turned pink as I heard the suite door open, immediately sensing Nour. I offered Ramsey a soft look, knowing that the two of us would no doubt still be… well whatever we were. Something, though, had changed. Just enough that I could feel my skin breaking out into shivers at his closeness while I tried to focus on the man walking towards us.

For a moment I was nervous. I knew that things were still tense between Nour and I. I also knew that this was his brother, not one of the other guys. Except, instead of acting weird, the demi-god approached and closed me in on the other side, examining my face.

"You haven't slept," he stated quietly, looking almost nervous… but more about my health than anything.

"I really did try," I mumbled as Ramsey frowned, looking concerned.

The two of them shared a look, and I followed as they urged me towards their suite. I shivered slightly, thankful when they offered me a blanket, and I curled up on the couch between the two of them. I let out a sigh of contentment and considered what to say next, because I knew they were waiting.

Looking around their room briefly, I noted the thick, dark closed curtains and warm fireplace that was lit with silver flames. The carved bookcases held tomes that looked like they'd been untouched for years, somehow, even though they weren't dusty. I was glad we had changed the space into their bedroom because I hadn't been able to justify them sleeping on the couch. I refused to admit that it was because I wanted the opportunity to do this. To be near them.

I avoided letting my gaze land on the bed for too long, because that would lead me to thinking about how they had to share a bed… which would make me think about being between them in a hot twin fantasy porno that was playing out in my head. I shifted slightly, really fucking glad for these couches because after that kiss, if we were on the bed, I'd be a lost cause. Even now I was flushed and so wet I was surprised they couldn't tell.

For the record, I hadn't even realized I had a twin fantasy until I had two sets of twins walking around being all handsome and muscular. That's not including their smirks and dark magic. Twins were absolute trouble. Alright, all my men were trouble, but you get my point.

Before I offered an answer for my peculiar behavior, I pulled my long sleeves over my palms. Damn it. I guess I hadn't had much of a plan, but sitting between the two of them had me losing my nerve. I wasn't positive what the hell to say, exactly.

Hey guys, since I can't seem to sleep, are you interested in delving into my scarred subconscious to rip apart my nightmares in the pursuit of truth? Pretty please? I also hadn't counted on both of them being up, which was stupid because Ramsey would have noticed me in his room and woken up, and Nour didn't sleep at this time.

If it had been just Nour awake, I could have suggested an early dawn walk and then bring up my concerns and thoughts. Not because I totally trusted his opinion or thought of him as my best friend… no, this was purely because he was a solid soundboard. Okay, I may have trusted his opinion.

After all, he'd seen my seashell collection, so therefore he

probably understood me more than most and would know…
you know what? I give up. I just trusted his opinion. I would
even admit to having a tiny massive crush on him. Denying
our friendship was like saying I didn't love Bora Bora.
Impossible. I just felt at home around him. Even now I was
leaning into him, comforted by his wonderful, familiar smell
and the way his hand rubbed my shoulder, allowing me to
process what I wanted to say. Ramsey looked impatient as
fuck, but he could chill out. I needed to think through this.

I played with the blanket over me, one that Ramsey had
put there, that smelled a lot like him. He totally hadn't been
sharing it before, but now that I was around he probably
didn't want to get labeled as a blanket hoarder. I mean shit,
that was enough for me to keep someone from my bed… not
really. He would totally be welcome, just don't tell him. I
mean, I wanted him to understand the hoarding tendency was
still a fairly serious offense and shit.

"Sunshine," Ramsey prompted as I put my head up,
closing my eyes and wondering if exhaustion would
randomly slam into me so that I could chicken out of my
plan.

"Everything okay, moonbeam?" Nour asked quietly,
rubbing his thumb over the top of my hand as he held it
gently. I would have totally moved my hand, but Ramsey had
pulled my legs over his lap so I was sinking between the two
of them very comfortably. Sometimes I felt like I had known
these men my entire life. It was sort of insane.

"Yes," I answered immediately and then muttered a curse,
correcting myself. "Alright. I'm actually a liar. Not everything is okay. Not at all. It's one of the reasons why I couldn't
sleep and why I have something to ask…" I trailed off,
feeling my pulse go off like a fucking firework.

Ramsey's brows raised at my honest confession. Ass. I didn't think I'd been fooling anyone with the 'nothing is wrong with Nova' show, but admitting that I wasn't okay was somehow surprising? I felt like I did weirder shit all the time. I scowled at him as his lip twitched.

"Nova," he rumbled, "you need to tell us what's going on --"

"I need something from you," I blurt out.

Nour frowned. "You know we will always help you--"

"This is a bit different," I mumbled, and Ramsey's eyes darkened in realization. Yeah. That didn't surprise me. The man had probably known I had wanted to ask for a bit now.

"I need to know." I directed my words toward Ramsey and then squeezed Nour's hand. "The nightmares are getting worse. More gruesome. I need to know if it's all true or if my imagination is running wild. I can't handle not knowing the extent of what she went through. I have no idea why she stayed through it all, but I need something. I need to at least know exactly what she endured."

Ramsey's eyes flashed with something as he looked past me to the curtained windows. I leaned forward and touched his face, drawing his gaze.

"You've seen them, haven't you?" Realization hit me hard, and I had no idea how to feel about him being there in that place with me. That vulnerable element of my childhood that was so up in the air. Did I trust him that much? Fuck. I guess I sort of did, didn't I?

His voice was rough. "Only if I am touching you--"

"Kinky," I teased, feeling like I could take a quick break as I broke the tension, unable to stay completely serious without feeling awkward as fuck.

"Sunshine." Ramsey gripped my face as Nour stayed silent, pressing his lips to my shoulder. "You know what you are asking, right? For me to be able to see them, they have to be something that's happened in your past. There will be no pretending that any part of what we see isn't real. In order for you to remember everything, I would have to interact in the memory, and you… well, that would cause a chain reaction and you would get all of those back. Every single one of them."

"Nova," Nour's voice was rough, "this is a dangerous hole to fall down…"

"I can't afford to live in ignorance," I mumbled, looking away from Ramsey's gaze and back to my silver-eyed demigod. "But you're right, it's a big decision… I'll think about it for now."

Neither man responded, and I closed my eyes, trying to pull on my reserves of courage. Last night had been odd, though. An odd night, and it was shaping up to be a somewhat weird morning.

I wanted so bad to be better at this. I couldn't explain myself to August, and now I couldn't seem to demand from Ramsey what I needed. I knew he would do it. Instead, I was acting like a damn coward. I sagged further into the couch, promising myself I would figure it out after a quick eye close.

Which was why I was shocked when I fell asleep. Maybe I needed to make a habit of sleeping between the two of them? I mean, a girl could get used to this.

I wasn't positive how long I slept, but when I woke to the brighter morning light coming through the open windows, I realized we had moved. I stretched against the bedding underneath me and shivered, feeling arms tighten around me from behind, the massive king-size bed smelling of both of my demi-gods. Ramsey, though, was missing, while Nour was spooning me.

Luckily, he didn't seem to be awake, so I let myself enjoy

how perfect it felt, rubbing my cheek against his arm underneath my head. I tried to not let it hurt my feelings that Ramsey had gotten out of bed while we slept. I had no right to feel that way, and for all I knew he was doing something productive.

Hell, I could be missing school right now and it wouldn't have mattered to me. Honestly, exhaustion still wracked my body, making me realize I probably hadn't slept all that long, unfortunately. At least it was something. Nour let out a soft exhale as his slight scruff brushed against the back of my neck, his hard-on making me squirm as he left a soft kiss on my skin that turned my body into melted butter.

Then I really got what I'd been asking for. *Ramsey.*

The bathroom door opened, and my eyes widened when I realized that I was looking at a very nearly naked Ramsey. Oh shit. I sunk into the bed slightly because he totally didn't realize I was up, and I needed to see more. I was saving this shit to the mental spank bank forever. I mean, this was literal muscle porn, and I narrowed my eyes at the towel he was wearing, willing it off.

I swallowed nervously as he ran a large hand through his damp hair, and my mouth dropped open because… holy fuck. First, the man was pretty hard, so I couldn't stop looking at how thick and big he appeared. Secondly, the man was literally. Nothing. But. Muscle. Like, did the body have that many muscles? Nour was cut, hell, all of the men were, but this was different. This was like pornographic in its own right. Fuck, I wanted to lick every single ab divet. He had a goddamn ten pack or something insane like that.

I licked my lips, noticing that his eyes were darker than normal as he scanned the room. I wondered, based on how turned on he was… if he was thinking about me. I shivered, thinking about him touching himself in the shower, his large hand wrapped around his... oh shit, he had that V cut that led to where his towel was tucked. My pussy clenched as I shivered, a whimper breaking from my throat that I couldn't have hidden even if I'd wanted to.

Nour's arm tightened around my waist as his massive cock rubbed against me, his teeth nipping my shoulder and making me emit a slight almost-moan. Oh hell. Do you see the shit I get myself into? I am so glad I didn't touch Nour this summer at all because the sexual tension crackling in his room had me wanting to strip naked for relief.

My whimper had Ramsey's heated eyes landing on me, surprise flashing through them before a dark smirk tilted his perfect lips. Cocky bastard. I scowled, muttering a curse and turning onto my back, not trying to hide my flushed face but needing my eyes elsewhere.

No.

I would not get this turned on before school. I would only get myself into trouble and then I would end up getting fucked in the cafeteria or some shit because of all this pent up tension... you know, it didn't sound like a half bad plan.

"What are you mumbling about?" Nour groaned, running his nose against my neck as if he wasn't fully awake. My pulse rate skyrocketed as I let out a squeak. So, what? This is what we were doing now? I swallowed as I felt his magic wrap around me.

"Nothing," I bit out, feeling like I was going to drown between them. Ramsey appeared above me, his shirtless chest entirely distracting. I narrowed my eyes as I looked over his body to find that he was in jeans... ah shit, that didn't help at all. I inhaled and tried to sit up to escape my position, because my magic was getting far too comfortable. Nour must have caught on because he locked me securely to him as Ramsey sat on the bed, his eyes filled with mirth. Bastard.

"Are you blushing, Nova?" Ramsey grinned, brushing a thumb across my cheekbone. Goddamnit.

"Am not," I growled lightly.

Nour propped himself on an elbow chuckling, "Wow you *are* blushing, Nova. It's as stunning as I imagined it would be." Alright. Now come on. What the hell was I supposed to do with that? The man's silver eyes were streaked with darker charcoal, and his hair looked mussed around his sleepy expression. He was perfect. Unfortunately.

"I think she's embarrassed," Ramsey noted curiously. "She was caught staring at me when I got out of the shower." I am going to die. I am going to die and then come back to kill him and spend my eternity in hell torturing him. If I am going to die of embarrassment, I am bringing him down with me.

"So, turned on?" Nour offered.

Ramsey hummed. "Now that's a thought, brother. Is it true, Nova? Is that why you're squirming all over the place? Are you turned on?"

Oh man, this was bad. I had always found them both attractive, but like this? Heated and teasing? I couldn't deal with this. I was practically panting.

"Not embarrassed or turned on." I narrowed my eyes. "In fact, I'm annoyed! How the hell do you look like that after waking up? Both of you. This is some bullshit. It's rude, frankly. Now I am going to be distracted all day. I will be awaiting my apology--"

"I think that was a compliment," Nour looked at his brother as I growled at the interruption.

"A compliment about your distracting looks," I clarified.

Ramsey's chuckle was dangerous. "Yeah? So you admit to finding us attractive?"

"Absolutely not." I narrowed my eyes. "Distracting, not attractive."

"Little liar," Nour purred. "Why are we distracting you, Nova?"

"Look at you!" I huffed. "All muscled and hot--"

"So, attractive?" Ramsey grinned smugly, his eyes all melted gold.

"Maybe to some," I waved my hand dismissively, "if you are into that type of thing. Hot muscles, that is…"

Nour sat up so that I was looking up at both of them, "Moonbeam, it's okay to admit you find us hot. You know, I won't be offended."

Ramsey smoothed a hand at the base of my throat. "I would even go as far to say the feeling is mutual."

"I have terrible taste, so I wouldn't trust me," I pointed out as Nour rolled his eyes, laughing as he stood up and strode towards the closet with an easy gait. I looked back at Ramsey. "And you find me attractive? I had no idea."

Besides his ridiculously hard cock that I totally needed a closer look at.

"Sarcasm, Nova?" Ramsey leaned down so that we were nose to nose.

"Never, scout's honor," I promised as his eyes lit up and he pressed a gentle kiss to my nose.

"Liar," he echoed his brother's statement. "Not just about being sarcastic, either. How much do you want to bet that if I tugged these tight leggings off you and ran my fingers along your tight little slit I'd find out just how wet and turned on your little pussy is?"

"Oh fuck," I mumbled as his lips twerked up. The bastard stood, adjusting himself and winking right as a knock sounded at the door. I growled, sitting up and promising I would seek vengeance.

Nour opened the door and River was there, his eyes immediately locking on mine in slight surprise before he arched a brow. "I was worried about you, butterfly. You are usually the first up and no one could find you."

"What time is it?" I climbed out of bed and walked past the twins, pretending I hadn't almost begged them to strip down minutes ago.

"We have about fifteen minutes until we need to leave--" I cursed out a 'shit' as I pressed a surprise kiss to River's lips and ran from the room. Smooth, Nova. Any sexy points you had gained were totally gone. Just saying.

"Where's the fire, baby?" Everett asked, confused as I sprinted through the house, passing him on the staircase and tossing him an air kiss. I closed my bedroom door, quickly brushing my teeth while stripping out of my clothes, and started the shower.

Yes, I know - very multi-talented. Normally, I wouldn't have been very focused on my looks today because who cared if I had an off day. Except! Today was the day of my epic party, so my hostess duties totally started at school.

I showered quickly, and when I got out I brushed through my long, wavy hair, quickly pulling it into two tight braids. It wasn't my favorite style, but it would work today. Putting on light makeup with thick eyeliner, lashes, and a purple-toned lipstick, I deemed it good enough.

I smiled at the outfit I'd laid out, knowing the guys would probably hate it. Well, they would love it, but it would get them all worked up.

Easily tugging on a black lace skirt that matched the dark bralette I would be wearing, I slid fishnets up my long legs. Add in a pentagram half top, an oversized dark hat, and laced up combat boots, and we were good to go, folks. I looked absolutely witchy, and I was honestly thanking humans' fascination with witch culture because their outfit inspiration for us was way cuter than how most witches actually dressed.

With two minutes to spare, I added a spritz of perfume and began making my way down to the foyer. I called out, "How is my party planning committee feeling today?" I grinned as the group of my boys that were ready to go snapped their heads up to look at me. My confidence spiked at their reaction.

"Fuck," Cassian snarled, looking down and seemingly trying to shake himself. I probably didn't help the situation as I landed in front of him and ran a hand up the back of his neck, his arms locking around me.

"Gorgeous," Fox chuckled softly, "what the hell are you wearing?"

"You don't like it?" I countered, because his cock would like to argue if I could base my judgement off how hard he seemed to be. Fox just offered me a dirty smirk as my eyes drew up from his cock. Alright, well, now I just wanted to see it again... or taste it.

"Baby," Everett approached me as Cass's chest rumbled, his arms tightening as Everett narrowed his gaze at my metal mage. "You are trying to cause trouble."

"Me?" I pointed towards my chest and then grinned at Auggy, who looked far more well-rested than I did and was watching me with a relaxed, amused smile. "Would I cause trouble like that?"

"Yes!" Rowan called while walking into the room and handing me a coffee travel mug. I kissed his cheek as he offered me that sweet secret smile I loved.

"Are we good to go?" I asked River as Ramsey and Nour followed after him.

"Fuck," Ramsey's eyes scaled my outfit. Nour's eyes

heated but he didn't say anything, making me want to know his opinion more than I cared to admit.

River inhaled and looked over me, mumbling "This is going to be a very long day, isn't it?"

Instead of responding, I hummed out a small laugh. A very *fun* day was what I heard.

FOX

I frowned, watching Nova's eyes flutter shut slightly as our math teacher droned on, the classroom bathed in dark shadows from the clouds outside. Cassian and I shared a concerned look as Nova shook herself awake. My hand twitched where it rested behind her on her chair.

I wanted to touch her, but I didn't trust myself to not take her into my arms to make sure she was truly okay. Especially considering how fucking edible she looked right now. No really, I wanted to sink my fucking teeth into the woman. Or bend her over to push up that goddamn skirt while sliding home and burying myself into her so deep that I never left. Either one. Preferably both.

Was it only me, or did Nova look like she was about to pass out? Like, I was well aware of what sleepy Nova looked like, but this was different. There were dark circles under her pretty gaze, and when she wasn't interacting with someone, she looked like she was slowly dozing off. It was times like this that I wished River was around in this class. As if reading my mind, Cassian shot off a message to our group text.

"Gorgeous," I whispered gently. Immediately her head

71

snapped towards me and she offered me a small sleepy smile. "You look exhausted, did you sleep last night?"

I think I already knew the answer, but when she shrugged it confirmed it. I wondered how many of the others had caught on to the fact that her nightmares were bad enough that she was scared to go to sleep. Not that she would ever admit that was the reason. Hell, I wasn't positive if she was even aware that it was because of that. I ran a hand through my hair as she went back to taking notes, her long delicate strokes of handwriting somehow turning me on… because I'm normal, clearly.

My phone buzzed almost silently, so I pulled it out, nearly laughing at how casually my twin had stated his concern about her looking like she was going to pass out. He rolled his eyes as a slew of text messages came in, and I would have smiled more if I hadn't been so concerned.

Cassian: Does anyone know how long Nova slept last night? She looks like she's about to pass out.

River: What the fuck do you mean?

I felt like he had been pretty clear.

Me: He means that Nova looks exhausted. Enough so she is falling asleep in class.

Rowan: She had two cups of coffee this morning like usual.

Everett: Leave class. I'll wait in the hall, she needs to go home.

August was oddly silent, and I had a feeling that he felt bad since the two of them had stayed up late last night. Nova let out a small sigh, her notes breaking off as she rested her pencil down. Cassian was leaning down and talking to her quietly, but she continued to put him off as if her health wasn't a big deal. I was thankful that the bell rang at that moment because I wasn't positive I could last any longer. I stood up immediately, Nova standing too quickly and her eyes closing as she swayed slightly. Motherfucker.

"Nova," I growled quietly, "you look like you're about to fucking pass out." I wasn't positive how many more times I needed to emphasize this to her.

She let out a soft hum of dismissal and turned to leave the room, the two of us following. My hand hovered right behind her because I really had a feeling she was close to the end of 'my body can stay up with barely an hour or so of sleep' mode.

"Moonbeam?" Nour frowned, making me know I wasn't crazy because he hadn't even been in the group text and he could see it. Nova leaned back against me as Ramsey walked towards us with River, making me nearly roll my eyes. The two of them should not be friends. For the sanity of literally everyone involved, that was a terrible idea.

"Nova," River barked as gorgeous rolled her eyes, making me chuckle slightly. What? She was fucking hilarious and had a lot of attitude in such a tight sexy body. Shit was like fucking crack to me. So much so I was wondering how many times she would have to come until she became a docile kitten again. I liked Nova wild, but I also liked holding back her orgasms until she needed me so much that only I could fix her frustration.

"Calm down," she yawned as Ramsey exchanged a look with Nour. "I am completely fine, just a bit sleepy."

River stepped towards her and I could feel his magic wrap around her. She hissed at the intrusion, but her magic was weak and tired, unable to fight it. My eyes widened as River's jaw clenched. "I know you are going to hate me for this Nova, but we are going home and you are going to sleep."

Ah shit.

"I'm fine, Rive…" And she was out, slumping forward

onto his chest as her entire body relaxed. Some days I wished I was a healing mage. That shit was useful.

"You knocked her out?" Everett asked as he approached. "Good, let's get the hell out of here." Without being asked, I swung Nova into my arms, her head buried against my neck as I walked towards the doors with Everett. I didn't really care if anyone else agreed.

I did find it funny that she would be fucking livid with River later. Her being mad was both terrifying and cute… terrifyingly cute?

Once we were in the car, her curvy body pressed against my own and I closed my eyes. A weird sensation rolled over my skin as the reality of how much my life had changed since meeting Nova hit me. Hell, how much my life had changed since finding my damn team.

The silence of the morning made me more fearful than not. I sat up, looking around the dawn-lit room as Cass offered me a concerned look. It was never good when silence permeated our home.

Our home reminded me more of a funeral home than anything else. The energy was stuffy, and no amount of opening windows would remove the scent of death that seemed to grow on every surface. Bleak, sad death. Except the one person that I wanted to die fucking wouldn't. Something that was becoming a very clear problem.

I stood up and stepped towards our bedroom door knowing that the house would creak. All eleven years of my life had taught me that she could hear anything in the house, even the smallest breath. My eyes widened as the creak sounded and the door opened, revealing our grandmother. Instant fear crawled up my spine, knowing her presence meant our mother was gone for the day.

It had always been like this. I imagined my mother had

assumed that going home to her estranged mother when she got knocked up and ditched would have been a safe bet. Little did she know that her mother's zealous religious attitude had only worsened after joining a church that worshipped the cosmos gods.

So our entire childhood had been filled with our metal mage grandmother using brand-like crosses that her church had stolen from an Earth realm religion. Believe me, both of us were very well-acquainted with the cross.

They hung everywhere in the house. They hung forcibly around both of our necks so that when we disobeyed she could almost choke us out with it. It laid on my skin where she had branded it on my lower back. Small, but painful as hell.

"Downstairs, now," she snapped, her shrewd eyes staring at the two of us with disdain. I really didn't understand what we had ever done to the woman, except exist. As she closed the door, I slumped slightly, feeling the burning of the cross around my neck, knowing she would slowly increase the tight-ness until we made our way downstairs.

We were fully dressed in uncomfortable suits. Ones that we would have to kneel in as she read to us from the large book she followed religiously. Then our mother would come home and go to her room silently, not bothering to stand up for us. Not bothering to tell her own mother that we weren't sinful creatures just because we'd been born into a situation we hadn't asked for. But she wouldn't.

No one ever stood up for us.

It was later that I learned why our grandmother hated us so much. One holiday we had come back from the academy without warning, and she had been livid about us appearing on her doorstep. So she had screamed about how we weren't welcome in her holy home because we were the product of…

rape. Yeah. So that explained a lot. It was also the last time we had seen our mother.

Outside of her and my grandmother, we had my mother's sister and her son, neither of which interacted with the family. My aunt Ava was sick, though. Stable, but suffering from essentially lung cancer. Luckily, our cousin Valerio, part of the command team for the Red Masques academy, had made sure his mom was taken care of.

They were the only family we had. Hell, we didn't even spend much time with the two of them either, so who the hell knew. We didn't really have a blood family. No, we just had our brothers.

Cassian offered me a look that made me think his thoughts had somehow gone in the same direction. That happened more often that we admitted. I wondered if it was a twin thing, a magic thing, or both. I narrowed my eyes at the cross Cass continued to wear. It wasn't because he was a fucking believer of the bullshit my grandmother was sprouting, either.

No, he wore it as a reminder of what we had been forced to grow up in. To remind himself and me, if we were being honest, that we weren't what she said we were. Just like how wearing the cross meant nothing, her words meant fucking nothing.

As we pulled up to our large house, I noticed the skies were still but darkening. If I had to guess, nature was confused on how the hell to feel since Nova was knocked out and had been considerably irritated before that occurred. Moving out of the car, Nova mumbled and River grunted, causing me to smile. The bastard was so screwed. I loved it.

Almost right on time as we entered the house and placed her gently onto the couch, her eyes fluttered open. I had a feeling River hadn't just made her fall asleep but also re-energized her because…

She looked pissed and annoyed as fuck. God I loved Nova.

Oh shit. I did. I fucking loved Nova.

NOVA

"**R**iver!" I growled as I sat up, feeling oddly far better than before. Fox was staring at me with a wide-eyed, confused look I didn't understand, but River was staring at me from across the room with his arms crossed. The others were moving around the house, but I knew most were watching us.

"Yes, butterfly?" He arched a cocky brow.

"You can't just make me fall asleep!" I demanded, standing up as Fox made a small complaining noise that almost made me smile.

"I did though," River pointed out as Ramsey chuckled, causing me to scowl.

"I need to talk to you." I narrowed my eyes as energy sparked his gaze.

"Yeah?" He looked down at me as I stepped into him. I couldn't help but smirk because you see, I knew exactly how to handle this and make sure he never did this again.

"Yes." I crossed my arms as his eyes flickered down to my lips before he seemed to come to some conclusion.

I let out an embarrassing squeak as he snatched me up,

and I found myself being pressed up against my bedroom wall upstairs, my pulse picking up as he dipped his head.

"What did you want to talk about, butterfly?" he goaded, his eyes filling with a heat that wouldn't have been there before. Actually, maybe it wasn't that it wouldn't have been there before. I just wouldn't have been as in tune to the massive man as I was now. You know, after he had fucked me senseless.

I was really trying to come up with a good reason to beg him to fuck me despite being busy.

"You can't put me to sleep without permission," I demanded as he chuckled softly with a dark tone. An undercurrent of his natural dominance seeped over me, and I found myself melting against him more than I would have cared to admit.

"And you can't survive on no sleep--"

"You do it," I pointed out as his jaw clenched, legitimate concern filling his gaze.

"It's not the same--"

"It is," I responded easily and then grinned, "Plus, if neither of us are well rested... I mean, then we won't have energy for... other things."

A low rumble broke from his chest. "Other things, huh?"

I smoothed a singular hand up his chest while intertwining my other fingers in his belt loop. "*Very* important other things."

He chuckled softly and leaned in to capture my lips. I moaned as his taste hit my mouth and a shiver wrecked through me, my fingers biting into his chest. I found myself nearly crawling up his body as he easily picked me up and wedged me against the wall, his movements demanding but controlled. I wasn't positive if I wanted to tease the beast out fully. Mostly because I felt bad for everyone else downstairs... I had a feeling we wouldn't be having a party if I started this shit now.

Then again, talk about a good stress relief method...

I had totally wanted to, but our lighthearted, sexy teasing turned into something more, almost as if he had heard my thoughts. More... serious? Yes. More serious as he devoured my mouth and I wrapped my magic tightly around us. We were just kissing, yet somehow it didn't feel like that simple act; this felt like something far more. This felt more important than any words that had been said between us recently.

It was no secret that I sucked at expressing my emotions, and River was no Dr. Phil over here. But maybe we didn't have to be. Maybe this expression of our feelings towards one another was big enough to fill that. I wasn't saying we wouldn't have to talk, but through the depth of our kiss and the interaction of our magic I could feel... everything.

I could feel his affection. His desire. The current of shame mixed with self-loathing that he hid beneath his controlled facade. I could feel the darkness boiling as it tried to greet my own monster. I had never felt more connected to the man, except when he had been inside of me, and it was just from a simple kiss. Something that should have been casual.

But when was anything casual between River and I?

When he pulled back, our breathing, mainly mine, was fast, and I couldn't help but stare into his darkening hazel eyes. Maker, he was stupid handsome. I mean honestly. My hands clutched his shirt as he pressed his forehead against my own, the sound of thunder outside rolling as rain pattered on the rooftop.

I knew others were around, but at this moment it felt like just us. And after what had happened in the Horde? The explosion of our emotions? This was needed.

"Nova," River rumbled as his magic tightened around the

two of us, tying us in what felt like was a very permanent manner.

"River," I replied softly as he kissed my lips gently.

"I feel like I am so out of my league here." His voice was rough and dark, as if admitting it was difficult. I could almost hear slight fear ringing in his voice, and I hated that. River didn't need to be scared of shit.

I found myself being protective of him, like all my boys, and it should have been laughable because… I mean, he was fucking massive. But what if I wasn't protecting them physically? I knew they could do that on their own. What if I wanted to protect them emotionally? Did I have the ability to?

Did the girl that had difficulty with her own emotions have the ability to protect others? *Stay tuned for this week's episode of 'Nova's Shit Show'…* Yeah, even that didn't seem very funny as a somber mood washed over me.

"You? No way, I have no fucking idea what I am doing River," I mumbled as his eyes examined mine. He grazed my lips once again, causing shivers to roll across my skin. What he hid behind those walls of his was dangerous and addictive, luring me in every moment we spent together. I was getting a bit of whiplash from our emotions, but I couldn't help but submerge myself further. His eyes held mine as I basked in being held against him.

"Feeling better?" a new voice asked, causing me to yelp and jump in surprise. I narrowed my eyes at August and Rowan, who were casually chilling in my bed, making River shake his head. Before I could respond, the door swung open and Ramsey and Everett stepped in.

"Why is she screaming?" Ramsey asked. I couldn't help but smile because it was sort of cute how worked up he got over me.

"And not like 'I'm getting fucked so hard' screaming," Everett added as I turned bright red and nearly lunged for him. I would have made it if Nour, who'd literally appeared out of nowhere, hadn't caught me around the waist, making me giggle.

I know. *Disgusting.*

It should have felt overwhelming with the eight of them, including Fox and Cassian who were trailing up the stairs, but instead it felt safe. It felt like home, and goddamn did that emphasize the point that I was out of my league.

"Oh!" I looked at my cell phone, tracking the time, "Now I have more time to get ready for tonight!"

"What are you wearing?" Fox asked, cautiously looking around my room. I was really glad that I had hidden my costume because I wouldn't be surprised if it had suddenly gone 'missing' while I was getting ready. Instead of answering, I just smirked as someone rumbled out a low sound.

"Nova," Cassian said softly.

"I am not showing you my costume beforehand," I said evenly before my lip tilted up. "I am positive you will like it, though."

"Like it, *like* I'll want to rip it off you?" Rowan asked, his eyes lazily roaming over my body. As always, his eyes flickered to my wrist possessively. I should give him a tattoo and see how he fucking liked it.

"Or like it, *like* you can keep it on all night without me killing someone?" Everett added, his eyes void of seriousness and instead filled with excitement at the prospect of others' pain. Yeah, it didn't surprise me that the notion excited him.

"Don't know," I shrugged as I looked up at Nour with a sugary-sweet smile. "You will support whatever I wear, right Nour?"

"Sure, moonbeam," he teased, his eyes warming softly.

Today the man was wearing a skin-tight blue shirt that literally highlighted every goddamn ab on his amazing body. I found myself wanting to run my fingers over each one… and you know, maybe lick them. If that's an option.

Fuck, what was with me wanting to put my mouth all over my hot boyfriends' bodies? That was weird… not. It wasn't fucking weird. Also, when the hell did these two demi-gods get grouped in as my 'boyfriends?' I really felt like 'monsters' was becoming a safer term.

"Liar," Ramsey muttered.

"Oh, so house rules!" I ignored the grumpy bastard and clapped my hands.

"House rules?" River asked, looking confused.

"Yes, like for example, I think we should make sure to ward off the upstairs. I don't want anyone fucking up here. Well, unless it's us. Anyway, we also need to decide what we are going to tell the humans, because I love dating you Ramsey but I really hate all those other hussies hitting on the rest of you. Maybe we should just tell them, I mean I can't be expected to *not* be myself in my own damn house. Plus, then you don't have to worry about killing humans because they will know I am taken, right? *Win-win.* Hmm. What else? Oh, the vendors should be dropping stuff off soon, so we need to direct all of that into the ballroom. It should be far enough into the house that no one will stumble out onto the front lawn drunk. I hope the cops don't show up, but we should expect that just in case--"

Fox started chuckling as he shook his head, making me realize the others were offering me stupid smiles. I mean, they were stunning smiles, but like, stupid. Stupidly beautiful.

"What?" I arched a brow.

"Nothing," River rumbled as his long large fingers brushed through my messy hair.

"No, it's something," Rowan teased, his blue eyes lighting up like lightning.

"Just have never heard you talk so possessively, Nova. We are rubbing off on you," August drawled.

Oh. I turned pink and shook my head. "No idea what you're talking about. That wasn't possessive, just a huge fan of honesty."

"So if someone was to hit on one of us?" Everett asked, looking far too amused.

"What are we talkin' here?" I narrowed my eyes.

"Tried to kiss one of us," Cassian goaded.

Outside, thunder and lightning crashed together, shorting the power in the house for just a moment. Silence reigned in the room as I tried to look somewhere else besides their shocked faces. Alright, it infuriated me.

"I would for sure talk to her about it." I paused, clearing my throat. "You know, just so she understood." *That she would be needing to arrange her own funeral.*

All of them broke out laughing and I realized I'd been talking out loud. Goddamnit. I groaned and walked towards my bathroom, slamming the door shut. I smirked then, reminding myself that I would get them back tonight.

If they thought I was possessive, just you wait.

NOVA

As steaming hot water fell from the chrome waterfall showerhead and rolled over my skin, I attempted to temper my amused smile of anticipation. I should not be this excited about their possible reaction to my outfit tonight. But I couldn't help it, even if I tried. They were just so fun to fuck with.

It was more than that, though, and the reason was extremely cheesy.

I was authentically excited to be celebrating a holiday together, even if it was just Halloween. It was our *first* holiday together. That was big, and I was wondering if stuff like that mattered to the boys. I hoped it did, because I loved celebrating, especially in a way that wasn't so goddamn boring like *literally* all of my childhood.

Tilting my head back, I let the water stream over my face as I took a relaxing deep breath. Any possible fear of being 'submerged' in water because of the shower was absent at this moment, and even the idea of sitting in a tub of water didn't make me as uncomfortable as before. Sure, being thrown into a pool would probably still send me into a full-blown panic attack, but I felt like I was getting better.

Or maybe *better* wasn't the correct word.

I think it was far more likely that my mind was simply more focused on the larger nightmares that awaited me when I closed my eyes. The new demons that seemed to have much sharper claws and a savage bloodlust. Yeah. I didn't think I was getting better. The world around me was just getting darker and scarier.

Somehow I'd become at peace with that change.

The one thing I could live without? These fucking nightmares. River wasn't wrong, I hadn't been sleeping enough, and part of that was due to the fear of what I'd see when I closed my eyes. I had no idea if finding out the truth via Ramsey would help, but it sure as hell couldn't make this any worse. I felt like I was losing my goddamn mind.

No. No, I was not doing this right now.

Pulling myself out of that particular rabbit hole, I finished showering and shaving. As I dried myself off, I muttered a small curse, realizing that I'd left my bag with my costume outside in the bedroom. Goddamnit. I would need to get that, but I could feel that there were too many of them out there to complete my mission successfully. The bag was hidden right now, and I didn't want them pulling out the costume and seeing it without full effect.

Trust me. The full effect would be worth it.

I didn't bother locking the door, knowing that if one of them got impatient they would probably just barge in anyway. I sort of hoped they did...

As I began to get ready, I found that my thick multi-colored locks were far more wavy today due to the slightly warmer weather and humidity. I considered fighting it but decided to instead encourage the natural curl with products.

Sometimes it was just better to listen to your hair. *It doesn't give a fuck what you want, anyway.*

Knowing that I had time and smiling as I heard some of my boys leave the room, I began to apply my makeup. I wasn't positive what kind of makeup sexy pirates wore, but I was going with a dark smoky eye and painted red lips. I slipped on a robe, and after looking over myself, I turned towards the door.

Operation 'retrieve sexy pirate costume' was officially in process.

Opening the door, I made eye contact with Auggy and Rowan, who were both laid out on my bed watching a video. I flashed them a smile as Rowan shook his head at me, unable to help his smile. I felt like the man had a sixth sense for when I was up to nonsense.

I had the urge to join them, but I knew I would probably never get up if I did. When it was just the three of us I usually became very relaxed and very, very turned on. I was glad that the tension between them seemed to have relaxed after our trip to Norway, and I felt like Rowan hadn't been nearly as weird about shit as before. Hell, even right now August had his arm behind him as they laughed about something on their phones.

I wanted to watch funny videos…

No! I could not forget my mission. As I walked towards the windows, I ignored Fox and Everett, who were both observing me cautiously with almost the exact same scowl. Ah. They were a psychotic bunch, weren't they? I loved them for it.

"That's not your costume, is it?" Fox narrowed his eyes at my silk robe, as if somehow it was offending him. If he thought this was bad…

I laughed while nearing the cabinet I'd placed the bag in,

right next to the two loonies. Now how did I grab it without them taking it from me first?

"You don't like it?" I arched a brow and let a bit of fake sadness fill my gaze. "Here I thought I looked good--"

Everett let out a low rumble as Fox growled, tugging on the belt of the silky material slightly. "No. I don't like it. It looks like you're naked underneath."

I quickly opened the cabinet and pulled out the black bag. Letting out a small amused sound, I walked backwards from them, making a hasty retreat with the bag behind me. I couldn't help but tease Fox just a tad bit. "Fox, it looks like I am naked underneath because I am..."

… And I slammed the bathroom door shut as he let out a growl and tugged on the handle. Oops. Everett said some-thing that made August laugh as I shook my head.

Honestly, Fox and Cassian kept setting themselves up to be frustrated. I mean, what? Had they not expected me to take this amazing opportunity to dress up for my eight smokin'… monsters? I was officially rolling with it. *They were my monsters.*

Shrugging my robe onto the tile floor, I unpacked the black bag and immediately grabbed the tiny nude seamless thong I'd bought specifically for this outfit. Can we just give it up for the freakin' genius design team that came up with the concept pantyline-less underwear? I mean seriously. How had we lived without them before?

Once on, I pulled out the black silky bodice that was meant to go under my costume. Its heart-shaped neckline and the way it cut across my butt cheeks promised to show off my best assets. It was essentially a Playboy bunny outfit, minus any of the other stuff. Although, for the record, I think I would look fantastic with a tail and ears. Just saying.

I shimmied it on and laced up the front, adjusting my

boobs and nodding at the girls in approval. We were looking pretty fucking good so far. No, really. Like, I didn't have that big of boobs, but in this? They were looking pretty fantastic. I unfolded the sheer black lace bodysuit that would go over the ensemble and cut off the tag, knowing that this wasn't going to make it the entire night. Honestly, I couldn't even tell you who would ruin it, but it was going to be one of them. I'd bought it realizing that it would indeed have a very, very short lifespan.

Worth it.

How did I know that? Well, let me be clear, the piece that went over the bodice? It was absolutely see through, the black lace highlighting my skin that was visible through most of it. I slid it over my legs and up my torso to where I attached it to the neckline. I shifted the material around slightly, glad it fit so comfortably before I looked up at the mirror.

Well, shit.

I mean, I had guessed it would look good, but hot damn. I don't want to be conceited but… *mama looked fucking hot.* My legs looked extra long, my arms looked toned and golden, highlighting my tattoo, and my waist looked tiny. This. *This* was the Halloween costume I'd wanted to wear all this time.

Attaching some gold jewelry, cuffs on my arms and a body set that started at my neck and looped around my back, I found myself nearly bouncing with anticipation. The time was growing closer to the party starting, and while I was nervous about hosting, I still couldn't check the thrill going through me. After brushing out my hair, I pulled on my thigh-high stiletto lace-up boots that gave me a solid few inches and did a turn, looking over everything.

Now I just needed my cute pirate hat and you had one sexy Captain Nova, ready to party! I grabbed the hat from the bag and placed it on top of my hair, grinning from ear to ear as I walked towards the door.

Opening the bathroom door and stepping into the bedroom, I kept my eyes down on my boots as if I was checking out the laces. When I finally drew my eyes up, I realized Fox and Everett were the only two left. Ah, shit. Two psychos and no buffer. This was going to be fun... no really, I was extremely excited. You had no fucking idea.

I'm just saying. If they got frustrated, there were a lot of ways we could handle that... namely with the bed only a few inches away.

Both men stared at me quietly, their eyes darkening and filled with a fuck ton of emotions as my smile grew so much I couldn't hide it. Wasn't it amazing when the reaction you wanted was even better than expected?!

"Do we like it?" I twirled as Everett, uncharacteristically quiet, tilted his head skyward and muttered something. Was he praying to the Maker? Oh. Now that was funny as hell.

Fox just continued to stare at me. Unblinking. Eyes completely dark and absent of any silver flecks. I honestly didn't know how to handle either of their reactions. It wasn't very often you surprised crazy people.

Everett stood sharply then and walked towards me with a predatory gait that had my pulse quickening. I swallowed as he wrapped a hand around the back of my neck and his other captured my waist. His eyes flickered over my face before he let out a low rumble.

"Baby?"

"Yes, Ever?" I asked softly, his rough voice running over my ears.

"You remember what I said about snapping necks if people looked at you, right?"

"Yep." I popped the 'p' as his fingers tightened and dug

into my waist. My heart was beating rapidly, and I could feel his magic caressing my skin in a way that could mean he either wanted to kiss or kill me. It was always a toss up with Everett. I was just glad the man loved me. Having monsters on your side was always a good move.

Plus, you know, because I was super into him and shit.

He narrowed his eyes as I saw the crazy that always rested under his skin jump to life, a smirk pulling at his lips. "And you are still wearing this?"

I shrugged, offering him a coy look as my magic rolled over my skin and pulled his close. "Come on, Ever. You won't really kill the little humans, they aren't worth it."

"Oh, I disagree," he chuckled softly. "I think killing anyone that looks at what's mine is very much worth it."

"Hm," I tilted my head, "I don't know if I believe--"

"Nova," Fox demanded in a warning tone.

What? Oh. Ohhhh, I was goading the crazy man? Yeah. That could be dangerous.

Everett's laugh was dark and soft, his hand gripping my chin and removing my attention from Fox's expressionless face. I was very much interested to know how he was feeling, but Ever's words had my ears perking up. "Nova, *puppet,* you have no idea what trouble you are asking for."

Then he was gone. I smiled as if I didn't just release his psychotic side, my gaze following his frame as he left the room. I looked back towards the other lunatic who was watching me like a predator. Was he going to hunt me? Maker, I hoped so. That would be so goddamn hot.

"Yes, Fox?" I asked because he'd demanded my attention moments ago.

The dangerous blood mage stood and I shifted slightly, my hands finding their way to my hips as I tried to ignore the excited and slightly nervous edge to the air. I watched him cross the room and his magic met mine, instantly tightening around me as I inhaled sharply.

All right… honestly? I may not have thought through their reaction to the fullest extent. I should have calculated the mix between their craziness, intensity, and possessiveness. I may have miscalculated.

"You. Cannot. Wear. That," he demanded sharply, his body shaking slightly with tension as his fingers dug into my hip, making me nearly moan. My fingers found their way to his chest as I gripped his shirt, my smile teasing despite how goddamn turned on I was right now. Maybe I should have considered how much their reactions would turn me on.

"Why not?" I arched a curious brow.

His nostrils flared. "You are practically fucking naked, Nova."

"I disagree," I stated, motioning down to my outfit. "In fact, most of me is covered."

He narrowed his eyes on me before stepping closer and dipping his head down to brush my lips. "Are you absolutely set on wearing this?"

"Yes." I let out a small whimper as he pressed a kiss to my jaw, his tongue flicking out on my neck as a shiver rolled over me, my body turning pliant in his arms.

"Fine."

His 'fine' was accented with my moan, almost a cry of pleasure, as he sunk his teeth into my neck. My head fell back as my nails bit into his shoulders, a low rumble breaking through his throat as his cock grew hard between us, making me want to rub the hell against him.

This was far more than any goddamn hickey. My thighs tightened and clit pulsed as a mini climax rolled over my skin at the simple action. My eyes closed as I moaned his name,

his arms tightening around me as I clung to him, not positive
I could stand on my own.

Holy hell.

Fox pulled back, breathing hard with my blood staining
his lips. "If you are going to wear that, then you are going to
have my fucking mark on your neck."

I nodded like a twit, feeling flushed and dizzy as he
tugged my hair back into a low ponytail, putting his mark on
full display. Where the fuck had he gotten a ponytail holder?
His eyes sparkled as he ran his thumb over the savage bite,
then bent to kiss the other side of my neck where my tattoo
rested. Of course he couldn't have done it on the same side.
Bastard.

My mouth popped open with a small laugh as he stomped
out. I tried to not find him fucking hilarious and adorable, but
I couldn't help it. Shit. Maybe I needed to just start walking
around in nothing all the time. Their reactions were really
boosting my ego here.

The sky rumbled outside as it grew dark, drawing my
gaze from my hot boyfriend to the window. Usually I was
ready ahead of time and was stuck sitting around forever, but
this time? I'd actually taken my time, which was good
because I was already impatient and ready for the party.

Walking into the hallway, I found Rowan staring at me
cautiously, as if he'd been waiting. August stopped himself
from going down the stairs, snapping his gaze toward me
with interest.

"Fucking hell," Rowan growled, looking furious and
turned on.

"Sunflower," Auggy groaned, "you look goddamn
edible."

"Thank you." I twirled on my toe, showing off my full
look. I giggled as Rowan caught me around the waist and

pressed his lips to mine. I whimpered at the taste of his magic as he caught my hands and pulled them from his hair to a spot between us so that I couldn't touch him.

"You cannot touch me right now," he breathed out, shaking his head. "I am not sure how long I'll last tonight before I need to see that outfit on the floor." August's hand pressed against my lower back as he nipped my ear, causing me to melt between them.

"How about, if we get through the entire night, you can take it off me... personally," I teased with a wink as Rowan's eyes darkened and flared with heat.

"I love the sound of that," Auggy determined as his hand trailed down my waist and firmly squeezed my ass, making me jump and let out a small sound of surprise.

"Those sounds," Rowan growled as he pulled at my bottom lip. I smirked, seeing my lipstick had rubbed off on his lips. I didn't plan on telling him. In fact, I reached forward and kissed his jaw, leaving a bright red mark.

"Are you marking him, sunflower?" August teased as I offered him an innocent look.

When a door down the hall swung open, I froze between them but couldn't hold back my laughter as River appeared. A man on a mission, that was what he was.

"Oops!" I slipped between them and towards the stairs, "Look at the time! I have so much to do -- River!" My voice broke into a laugh as the healing mage threw me over his shoulder and jogged down the steps with me. I shivered as he smacked my ass, his low voice echoing curses in different languages. Why was that so goddamn sexy?

"Let me go!" I squirmed as he shook his head, entering into the kitchen before plopping my ass down right on the counter. I offered him a smile as he stepped between my thighs before looking over my entire outfit. I sighed into the brush of his lips against mine.

"I am torn between telling you that you look gorgeous, which I am positive you are well fucking aware of, or demanding that you change so I don't take you over the goddamn counter," he grumbled.

"But if I changed, it wouldn't match my pirate hat," I blinked and spoke in a mournful voice as his lips twitched with amusement.

Muttering something, he turned towards the fridge and took out a bottle of water and some fruit. I had no idea what he was saying to himself, but if I had to guess, it was something like 'goddamnit Nova is so right and so perfect all the time.' He handed me both items and walked out of the room without another word.

"I am guessing I should eat these?" I called out as he grunted a reply.

I grinned and turned on the counter so I was facing the doorway as I began to eat the fresh fruit. I think I drank almost the entire water bottle in less than a minute, making me realize just how dehydrated I was. Also, when was the last time I'd eaten before this? I frowned, feeling a bit off at that thought.

I had been eating far more than I used to, and I tried to eat even when I wasn't feeling it... but with all of this insanity going on, the temptation to control that element of my life still persisted. I know that my true nature laid in chaos and that it wasn't healthy to restrict myself like that, but habits like this didn't change overnight.

I nibbled my lip in thought, glad that I at least felt more well-rested. Whatever River's magic had done had really made me feel much better. Maybe I could have him do it all the time so I would never have to sleep again...

Or, and this was a concept, I could handle the issue like an adult.

"Nour?" I asked curiously as he walked in through the back door, his black hair damp and his silver eyes roaming over me. I saw heat, surprise, and then mirth flash through his gaze as he set a bag on the counter.

"You," he tsk-ed before caging me on the counter between his large arms, "are a troublemaker, Nova. I love it. You look beautiful, moonbeam."

I blushed as I tried to cover it and rolled my eyes. "I try." I had to fight the urge to brush back his wet hair as raindrops slid down his umber skin.

"You very much succeed." He flashed a boyish smile before winking and opening up the bag he'd brought in. I was caught off-guard by the wink, so much so that I didn't process that he was trying to hand me something until he said my name with a slight amount of laughter. Bastard. Adorable, perfect, handsome bastard.

"Oh!" I grabbed the bottle from him as he took a few more items out of the local liquor store plastic bag.

"I know you ordered kegs and some other stuff, which by the way Cassian told me to tell you have arrived and are in the ballroom, but I figured I would grab this when I saw it. I hope you still like reds."

I bit my lip, smiling slightly. "This is from that one night, right?"

I already knew it was. I couldn't forget the wine, and not because of how good it tasted. No, this was because that night had meant so much more to me than he probably even realized.

It had been right after a big coven dinner. Nour had only been there one or two weeks, and I had left early to go on a walk. Usually we didn't meet up until late in the night, but it had all been too much. I had needed to get away. Plus, it wasn't like anyone would notice I was gone.

The cool summer evening air brushed over me as I tightened my light pink cardigan around my shoulders, wishing that I'd changed out of this dinner dress. At least I was barefoot. The forest and heels were not a very good combination. Literally ever.

I couldn't believe I'd managed to sit through that bullshit. I mean, mind you, I may have been gazing a bit at Nour. I hoped he didn't notice me being a creep, but after some point, I stopped giving a fuck. Can you blame me? He was smart, sarcastic as hell, and stunning. Everything John wasn't.

Why did I have to be with John?

Oh, wait, because your life is boring as fuck, Nova.

I knew Nour wouldn't be around forever, and when he did leave it was going to hurt even more if I gave into those feelings. Shaking my head, I wondered if I should even be out here tonight.

"Moonbeam," a voice echoed through the space as I turned around, coming face-to-face with the man in question. Shit.

"Hey," I said, feeling awkward.

"You seemed upset at dinner. I came bearing gifts." He winked and held up a bottle of wine and two plastic cups as a peace offering. I couldn't help but laugh as I motioned for him to follow me.

One more night of spending time together wouldn't hurt - right?

I moved my gaze up from the wine bottle, trying to not let myself dwell on the summer, when everything had been different and a lot sadder. Less dramatic no doubt, but a lot sadder and more empty. Here and now, though? Well, I had no restrictions on how I had to feel about Nour, and trust me, my brain and heart had one hundred percent received the news.

"I just remembered how much you loved it." He shrugged and offered a soft smile. "Plus you told me you get nervous hosting stuff, so I figured it would help at least some bit."

Damn this man.

Damn him to hell.

He knew me. He really fucking knew me and there was no denying it.

I moved closer to the edge of the counter, taking a chance and wrapping my arms around his neck as he took the invitation to step closer to me. My breathing increased, and I tried to tell myself that this wasn't new. We'd been this close before. Hell, we used to fall asleep together sometimes in the forest before we'd walk back. It would only be a quick nap, but I had woken one time with my head on his shoulder. I still had no idea if he had known because I'd literally jumped away, alarmed with how comfortable I'd felt.

I wasn't alarmed anymore.

"You know a lot about me, Nour," I whispered as his silver eyes examined my expression.

He exhaled slightly and nodded. "Yeah. Yeah I do, moonbeam. I mean… you're all I thought about and focused on this past summer."

"Just this past summer?" His admission had me feeling nervous as his thumb brushed over my jaw, making shivers break out across my skin.

"Ever since I met you, you've been the only thing on my mind. Consistently."

Nour's words hit me like a freight train of excitement, adrenaline, nervousness, and a fuck ton of affection. I felt like I just found out my crush liked me back. Nour, sweet, sexy Nour, totally had a thing for me despite me being batshit crazy. I was starting to think I'd been right showing him my seashell collection. Scratch that. I knew I'd been right.

I froze, not trusting myself to not throw myself into his arms. Couldn't the man just fucking kiss me already?

Almost as if he heard me, his head dipped slightly as he looked at my lips. I was going to get my wish, I promise you, but... then someone walked into the kitchen. I made a soft squeak realizing who it was.

Oh, no.

"Absolutely not," Ramsey's eyes honed in my outfit as Nour chuckled, nipping my nose and winking, his body taking precious heat away from mine in his absence.

One of the benefits of being with multiple men? The fucking body heat. I was almost never cold anymore, and it was amazing.

"You can't." Ramsey's voice almost had an edge of pleading as I offered him a full blown smile.

Before I knew it, the man was in front of me, his brow furrowed and his fingers rubbing the lace material before muttering something unintelligible. Clearly, he wasn't waiting for a response from me, which was good, because I didn't have one he'd like.

"I am," I finally answered and then ran a finger down his neck. "Don't worry, Ram. Remember, you are technically my boyfriend... so you can touch me as much as you want tonight."

Nour barked out a laugh as Ramsey's eyes flared, his demeanor going from frustrated to something far more intense. I shivered as his eyes lingered on my prominent cleavage before his two large hands ran down my waist and grabbed my ass lightly. Oh Christ. He pulled me close so that we were nearly nose-to-nose.

I had totally been joking. Totally teasing… totally getting myself into something I probably wasn't ready for.

"Is that so?" he demanded softly. "What else does your 'boyfriend' get to do?"

My voice was a bit breathy as I uttered, "Well, I would imagine you would get to kiss me as well… I mean, only if you want to, of course."

Ramsey let out a low rumble as his eyes flashed. "Oh, I don't think that's ever in fucking question, sunshine."

My mouth opened as he turned on his heel and walked out. Why the fuck did everyone keep walking out on me? Next time, I would be the one to walk out. I promise you.

Nour shook his head, popping a grape in his mouth before arching a brow. "Nova, you better be ready for all of that."

It should have been weird that I'd nearly kissed him and his twin within minutes of one another, but Nour didn't seem bothered by it at all. In fact, if anything he seemed amused and pleased.

I frowned, needing clarification, because 'all' of anything with Ramsey sounded sexy as hell. "All of *what*?"

"My brother isn't nearly as laid back as I am, Nova. Something you've probably cued into. He has never given any woman the time of day, so if he is playing this game with you, it's not because he considers it fun, moonbeam. It means he is very serious about how he feels about you. The guy is a bit intense, and that's understatement. Just be careful and know that he is very much *all or nothing*."

Oh.

He kissed my temple as I stared at him without response, his lip twitching and eyes sparkling with mirth as he walked out of the room as well. All these damn kisses and walking out on me. I looked down, frowning a bit as I considered his words.

Was I concerned about Ramsey's intensity?

No.

No. I really wasn't. I actually rather enjoyed it, if we were being honest.

"Oh well," I hummed, shrugging to myself as I slipped from the counter.

Making my way towards the ballroom, I felt Cassian's magic reach out to me like a cool brush of air, and the scent of metal filled my senses. I came to the door and watched as tables, chairs, kegs, and a bunch of other stuff was lifted and placed on the outside covered patio and the recently decorated space. I knew that people would spread out through the rest of the house, no doubt, but this was going to be the main area. Contain the damage, as they say.

A bonfire was lit further out, a pale yellow flame that seemed to never go down despite the sprinkling of light rain. Interesting. I was so enraptured by everything going on that I didn't notice my metal mage had neared until I heard a strangled, almost feral noise.

"Cass!" I squeaked as my back hit the ballroom wall, his cool mountain air scent flitting across my nose before his sculpted lips dipped to devour mine. I moaned at his ravaging move as his hands roamed my body, his length hardening between us, making me somehow more wet than I had already been before. I hadn't realized that was possible, but leave it to this man to make it happen.

When he pulled back I let out a whimper as his large hand grasped my jaw in a tight and possessive hold, not allowing for any movement.

"Fucking hell, baby girl." His body was tight with tension, and everything - and I do mean everything - hardened to an extent I had to imagine was painful. "You are doing this on purpose."

"Maybe," I teased.

"You're not going to win this, Nova," he proclaimed softly, his gaze heated but becoming more controlled. "You are going to be begging me to fuck you before I break and give in to it."

Was this the time to essentially beg him to fuck me?

I put on a sassy smile. "Wanna bet?"

Okay, come on! We all knew I had a competitive steak!

"Absolutely," he growled, nipping my lip and pulling on it in an erotic gesture that had me moaning. There was a solid moment where I almost did before I shook myself and got it together.

"Fine," I shrugged, trying to not show my weakness. I broke away from him and began strutting out of the ballroom, calling out, "When I get you to break Cass, it will be because you're begging, not me!"

He chuckled softly at my retreat as I felt determination roll through me. *I was totally going to win this.*

ROWAN

I knew Nova was standing in my doorway without looking, but I met her gaze and couldn't help but smile as she nearly shot across the room and crawled up onto my bed with me. My cock had been hard since I'd met Nova, but particularly so right now. Her little outfit and thigh-high boots were driving me crazy. I wanted those long legs wrapped around me, and I nearly rolled her so that she was underneath me, but I was in the middle of something that limited my ability to move.

"What are you doing?" she asked quietly as I paused the pen I'd been using to add runes within one of my tattoos on my arm.

I didn't have to do it very often, considering how often I put ink on my skin, but this one had needed a touch up for a while now. It had been one of my first, and knowing that we were meeting with a demonic king, I figured it was better to be safe than sorry. As it was, ink mages weren't fantastic at using their magic in defensive situations, which was why I had to train to be a good fighter. However, it did help when you could literally ink protection spells into your skin.

"Placing some protection runes within an older tattoo I'm touching up," I explained softly. "Sort of like the ones on your wrist."

She scowled, but her eyes jumped with humor. "I never even told you that I was okay--"

"Didn't need to." I switched to a different color pen and smirked slightly. "Wildcat, I would have marked you somehow, someway, as it was. I just figured there was no point in waiting."

"Hm," she made a sound, and I watched as she grabbed a pen from my little pile. I knew that she was blowing off time right now because she was impatient as hell, which was adorable, but I loved that she was in here. Just the two of us.

I was hoping that when all of this was over we would get to spend every day like this. Relaxed and happy. She could wear any fucking costume she wanted at that point. Or nothing. I was very much okay with that concept as well, and definitely preferred it.

Nova didn't say anything as she laid down on her stomach, focusing in on my muscular side, my lips twitching. Instead of saying anything, we laid in a comfortable silence that echoed with the rain outside. I watched as she grabbed a pen and uncapped it. I nearly groaned when she started drawing on me. If she only fucking knew what that did to me.

My magic was elated. Fucking thrilled at her marking of us.

"Hey, Rowan?" she asked curiously. "When did you start tattooing yourself?"

I swallowed, trying to not relive that particularly painful memory. I knew that I needed to tell her something, and I could have played it off like it was nothing, but this was Nova. Not only did I think she would know if I lied, but there really wasn't any point in hiding shit from her. I could feel her smooth sketches and lines, and I had the urge to see what she was drawing but continued to work, wondering if she would let me mark her again after this.

One tattoo of mine on her stunning body wasn't enough.

"Row?" she asked softly.

I swallowed. "The first tattoo I received was from the ink mage that determined my powers. My father is a naturalistic mage, so he wasn't happy about that at fucking all. He had always said that ink mages were useless because his own brother was one, and to say they don't get along is an understatement. So yeah, that was my first tattoo, but when my father sent me off to the Red Masques academy at thirteen to get some training, I finally learned how to use my magic since it had been banned in my house."

Along with everything fucking else.

"My first tattoo was this one," I said, stopping my work and pulling up my sleeve to show her a black circle that almost looked like a wheel with six spokes. Between each was a different symbol. She tilted her head and smiled slightly.

"Is that for the team? Like all six of you?" she asked with a big smile.

"Yep," I smiled and went back to work as she switched to a different color pen.

After a moment of silence I took a bit of a leap. "It was the first time I felt like I actually had a family. People that were cool with me being me."

"Your father isn't like that?" she asked softly, but I had a feeling she knew. Or at least could assume. I wasn't exactly fantastic at covering up my emotions.

I grunted, "No, wildcat, he is most definitely not."

"So it isn't just about your feelings with Auggy?" she voiced softly, almost hesitantly.

"No," I admitted. "It's about any emotions. Any feelings. Anything that wasn't what he defined as being a man. Well, I suppose he still defines it that way. I don't see him very often, though."

"Good, he sounds like an ass," Nova admitted as I chuckled, feeling a bit of the weight from his negative memories lift away.

"He is, and you being around us? Coming into our life? It's made me realize just how much I cared about his opinion despite him not being in my life."

Nova blushed and continued working. "Why is that?"

"Because you live life fearlessly, Nova."

She looked up at me, her eyes filled with emotion as she twisted her lips. "It doesn't feel that way lately."

"Your nightmares?" I questioned. It was weird that our mood was so serious. We'd never had a conversation like this, and I was finding it therapeutic and very needed.

"Yeah," she mumbled.

"I don't think you're afraid of the nightmares, Nova," I answered honestly. "I think you're afraid of what you will do when you remember all the details."

She looked up at me after finishing a stroke and caping the pen. Something flashed across her face as she nodded and offered me a small smile. "You know, I think you're right, Rowan."

"I tend to be," I flashed a smile.

A small laugh escaped her as she stood up and rounded the bed, pressing a light kiss to my lips. I pulled back and decided to ask her something that I'd been a bit nervous to.

"This Christmas, sometime around the holiday, my father wants me to visit. August was going to come with, I would love for you to also--"

"Yes."

Her firm acceptance had me smiling and I kissed her again, only breaking away when Fox called her name. Rolling her eyes but blushing, she walked backwards towards the door.

"Hope you like your tattoo," she winked.

I chuckled and finished up my rune before placing the pens down and standing up. Damn that woman, she was just so fucking perfect. My heart squeezed because I knew that with each day passing I fell further and further for her. But who could blame me? Who could blame me for being goddamn obsessed with someone so strong and so full of life? It was like Nova had destroyed all sadness in my life and filled me with strength. It made me want to be the person she believed I was.

Walking over to the mirror, my brows went up as a chuckle escaped. On my side, right above where my jeans rested, was the outline of a jungle cat. She'd added the dark eyes and nose in purple, but the rest was a black outline. It was fucking perfect.

Normally I liked my tattoos shaded in, but using a dark pen, I wrote a scripted *wildcat* and let my magic set it permanently. I couldn't wait until she saw that I was keeping it.

Was I worried about having a woman's name on my body? Nope. Even though we hadn't said 'I love you' or made any fucking commitments? Nope. Why?

Because even if Nova left tomorrow, I would still want her name on me as a reminder that we'd been close enough for her to do that. I was well aware that I would never feel the way I did about Nova ever again.

She was a chaotic storm that had torn everything up in my life, and instead of hunkering down and trying to maintain sanity, I let myself get destroyed by it. By her.

I'd never felt more at peace with a decision in my life.

NOVA

I *was totally not going to win this.*
Well, not the battle with Cassian's control, at least,
because the man seemed to have the patience and control of a
saint. No worries, I would get him. For now though, I would
win literally best fucking hostess of the year. Hostess with the
mostess? Yes, that would be me. I watched the room explode
with activity as I sat on top of the large grand piano in the
ballroom.

The night was warmer than usual, and despite the skies
rumbling, very little rain fell, allowing for the entire space,
both outside and in, to explode with people. Candles dripping
with wax hung from candelabras on each wall. Skulls sat
randomly placed amongst black silk and festive gothic fall
decor. Dark club music played over the sound system as
humans scattered around talking to friends, pouring beer from
the kegs, hanging out by the bonfire, and dancing.

In a word, it was perfect.

I sipped on my wine as my eyes followed Cassian once
more. I would give him this - the masks? They were scary as
fuck.

No, really. Each of my men was wearing all black with those wicked silver monster masks in place. They were hovering nearby but also allowing enough space so that people felt they could socialize. I didn't fully buy it. Nour leaned next to me against the piano as I ran my hand through his hair, narrowing my eyes once again on my target.

I knew that Cassian wasn't completely relaxed. I could tell. His eyes kept moving towards me whenever I looked away, and his magic was running loops around my own in a teasing pattern. He was a damn good faker, though.

Laughter rang out as the room pulsed with the only type of magic that humans did have... sexual tension. Literally, this room was everything that embodied high school, and it was glorious to see. It was also why everyone was paying attention to my interactions with my men. It was unique and gossip-worthy. Very, very high school.

I'd given up on hiding our relationships, because who the hell knew how long I'd even be at school. It wasn't worth staying away from them and risking other women talking to or hitting on them, frankly. Plus, the guys seemed to love it. Even Ramsey, despite my teasing from earlier. In fact, I think he may have felt it as almost more of an incentive to touch me. I think he was a bit competitive, whether he would admit to it or not.

I could tell it made Fox happy, his eyes finding mine from where he sat looking absolutely lethal with his brother. I tried to not smirk as I watched the two of them say something in a quiet tone, wondering if Cassian had told him about our little bet. Honestly, having Fox join in could only make it even more fun.

After all, *three is a party,* right? So what the hell did that make nine?

Rowan stood with someone from our highschool, I

wanted to say his name was something that started with a 'B,' but I wasn't positive. I inhaled and realized that he was a shifter of some kind. Not one I recognized, but his scent had a similar tone to Maya and her mates. Interesting, I hadn't realized that there were a lot of shifters at our school. Then again, up until a month ago I hadn't known anyone but my coven, really.

August was sitting with River as the two of them relaxed into some of the comfortable seating I'd rented for the night. It was plush, and the blood red added to the very 'vampire-ish' vibe of the party. Or maybe that was just me hoping Fox would become my Dracula again?

Ramsey caught my gaze as he walked across the ballroom carrying a drink for his brother and himself. I smiled as he handed one to Nour and ran a hand up my leg before squeezing it firmly. See? Like okay, Mr. Touchy. Not that I minded, but I call shit on it being 'protective.' I think the bastard was possessive, just like the rest of us.

See? I was being fair! I even included my fucking self.

"I'm going to walk around the perimeter," he told Nour as I scowled.

"Ramsey," I complained, deciding I liked him where he was. "Stay here and party."

He grinned. "Tell you what, sunshine. After this run, I will."

Liar. I watched him walk off and wondered what it would take to get the man to loosen up. I had to say, though, ever since our conversation earlier, he seemed to have relaxed a tiny bit. His energy seemed stronger, as if he was motivated. It was hot.

Side note, *where the hell was Everett? No. Really. That was a massive fucking concern.*

I slipped off the piano as I told Nour I was going to

look for him, and he headed towards the twins. Oddly enough, the three of them seemed to get along fairly well. Actually, everyone seemed to like Nour, so that wasn't very odd, really. He was so lovable... *likeable*, he was totally likeable.

"Nova!" A charming voice called out as I turned to see *what's-his-name* from the other day in the lunchroom walking over to me. How could I not remember his name? He was the kid who wanted me to sit with Tara and the others... Maker! I was literally the worst at this.

"Hey," I offered with a slightly forced smile. I could see that he looked a bit tipsy, which had me crossing my arms, not liking how he swayed towards me.

I hadn't interacted with a lot of men before the mages came around, and any I did tended to make me feel uncomfortable. Yes, I know it was shocking considering how I acted around my men, but it was true. With that being said, now that I was aware of them, I felt even more fucking uncomfortable around other men. I blamed my magic, because she made me feel almost twitchy, as if she knew their energies weren't familiar nor the ones we wanted.

"I just wanted to let you know," he grinned, downing his beer, "how fucking awesome this is."

"I am so glad you are enjoying it," I replied as I felt the air around me tighten. Oh man.

See? Here I had been worried about where my psycho was. It was very clear that he was on his way over to me right now, and I didn't even have to fucking look.

"No, really," he moved closer, putting a hand on my shoulder and making me realize he was *way* more than tipsy, "you should have invited me over sooner."

Did he not realize I lived with not only my 'boyfriend' but seven other men? Also, can we talk about what a lightweight this kid was? Or maybe he was just using it as an excuse to touch me. That seemed far more realistic.

Before I could respond, a solid arm wrapped around my stomach as Everett let out a low growl. There he was! Found him! I tilted my head up and tossed him a smile, his eyes relatively amused at my expression.

"I missed you," I teased softly as he kissed the top of my head.

"Wait..." The kid frowned, making Everett's jaw harden as he looked at him. "Is it true? Are you fucking all of them? Hell. I didn't realize you were into that. The boys and I on the team would fucking die for a chance at you--"

Ever froze as I closed my eyes and exhaled. Oh, *what's-his-name.* Why did he have to go there? Also, can we talk about how this man was an expert at turning women off with two sentences? Who said 'would fucking die for a chance *at* you'? Like, not 'with' me but 'at' me. He was gross.

"Nova," Ever warned softly.

Yeah, I wasn't going to deny him this one.

"No killing," I chided as I met him with a stern gaze. He narrowed his eyes at me before nodding sharply, grabbing the kid by his shoulder. I watched as Rowan and Fox followed him, looking thrilled, leaving me shaking my head in amusement.

What?

They probably wouldn't kill him. Probably.

Hey! At least I knew they could dispose of a body properly. It was an important element of manners as a serial killer, after all. Because let's be clear... we could call this whatever we wanted to, but half the time? We killed people for fun.

I mean, usually they deserved it... but restraining them would have probably served a similar purpose. Not for us though. No, our natural instincts called for blood, so they died. Brutally. I wasn't judging, rather condoning if we were being honest, but I just didn't think we should bother lying to ourselves.

Intertwining my fingers and looking back over to where Cassian sat, my lips tilted up. Nour was talking to his brother, who had returned from his perimeter sweep, so I sauntered over to Cass, standing in front of him and leaning down to kiss him lightly.

"Nova," he chuckled.

"What?" I teased. "I can't kiss you?"

"Kissing isn't the problem," he growled, tugging me onto his lap. Maker. Now I was straddling him in the middle of our party. This was bad.

"What's the problem?" I asked curiously.

"The problem is that if you keep it up I may fuck you right here in front of everyone," he smirked. It was dirty and hot.

"I thought you were very confident about your control?" I countered.

"I was more referring to when you beg me to cut you out of this little outfit," he grinned, his hands gripping my waist and pulling me against him so that we were almost flush against one another. I wasn't positive, but with the slight shift of magic I sensed, I was almost damn positive my other guys were spread out near us as a cover. Not that I was worried in this shadowed corner out of view from a bunch of drunk highschool students who were partying obliviously to our actions, but it was still appreciated.

"Cut me out of it?" I let out a small sound. "I don't want you ruining it--"

I let out a moan as his lips met mine, my hips rolling against his hard length I could feel through his jeans. My breathing was fast as I felt his one hand reach up to grasp my hair in a firm hold, rooting me in place as a wave of dominance seemed to crawl over me, forcing me to listen to him.

"I don't think you are really worried about that," he whispered, my control faltering as he ran his fingers down my spine, causing me to arch into him.

"You don't know that… Cass," I moaned and shivered, his lips trailing down my neck as I felt myself nearly uttering the words of what I needed from him.

"Baby girl," he chided, "if you aren't quiet, how am I supposed to fuck you in public?"

Holy hell.

"Cass," I whimpered as he offered me a grin and moved his hands down my thighs, running up them before his right hand cupped my breast, his lips trailing my cleavage.

"Yes?" he asked, his eyes filled with knowledge of my soon to be defeat. I needed him to fucking touch me, someway, somehow. Skin to skin.

I leaned in closer, and with all the strength I could manage, I uttered the words, "I still won't beg."

The growl that ripped from his throat had me letting out a laugh as I tried to pull away from him.

This was victory, folks!

I let out a legitimate surprised sound as my back hit a tree. What in the fuck? I blinked, finding Cassian in my space caging me against one of the many trees of the forest behind our house. Well, we were a bit speedy tonight, weren't we? Hopefully no one saw us disappear. The noises of the party were distant, and my fast, light breathing no longer portrayed my small win.

"Nova," he chided as I let out a small yelp, his fingers coming to the top of the delicate lace bodysuit over the rest of my costume. He ripped it like it was fucking paper, the material falling down my legs. "You should know better than to tease me, baby girl."

"*You* were teasing *me!*" I accused as he chuckled and flashed me a cocky smile.

"Be a good girl and turn around," he demanded, his lips melding against mine before I could respond. I let out a moan as I turned and he ran his fingers up my silk undersuit.

"What are you doing?" I moaned as his lips traced my neck. I jumped as I felt something cold press against my skin, causing me to freeze.

"I told you," he drew what I realized was a blade across my skin and to the start of the outfit I wore, "I was going to cut you out of this."

Lust rolled over me at the prospect of danger as I let out a small whimper, his groan worth it as he began to drag the sharp edge down the material, the pieces falling off my skin with ease. I knew he wouldn't hurt me, but the chance he could knick my skin had me wanting to see my blood on his lips as his twin had earlier.

"Maker," he snarled as he easily snapped off my thong, leaving me in nothing but my boots, pressed up against a tree, his hands teasing my skin. I was so wet I could feel it dripping on my thighs as I shook with the anticipation of what he would do next.

"Cassian," I whispered and finally gave in. "Please?"

His entire frame froze as I felt his smile against the back of my neck. "Please what, Nova?"

"Please fuck me," I moaned. "Hell, just fucking touch me at this point."

My eyes nearly rolled to the back of my head as his large fingers skimmed my center, causing my knees to nearly go weak. His voice was rough and edged, "Have you been soaked like this all night, Nova? Soaked and wanting to beg me to fuck you?"

Yes.

"No," I growled as he let out a dark dangerous laugh.

"Liar." I tried to turn to see him but instead he tugged me against him, his now bare length sliding between my parted thighs as I arched my ass back into him. Oh shit. I looked down as his length nudged against my clit, his metal piercing making my eyes flutter shut.

"Cass," I groaned, feeling literally pained at my frustration.

"Tell the truth, Nova," he demanded. His voice held a thread of warning and dominance, something that had me giving in almost immediately.

"Yes, I've been wet all day wanting you to fuck me," I snarled slightly as I felt his magic collapse over me as if that was exactly what he wanted.

"Good, baby girl. Now stay quiet as I fuck you until you pass out." He accented his words by slamming home and making me cry out his name, my face turned to the side against the tree. Holy hell. He was fucking huge. I arched further as his hands gripped my breasts tightly, making my pussy convulse with pleasure.

"Holy fuck, you feel amazing. This feels fucking great," I admitted, my breathing rough.

"Fuck yeah it does, baby," he snarled, his hand wrapping around my hair. "And you're going to let me have this whenever I want from now on, right, baby girl? Even if it's in the middle of the fucking cafeteria, you're going to let me slide into this tight. Fuckable. Pussy.``

I started to cry out his name as he covered my mouth, his movements sharp, deep, and demanding. I had no idea Cassian would be so into dirty talk… lies, I did know that. I could feel the man molding my fucking center to his cock as he bounced me off of him, my ass slapping across his abdomen as he gripped my throat, making me tip my head up to kiss him. I moaned into it and whispered his name.

Something about his name on my lips clearly triggered him. The bastard spun me around so fast I barely had time to realize he'd picked me up before he was slamming back into me.

"Shit!" I gasped as he began to bounce me on his cock, my back against the rough tree, something that hurt but accented how fucking good he felt buried inside of me. My magic tightened on him possessively as I felt something very dangerous building between us, as if an explosion was about to go off. I gripped Cassian's face, my hands pulling him forward so that his lip ring pressed against my searing skin.

"Nova," his voice was rough as all of the cockiness from before slipped away, leaving just the two of us. I pressed my forehead against his as he continued to drill into me, his mouth holding back my screams as my legs began to tremble. I could feel my center tightening as that magical fucking climax grew.

Before I realized what I was doing I'd wrenched my fingers into Cassian's hair and was biting down on his lip, causing something in him to set off. No really. Motherfucker lost it. I cried out as my back hit the forest floor and he began to slam into me. My back arched as he bit down on my neck, causing me to reach that fucking pinacle. I exploded on his cock as he let out a low, dangerous groan.

"This is mine," he snarled, rubbing my clit as I let out another moan at the overstimulation. "You're fucking mine, Nova. Tell me you know that."

"I'm yours and you're mine, Cassian," I whispered as he growled and continued to fuck me. I had no idea where time even went as I gripped onto him hoping that I wouldn't be lost in the fucking explosion that was us. Because it was totally possible that I would lose myself forever in him.

"Nova!" he roared into my neck as he slammed home one last time, balls deep and causing my eyes to flutter shut. The tress around us felt as though they were shaking as I let out a soft, tired moan from underneath the muscular sex god bastard.

Oh wow. Just wow.

"Cassian," I whispered after a few moments of silence, "that was fucking amazing."

His voice was dangerously soft as he nipped my collarbone, still buried inside of me. "Nova, amazing doesn't cover that…"

No it didn't. He pulled back, his hard cock trailing cum out of my pussy as he held himself above me, smirking as my eyes darted down. One hand grasped his face while the other moved down his chest, my fingers closing around the cross dangling from his neck. His eyes closed as something dark passed over his face.

"What is this?" I asked softly, feeling like now was as good a time as any to ask.

"My grandmother made me wear it growing up," he answered truthfully, his eyes meeting mine.

My head tilted, "Was she important to you?"

A shadow crossed behind his gaze as he shook his head. "More as a reminder to not be her. To be everything that she wasn't."

Oh.

Before I could respond, a rustling of leaves sounded and Cass, in an impressive move, had his shirt pulled over my body and his jeans belted with his amazing cock put away. *Sad. Very sad.*

I relaxed a bit when I realized that it was August. His amusement was obvious.

"Hey you two love birds," he chimed, looking over me with heat before Cassian helped me up. "You can probably guess who is freaking out about you leaving the property wards, but they would like you to return."

Cassian muttered something as I let out a small knowing laugh. I reached down and ripped out the rest of my lace bodysuit from my boots and collected the pieces, scowling.

"What the hell am I going to wear for the rest of the night?" I demanded of both boys, who looked suspiciously thrilled at the destroyed scraps.

Also, could we just go back to that little bit of knife play action Cass did? Like, could we do that again? I would like to explore that option, thank you very much. I promised myself next time we would take our time and also that I would do some research ahead of time. I wasn't saying that I wanted Cass to hurt me, exactly… but I wasn't opposed to experimenting. I was a total adrenaline junkie, and having that knife so close to me? Well, that danger and the trust I had in him was fucking addicting.

"Guess you will have to put on something comfortable," Cassian suggested, grinning.

I narrowed my eyes. *Game on.*

NOVA

"T his is worse," Ramsey determined with a slight growl to his tone. "Somehow this is worse."

"You are so cranky." I bopped him on the nose as he let out a dangerous rumble. "Lighten up, it's not even eleven yet." But man, were people fucking wasted.

"You are wearing lingerie," he snarled as if I was the crazy one.

"You're being dramatic," I smirked. He wasn't. I was wearing very much exactly that.

As I mentioned, I loved lingerie, and my collection had only grown more colorful the longer I had been with these guys. Right after returning from the Horde, my package delivery had come from one of my favorite shops out of Milan, and now I had literally fifty or so different options. Every color of the damn rainbow.

Plus, my new outfit wasn't that bad. Half the girls here were wearing less clothes than I was now, so I was hardly worried.

Deciding I was going to go as a Victoria's Secret angel, I had slipped away to my room, seeking vengeance for my amazing pirate costume that had been destroyed at the hands of a knife-wielding metal mage. My entire body was still rolling with heat after his intense use of it, and I couldn't help but feel like I'd won our bet a bit. Like, okay, I'd begged, but he'd slammed me up against a tree after cutting me out of my costume so he could fuck me faster? Chicken or egg, am I right?

Ramsey grasped my jaw and motioned to my outfit. It was a pair of bright purple stilettos and a tiny silk slip dress that was a black, dipping to my lower back with high slits on either side of my hips. I unfortunately didn't have the wings to go with it, but I had sprinkled some glitter on me for good effect.

Alright, so I was essentially wearing heels and a night-gown. Oh well.

"Tell that to Cassian," I pointed out as the smug bastard smirked at me from the couch. "He ruined my pirate costume."

Ramsey grunted, sitting down as if giving up. Well, I thought that was the case, until he pulled me down on top of his lap. My eyes widened as he offered me a 'deal with it' look. I couldn't help but smile. Looking around, I realized that Fox, Rowan, and Everett were suspiciously absent. Cassian, as if realizing my train of thought, chuckled and poured another drink for himself and Nour.

"River," I caught his attention from where he was looking outside in thought. August was standing out there, his magic floating through the space, and I could tell the men were keeping tabs on everything tonight. Probably because of what John's mom had warned us about. I nearly shook my head at the thought of her. How odd.

I had to appreciate that she would go out of her way to even offer me that vague warning. It made me want to destroy the patriarchal restraints on the coven all the more. I promised myself if I ever took over after killing my dad, I would ban that bullshit. It was only fair.

"Yes, butterfly?" he asked, crouching down because of where I sat perched on Ramsey's leg. I think the demi-god had been attempting to cover more of my body by having me sit, but instead the slit on the side had risen up more. Don't think he didn't know, either, considering his massive hand was wrapped around my thigh.

Protective my ass.

"Where are the crazies?" I tilted my head in interest. If they were off doing more crazy things, why had I not been invited? Besides the obvious that I had been being railed into a fucking tree outside.

He ran a hand through his hair. "Are you actually asking?"

"No, I am fake asking." I blinked innocently as he shook his head, looking amused.

"They are upstairs with Jason and some of his friends, who were talking about you in a not so," he exhaled, "polite light."

Ah, so that was the name of the asshole who'd wanted a chance *at* me.

Oh man.

I stood up, kissing his cheek before promptly leaving the room. What? Someone had to save the stupid humans, because let's face it, if I left them with Everett, Fox, and Rowan? I might as well kill them myself.

As I walked towards the stairs, I began humming to myself, wondering where exactly they'd chosen to go. I was distracted enough that when I nearly bumped into someone I'd been authentically surprised.

"Tara?" I asked curiously. Had I invited her? Well, I

DESCENDANT OF SIN

suppose I'd sent out a mass invitation to everyone but the children of my father's coven... but still. Weird that you would show up to the house of the woman you tried to kill, right? I just felt like that shit wasn't polite.

"Nova!" she smiled. Her eyes were bloodshot but her smile was friendly. "I just wanted to tell you what a fantastic party this is. Truly amazing."

I stiffened as she grabbed my hand, squeezing it tightly between hers, making me feel almost sick to my stomach. Was I crazy, or was there something seriously off about this chick? Tara McGaffrey gave me honest-to-god chills. I wasn't just saying that because she tried to kill me, either. No, this was way more than that.

Like, by all means, she should have been very un-scary, considering she was my size and very human... but my instincts were telling me to be wary.

"I am so glad you are enjoying it." I tried to tug my hand back, but she kept it and moved closer. Ah. Shit. What the hell?

"When I got your invite text, I was so thrilled," she said wistfully. "I know we got off on the wrong foot, but really, I've always wanted to be close to you."

I blinked, my eyes flickering down to her grip on my hand. Was this the time to bust her ass with lightning? I mean, hell, am I crazy or is she hitting on me?

"Baby?" Everett's voice echoed as my head snapped up. Tara made a frustrated noise but immediately let go of my hand, all but disappearing. My mouth popped open as my psycho offered me a confused look.

"What was that?" he asked roughly.

I inhaled, shaking my head, "No idea, babe. Oh -- wait."

Leaning up on my toes, I slid my thumb across a blood

123

splatter on his otherwise clean face. I smiled and pulled back as he offered me an expression of pure affection.

"Are they dead?" I asked curiously. I was semi-hoping not. That would be a lot of deaths to hide. Plus, I didn't think they really deserved it. I mean, the guys were total assholes, and not even just today. I knew that from being in school with them. But death? Nah.

But you try telling that to my crazy bastards.

"No, unfortunately," he chuckled. "Rowan and Fox are just fucking with them. Those guys are such dicks, the shit they say about people is disgusting. And that's coming from me, so it's well deserved."

"Were you feeling a bit stabby, Ever?" I asked sympathetically.

Come on, we all knew this was larger than just the guys upstairs. These men weren't made for human life and high school. I was starting to think that I wasn't either. We were just built differently. More savage. More wild. Far more exciting.

His lips melted against mine, and he kissed me so hard I got dizzy. When he pulled back, his voice was filled with honesty. "This is why I love you, Nova."

"Because I support your homicidal tendencies?" I just needed to make sure.

"Yep." He popped the 'p' while leading me back towards the ballroom, my body relaxed against his. Alright, I could live with that answer.

Before we turned down the back hallway, I heard someone call Everett's name. I frowned as he made a confused noise, both of us turning back to a woman who was returning from using the bathroom. She was in this tiny little sparkly dress with white fluffy angel wings and a halo. She was also wasted.

"Oh my god!" She smiled, out of breath and flushed. "I have been wanting to talk to you forever! My name is Claire, from your history class."

Ever blinked at her as he looked down at me. I cracked a smile, realizing he had no idea what to do. I patted his shoulder and stepped up to Claire.

"Hey Claire?" I asked as she looked down at me, swaying and frowning.

"Oh, you're Nova, right?" she asked, confused as her small nose twitched. "You are the one everyone always talks about. You're not that pretty."

This bitch.

"Right," I nodded, not feeling bad about what I was going to do next. "You know what, I have something really special to show you. Don't worry, Ever's coming with."

Leading her forward toward the front door, I ignored her attempts to hit on my mage. As I reached the door I took her wings off her, and she frowned. She didn't try to stop me, though. Instead she just stared at me like I was the weirdo.

"What are you doing?" She tried to tug back as I handed the wings to Ever. I then promptly opened the door, pushed her out, and watched as she stumbled onto the grass. I proceeded to shut the door and lock it for good measure. I heard her yell something, but I just smiled, taking her wings and shimmying them on.

"You have no idea how upset I was that I didn't have wings for this," I mentioned to Everett as he offered me a big smile.

"Nova," he chuckled, shaking his head.

"Not pretty, my ass," I mumbled, putting my head up high. "Come on, let's go back to the ballroom so I can kiss and dance with each one of you. I'm tired of people being confused."

"Yeah." He nipped my ear as he followed behind me, an arm wrapped around my waist. "You know you could just make honest men out of us, Nova, and marry us in the Horde. Then no one would be confused."

I looked up at him, shocked. "That's a thing? You can marry multiple people?"

"Yep." He looked happy at something… *oh fuck.*

"Hey," I wiggled my finger at him while walking backwards. "I was just curious. No one said anything about marriage, you lunatic."

"You didn't say no. Still haven't," he pointed out with an innocent shrug.

I shook my head, laughing, and refused to respond to his insanity. Good to know, though, that I could marry multiple men… I mean, if I ever wanted to. I should have probably realized that already considering Vegas's and Gray's situations.

As we entered the ballroom, Nour offered me an interested look. "Nice wings, moonbeam."

"Thank you." I twirled and sat down next to him, tucking my leg beneath me and leaning against my arm. Everett was relaying what happened to the others in far more detail than I was about to. "I stole it from some chick that thought Ever and probably the rest of you all were single."

He turned towards me so that we were facing one another. "I'm not single?" Nour asked, smiling at my slip. I bit my lip and let out a small hum, wondering if I would take the leap. I mean, frankly, I was wearing wings and feeling pretty fabulous, so it was probably going to happen.

"Do you want to be single?" I hedged, still feeling a tiny bit insecure.

Nour brought a hand under my chin as I looked up at him trying to appear relaxed even though I felt anything but at the moment. I had been lying to myself when it came to Nour. I didn't just like the man, I had a massive crush on him, and now that I wasn't mad at him... well, I had no idea how to deal with this.

"No," he admitted quietly. "I don't want to be single when it comes to you, moonbeam."

A moment of hesitation occurred on my end as I absorbed his words. Then I took a leap, my lips pressing against his as I leaned forward. My fingers slid through his dark hair as I finally let the emotions I'd been feeling for him flood my magic. His low, simmering magic began to bubble as his lips moved against mine, his hands instantly gripping my waist.

I couldn't help it. The truth was? I didn't want Nour to be fucking single either. He was mine.

Holy hell. I was kissing Nour. I was literally fucking kissing him. After a summer filled with sexual tension and angst, my lips were against his. His hands and his familiar scent rolled over my body as my hormones began to go haywire. Suddenly, I could not get fucking close enough to him.

Damn. I was a mess today.

The rolling heat under my skin was like a fucking wildfire. Affection, desire, our history together all fueled it like oxygen to an open flame. Before I knew it I was on Nour's lap, my legs on either side of his large frame and his taste exploding against my lips. This was all before his magic slammed into me, his control dipping as I felt a solid wall of fire sear my skin in a pleasurable hit.

His god magic was filled with power and intensity. While the mages' magic contrasted mine in an intoxicating way, Ramsey's and Nour's complemented mine and snapped a connection into place in a way I would have never expected. I shivered as his tongue traced the seam of my lips, deepening the kiss even further as he explored my mouth. I rocked against his steel-hard cock underneath me, feeling on the verge of letting out a moan.

I pulled back finally, needing some air, as my face turned pink from the eyes I could feel staring into us. Nour watched me with wide eyes for a moment, pressing his head against my collarbone and pulling me close silently.

"Wow," I admitted quietly, feeling nervous at his silence.

Nour gently placed me down next to him and pressed a kiss to my forehead, his long frame expanding up as he stood. Without another word, the man walked towards the patio, running a hand through his hair and looking... distraught?

"If anyone else walks away from me today, I'm going to lose it," I mumbled, trying to hide the insecurity that washed over me.

I felt confusion and hurt swarm me as I watched him walk outside. Why did he walk away? Had I done something wrong? I felt tears prick my eyes as I shook myself, trying to gather myself before someone like... River saw me. Who was now sitting where Nour had been, his firm hand cupping my jaw.

"Butterfly?" he asked quietly, his eyes flashing with a darkness that I knew had nothing to do with me. I inhaled, shaking my head as a surge of dizziness ran over me. I didn't exactly trust myself to say anything right now, so I focused on controlling my emotions.

"Do you want to get some air?" River asked, looking concerned as I heard Everett say something sharp, probably in response to how I was acting. I tried to shake myself. This wasn't their problem. This was my own. I swallowed and stood up.

"I'm good," I mumbled and brushed imaginary lint off my dress before looking up. "I'm going to go, um, step outside…" I didn't finish my sentence as I walked towards the open patio door. Instantly, I let out an exhale as the cool air hit my flushed face and made me feel a bit less dizzy. Thank the Maker.

What did I do wrong? *Had* I done something wrong? I think the mood of the night had just caught up to me, and, well, his fucking words of course…

Ramey's warm scent surrounded me. "You didn't do anything wrong, Nova."

"Yeah," I offered with a dry smile, looking up at him. "I'm sure he was just so overwhelmed by my kissing skills that he needed a moment, right?"

See? I was doing fucking great! Could someone that was not doing great be *this* sarcastic? Of course they couldn't! Yeah… I was bullshitting myself.

"Sunshine." Ramsey hedged, his hand resting on my back.

"I just need a minute," I said with a tight smile before stepping towards the growing bonfire. The thick forest sparkled with mist as rain fell, the thunderstorm growing as my emotions turned. I could feel my men's eyes on me, but as I sat on the cement bench outside and breathed in the cool air, I began to feel a bit centered.

Had I read that situation wrong?

He had been saying that he liked me, right?

I mean, he said he didn't want to be single when it came to me… how else was I supposed to take that?

Hell. How had I messed that up?

I groaned, putting my hands over my eyes as I closed them. See what I got for making the first move? Awkwardness and insecurity. So much flippin' awkwardness.

"Wildcat?" Rowan's voice rang out. I looked up at the man rounding the bonfire. It was clear he didn't know what was going on because he seemed confused. I put my arms out as he scooped me up and I let out a soft hum, running my nose in his neck.

"Row-baby," I sighed. "Thank you, I needed that hug."

I know it was weird to say, but I felt inexplicably closer to Rowan than before. While he hadn't said much earlier, it was a hell of a lot more than I'd known before. It felt so good to know he trusted me like that.

Didn't change the fact that I wanted to kill his father.

"What happened?" he asked confusedly, pulling back as my toes touched back down.

"Nothing." I shook my head and ran my fingers along his dark shirt collar, wondering where his mask went. I smirked slightly, trying to hide my feelings. "Did you have fun upstairs?"

His eyes sparkled. "Didn't even use my magic, but that asshole deserved more hits than I got in. I told him if he didn't admit to roids to the faculty and football team, I would find him again. Then he cried."

I let out a soft smile. "You guys are insane."

"About you." He nipped my nose. "Now what is going on?"

How did I explain that this party, despite what I thought originally, wasn't really what I had needed? Don't get me wrong, it was fun, and teasing the boys had been even funner… but the party was going to end soon, and then what would I be left with? A dark past that I was avoiding dealing with by pretending I was having over-the-top nightmares and not legitimate flashbacks… oh, and apparently several assholes that were draining others' magic.

Yeah. So, you could say I was feeling a bit odd. Honestly, right now I wanted pajamas and cuddles. I sounded like a total baby, but that was the truth of it.

"Nova." Rowan cupped my jaw as I met his baby blues, bringing a hand up to touch his dark eyebrow piercing.

"You are so handsome," I said softly.

Rowan grinned, his ears heating as a pulse of affection went through my head. "Thanks, wildcat. But come on, tell me what's up."

"You're persistent," I grumbled softly, not bothering to hide my obviously hurt pride. "Alright. So I kissed Nour, and then he walked away without saying anything, so now I just feel... weird? Yeah. Weird."

"Nova," he offered an understanding look, "maybe he just needed a moment?"

"Do you want to go on a walk?" I tried to distract from it as he nodded, his hand wrapping around mine. Turning, he motioned to someone, I assumed the others, as we walked around the large estate.

I let out a soft hum as our hands swung between us, our path taking us towards the side of the house and the forested tree line. I slid off my heels before stepping through the thick trees, just enough to find my way to a comfortable branch that had fallen over that I could sit down on.

How did I explain that the thing with Nour wasn't just about him? That it was about my own insecurities? Honestly, I was worried about my part in their lives. I didn't have a mating bond like Maya seemed to have with her mates, nor were my men like Gray's royal guards. Hell, I didn't even have a lot of history like Vegas did with her men.

It was just us. At this moment. In this insane plot of fate we'd found ourselves in. There was one very real question rolling through my head. One I normally ignored... *how could I make so many men happy?*

Obviously I was awesome and shit, but sometimes it felt like... maybe I wasn't as badass as I thought. Eight men's hearts were no joke, and as much as I teased, I didn't want to play games with them. Just how I hoped they wouldn't play games with me.

"Row?" I asked softly as he watched me, waiting patiently for me to get my thoughts together. "You guys aren't going anywhere, right?"

Rowan reared back slightly before snapping to right in front of me, crouching down. "Fuck. Of course not, Nova. Why would you ask that?"

I shrugged. "I don't know. I mean, hell, I don't usually do this insecure bullshit, but... I guess I'm just worried this is a lot more than you signed up for. All this god shit? We all know where this is headed, and I don't think this is going to get any less complicated. I don't want you to regret getting involved--"

Rowan pressed a thumb to my lips, a low rumble breaking through his chest. "Nova, I can only speak for myself... maybe Auggy also." I couldn't help but meet his smile at that before he continued.

"I would follow you anywhere. I don't want you to think for a moment that my loyalty or emotions are dependent on the fucking predictability of our life. Of situations we can't control and wouldn't want to anyway. Whether you want to go to the God realm or stay here in Seattle, I am one hundred percent behind you."

My eyes pricked with tears as I buried my nose in his chest, asking my question in a muffled tone. "Why?"

His magic tightened around me like dark ink brushing over my skin before tilting my head up so that I had to meet his gaze completely. I could feel his thumb running over my wrist as a vulnerable look flashed on his face, making me feel like both of us were very young in the moment. Or maybe it was that we had so much responsibility that, for the first time in forever, I felt like an insecure eighteen-year-old. It was fucked up.

"I think you know why, Nova."

I think I did as well.

Before I could respond, the air charged. Immediately, I turned towards the emptiness of the forest… that was no longer empty. I let out a curse as a pulse of power from multiple witches hit the wards hard enough that they wavered, making Rowan growl.

I felt as though everything happened so fast in that moment - the sky crackled with thunder as the witches' power breached the wards, causing the earth to buckle underneath me like a wave, which sent me flying into the air.. My head cracked against one of the trees as I groaned, a current of magic hitting my chest immediately after as I let out a scream.

"Nova!" Rowan's roar echoed in my ear as my eyes fluttered shut. I could hear his grunt of pain, and suddenly it felt like everything went fuzzy.

They were hurting him.

Lightning flashed behind my eyes as my body began to convulse, my heart seizing as my nails dug into the earth. A scream broke through the space as I realized it wasn't Rowan. It wasn't me either. No. It was my magic hurting others.

My magic was doing what it did best.

It created chaos and destroyed everything in its path. Every inch of my body warmed as the ink embedded into it by the gods literally sparkled and began to spin, faster and faster. I could feel them twisting and turning under my skin like writing snakes. Energy coursed through me in rippling waves as my newly acquired death magic jumped to the forefront of everything at once.

Painful cries screamed in my ears as I felt myself latch on

to the witches around me. I dragged them down as I opened the earth, and my eyes closed as the ground broke around me, instantly swallowing them. Thunder vibrated the earth as black fog surrounded me, whispering against my skin and making me shiver. I could feel demonic claws pulling at me but I resisted, knowing that the earth wouldn't consume its own.

Finally, when all of those transgressors were swallowed, the night was preserved. My eyes opened to look at the forest canopy above. Immediately, my vision was filled with warm blue eyes that I knew to be Rowan's.

Blood covered his face, but his life force felt healthy as he clasped my cheeks. He was talking, but I couldn't hear him. Ink covered his hair and his fingertips, the magic brushing over me in comforting waves.

He was safe.

He was alive.

"--- Nova!" Rowan's voice finally broke through as everything came back to me, my ears popping as I winced. "Wildcat, you have to tell me you're okay. Please Nova--"

"I'm okay," I whispered, closing my eyes as he shouted something. I couldn't hear it though, because the world began to spin around me. I fell into the deep subconscious of my mind, and everything went black around me. Comforting darkness took the place of my consciousness.

See? I was totally fine.

RAMSEY

"Where the fuck is Nour?" Everett snapped as I met his gaze quietly before looking back down at Nova's sleeping and peaceful expression. I brushed her wavy hair from her face while resisting the urge to pull her into my lap so that I could ensure she was comfortable. Ensure that she would never be as goddamn pale and sick-looking as she was when I had first lifted her off the ground.

I think that image would forever be ingrained in my head. Her multicolored hair covered in dirt and her costume wings covered in blood and broken underneath her body. Her small frame bent at an angle that sure as fuck wasn't natural.

Everything about the moment had caused pure, unadulterated fear to course through me. She looked so delicate, so breakable in that moment. You know, after she slaughtered a dozen or so witches and allowed the earth to consume them.

I couldn't fault the other men on how protective they were because I fell into the same hole. Most of the time, the power coursing through Nova had me knowing she could handle everything and anything. She had so much life to her it made her seem ten times larger than she actually was. But then there were moments like this, when I remembered just how small she was. She may be immortal, but that didn't mean she couldn't be severely injured. Broken. Something I planned on preventing on every level possible.

I rubbed my chest, feeling a slight squeeze because of the fucking fear of Ra I'd felt hit me right in the chest at the sound of Rowan's demand for help as Nova screamed.

Needless to say, Nova's party had been forcibly cleared out in seconds.

"I have no idea," I answered truthfully. It wasn't that I didn't care where my brother was,, but I knew the man well enough to know that he would return after he thought through whatever was plaguing him. Because mark my words, something was bothering him, and it was fairly easy to assume what. I just didn't know if he would return tonight or not.

Nour and I had never been particularly similar in personality, but that was just our dynamic. And while we weren't extremely close, he was still my fucking twin. I knew him really fucking well, and I also knew that he wore his emotions on his sleeve. He was hopeful, optimistic, and a goddamn romantic.

Nour had spent his entire life training to be one of the best fighters in the Scarabs while trying to earn the affection of our father, a man who only respected one thing- violence. A military unit that existed to protect someone didn't fall under that category, apparently.

I knew all of these things about Nour. Just like how I was very well aware that he loved Nova. More than he had ever loved anyone before. It was clear as day to probably everyone but her.

That was mostly because I was pretty damn sure I knew why she had been so angry with him originally. Why she'd been so upset when he'd left and then come back into her life without explanation. She hadn't been upset as much as heart-broken. It explained why my brother had stayed in Seattle for such a long time this summer, and after meeting Nova, I couldn't blame him in the fucking least.

When Nova kissed Nour tonight, I knew he had freaked out. Not because of the kiss, but he probably had to force himself to leave before he admitted he was in love with her. That was my best guess, at least. It didn't remove the urge I had to hit him over the head, though.

I sighed. "My brother isn't the best when dealing with emotions that are more intense than what he is used to. He'll be back, but not until he's ready."

River sighed, sitting on the other side of Nova, as he looked over the rest of the room. Rowan passed out, his skin nearly green because of Nova's death magic that had begun to affect him, as August paced back and forth, looking at Rowan and then at Nova. Fox and Cassian were staring into the fire-place, occasionally talking but otherwise silent. The entire room was tense and worried. Everett and his fucking crazy didn't help.

Everett let loose a low growl. "If he hadn't been such an asshole, Nova and Rowan would have never gone on that goddamn walk to begin with."

But they had, and Nova had countered the attack that had been thrown at them. The woman was growing more lethal and dangerous with every single day that passed. If it wasn't so fucking beautiful, it would be scary as hell. Alright, it was possible that it was both.

"And I can assure you that when he comes back he will beat himself up about that," I snapped, feeling defensive over my twin. "You know he'd never put Nova in harm's way purposefully. None of us could have guessed they would have attacked or that they would find a way to breach the wards. They've upped their game, and we essentially gave them the perfect fucking opportunity with this party."

Everett snarled, and after River offered him a look, the death mage stalked from the room. We heard something shattering upstairs. I would always stand up for Nour, even if Everett found it annoying. And despite my twin doing stupid shit, I would always be there for him. It had always been that way between us.

Sure, I would call him on his shit, and trust me, when he showed his sorry ass back here in a few hours I was going to probably hit him.... But growing up together? In the God realm where everyone was either violent or a complete asshole? Yeah, we had to rely on one another for strength in the face of having almost no one on our side.

"Ram," Nour's voice was soft and concerned, standing next to me looking nervous. "What if he doesn't like us?"

"He's our father," I stated grimly and clasped his shoulder in a hopefully comforting way. "He has to like us." He didn't actually have to. He honestly probably wouldn't.

At eight, we were both tall and lanky, holding lightweight swords as we stood with other boys and girls our age. Other kids that were descended from minor gods and demi-gods throughout the Egyptian sector of the God realm. I could feel how nervous my twin was, and I hated that. I hated that we even had to attempt to interact with a man that was supposedly our father.

I mean, we'd never met the man, so while we were related biologically, he was far from being someone that I considered a father figure.

A hot wind ran over us, the realm particularly warm today, as I shifted slightly on my feet. When were they going to get here? I was wasting time that I could be using for training, and on top of that, there was a chance that the guy wouldn't even show up.

"I bet your dad won't even show up," a kid next to Nour bit out, echoing my thoughts. Nour let out a growl as I narrowed my eyes at the unimportant asshole, making a note to kick his ass later. He was just bitter because no one recognized the name of his father, being that insignificant, whereas everyone knew who we descended from. In fact, sometimes that legacy felt more like a burden than a blessing.

"Our father will show up," Nour stated, seemingly assured of the fact. I honestly didn't care if he did or not, but I knew it was important to my brother.

A horn sounded as the gates to our training academy swung open, allowing chariots to enter the grounds. The Scarabs academy, founded by the god Set, was a prestigious institution created to protect his legacy. It had been easy for the two of us to get in, and ever since the first day I'd learned to use a sword, I'd been devoted to the cause.

I may hate most of the gods, but I could say that I respected Set. He seemed to have his crap together far more than anyone else here.

I watched as kids scrambled from their neat lines to find their fairly absent father- and mother-figures, begging for some form of attention. I stayed exactly where I was and found myself completely unsurprised when we were the only ones left standing in the waiting formation, no one else entering into the lands.

"He's not coming, is he?" Nour asked softly as I saw him try to blink back disappointment and tears. I offered him a small, sad look as I swallowed back any emotions I'd had towards hoping that our father would give a damn about us.

"Come on," I nudged his shoulder. "We can use the time to practice, he's probably busy with important stuff."

Nour nodded, but we both knew why he hadn't shown up. We were two out of hundreds of children he had. We probably hadn't even made it onto his calendar. That was fine. All that was important was that we had each other and our mom.

At least we could count on that.

Closing my eyes and running a hand down my face, I briefly considered what it would be like if my mom were still around. She would probably be proud of where we had gotten to and surprised we'd done so as fast as we had.

Like ourselves, she'd been a commander in the Scarabs, and when we were around seventeen, we'd received the news that she'd been killed on a mission. It had been painful, because she truly was the only person we had in this world. Well, at the time. Now though? Now we had Nova, and despite being stubborn as fuck, I couldn't deny that Nova was starting to mean... well, everything.

I had faced most of my life without fear. When it came to her, though, I felt like I was plummeting right down to a fate that I knew could only end badly. That type of risk was almost intoxicating, and she herself had an addicting quality. I was obviously attracted to her, but hell if it wasn't far more than just that. There was something about Nova and her magic that just fit like a puzzle piece against my own. It was why she fucking frustrated me so much when she wouldn't just listen to what I was saying.

I didn't expect that to change anytime soon, though; rather, I planned on tying her up at some point just so that her sweet ass would have to listen. Well, that and so I could fuck her all the ways I'd been dreaming of. My cock jumped to life at that thought as I inhaled sharply, trying to not let my thoughts go there right now.

Nova let out a small sigh as she rolled into me, exposing her elegant neck and the symbols that ran down it. My jaw tightened, knowing that when we finally went to the God realm, several things were going to happen. None of them were good.

For one, she was going to garner an insane amount of attention. Not only for being Set's descendant, but because the woman shone like a fucking beacon of light. A stormy, intense beacon that may fry you with lightning. But the key with Nova is that she was… well, so fucking *Nova* that you wouldn't even mind.

I had known a lot of gods and goddesses in the years I had been in this universe, and I could tell you straight and simple… *Nova was the type of woman men died for.* She just had that quality about her. You couldn't help but obsess about her, because she unintentionally filled the space in your soul that was empty. Every breath she took and movement she made spoke to magic and chaos, a tornado you couldn't help but throw yourself into willingly. It was so fucking beautiful. But it was more than that, more than my obsession, that had me worried about the God realm.

I was well aware of just how many cocky assholes lived up in the God realm. If the mages thought the attention Nova received here was bad… they had no idea. I shook my head, feeling a surge of possessiveness and protection that usually came hand-in-hand with any feelings regarding Nova.

Finally, I had a feeling our father was going to make an appearance. Shortly after our mother's death, we had been invited to a party with other members of our command level because we'd made rank. It was the first time we'd ever met our father.

To say we were disappointed was the understatement of the century.

It had been clear right off the bat what a selfish bastard he was, and I had found myself thanking Ra that we hadn't grown up around him to influence our view of the world. It was why most children of the God realm were petty and immature, filled with the same attitude as their power-hungry parents. Upon realizing our relationship to him at the party, he'd begun to brag about us. As if he'd played a role in our achievements. As if he'd even spoken to us before that moment.

He was sorely disappointed to find that I didn't give a hell about what he wanted, including his bragging rights, when I outright rejected him and told him exactly how I felt in front of everyone. It was rather awkward, if we were being honest, but it only seemed to fuel the party, not ruin it.

I shook my head, knowing that the minute Nova came into the equation he was going to try to be part of our life once again, because he would do anything to climb in the Egyptian sector. To say that the revelation of him being Greek had hurt him socially would be an understatement as well.

"Ram." Nova's soft whisper had me looking down to find her lightning eyes focused on me. River's breathing was calm as he slept next to her. I realized a good amount of time had passed and the lights were now dimmed, everyone spread throughout the room sleeping.

"Yeah, sunshine?" I asked softly as she wrapped an arm around my abs, her small yawn against my chest making me smile.

"Promise me," she stated as her eyes filled with a bit of sadness, "if I have a nightmare tonight, that you will make me see the truth. I can't keep living like this."

I tensed. "Nova, are you sure--"

"I'm positive," she nodded, her eyes turning dark. "I need to face the truth. I am so tired of being scared."

As she drifted off at my silence, I considered the implications of what she was saying. The concept of being the one that would release these memories made me sick to my stomach. At the same time, I didn't think I had it in me to tell the woman no. I told her she could trust me and that I would do anything for her. I had to hold true to that, even if it was going to hurt like hell.

I sent a small prayer to the Maker that she wouldn't dream, but almost immediately, I was pulled into her subconscious, slipping like a shadow into the corners of her nightmare. Darkness closed over me, and a cold chill rolled over my skin, revealing the thoughts streaming through her head.

"Mommy?" Nova's soft voice echoed in the space of a bedroom. It appeared to be hers, if I could trust the small bed and finger paintings hung everywhere on the walls. Looking at the small figure, I had to guess she was maybe around five? Possibly younger? In the distance, I could hear screaming ringing through the space. I assume that was what had woken her up to begin with.

I watched as Nova left her bed, my brow creasing as I followed her, knowing that this was going to be fucking torture. Literally. I wanted to stop the dream now, but as she walked down the hallway, already sniffling as if she knew what awaited her, I followed.

Nova had known she wasn't supposed to see what was happening.

How did I know that? When we reached the room with the screams, she turned in the hallway and went down to where a vent connected to the room. I watched in shock as her little hands pulled at the grate, nearly silent over Earnest's yelling and her mother's screams. I followed her through, passing through the wall as we found ourselves back in the closet from before.

I take it that this was a normal place, then, for torture.

"You fucking whore," Earnest growled and hit her so

hard that I could practically hear the rattling of her fucking brain. Nova whimpered but covered her mouth and tucked her chin over her knees, curling into a small ball.

I stilled as her mother laughed, rough and low. "You say the same shit every day, Earnest. Every single day. Does it get you off? Beating me up? You sick fuck."

I stopped myself from pulling Nova out of the dream, feeling like there was something larger here. Call it instinct, and maybe it was, because I'd never heard her mother talk before, but I was starting to believe that their relationship wasn't simply an abusive one. There was a tone to it that made me think back to when we'd interrogated captors.

Earnest roared out and a metal bat sounded as something hit the floor. Her mother laughed, despite the sound of her coughing up blood.

"I will never tell you, Earnest." She was grinning, I could tell. "I will never tell you, and one day, when they come for us, you will be slaughtered."

A gunshot rang out as Nova began crying softly. I didn't hesitate to pull her out of this hell-hole memory, the dream automatically fading...

Nova's small, almost inaudible whimper sounded as she buried her head on my chest, shaking. I had no idea what to do, so I just wrapped my arms around her, pulling her against me as close as possible. I hoped for the fucking both of us that she didn't want to go through each and every goddamn memory. Tears hit my chest, soaking through my shirt, as River's eyes opened in concern. I shook my head as he frowned, seemingly wide fucking awake now.

I wanted to explain, but I felt like that was Nova's place.

Plus, half-asleep Nova, while mourning the loss of her mother, was coursing with another type of energy as well. Angry, seething energy that seemed to pulsate on her skin. If I knew her as well as I thought I did, this would only solidify her plans moving forward. Maybe that was what she'd been afraid of all along. Afraid that she would remember the truth, and all of this, from her father to her past, would become clear. That her path would become clear.

My sunshine was strong, and while I hated putting her through this, I never for a second doubted her ability to deal with it. Nova's bloodline fueled chaos itself, and she breathed magic. Once she detached from any human concepts, which I had a feeling she'd mostly done, there would be nothing stopping her.

I had no doubt the woman was going to bring the God realm to its knees.

I couldn't wait to fucking watch.

NOVA

My eyes fluttered open, feeling gritty and sore, as if I had been crying. I hadn't been, right? Shit. What the hell had happened before I passed out? I let out a small concerned sound, noticing that the normal smells and sights that accompanied my environment were completely absent. Where the fuck was I?

No, seriously, where? I tried to look around, but my body sunk further into the soft texture underneath me, so I froze. Swallowing nervously, I considered the few possibilities that existed.

One: I had died, something that seemed highly unlikely since I'd survived a bullet to the stomach and was supposedly immortal. I would kick Ramsey's ass if he'd been wrong about that.

Two: I had expended so much power that I had fucked it up somehow and was now hanging out in some weird magic in-between. Yeah, those were really the only two viable options. I was betting and hoping on some weird magic fuckery.

The skies above me were far different than Earth's, yet

they were familiar. The reason hit me as I sighed a bit in relief. *This was just like the dream realm I'd been in with Isis.* Although I had to admit that it didn't feel very much like a dream, despite appearing as one. No, I actually felt rather grounded.

The hot sand underneath me shifted further as I rolled to the side, glad that I didn't find myself in quicksand or some bullshit. I looked around as a silent energy vibrated around and through me, making me realize that other than my breathing, the space was absolutely devoid of noise. *This was trippy as hell.* Honestly, the silence was terrifying in a weird way. Almost intoxicating in its depth and power.

A mirrored moon slowly rotated above me as stars twinkled and pulsated like flashing lights in the distance. My eyes tracked the barren, dusty landscape around me, pyramids standing out in the twilight light of the horizon. It was stunning. Picture perfect. And therefore no doubt not real in the least.

"Cousin," a voice purred from behind me and I felt myself relax a bit, turning to meet a familiar face. I never thought I would be so damn pleased to see the god of the afterlife.

My lips pulled into a smile as a serene feeling invaded my bones. I should have guessed that the weird bastard would pull this shit. Maybe I really had died. I mean, I'd passed out from using death magic and then landed here... right?

I felt like I was forgetting something vital between those events, though. Something that tugged at my heart, dangerously sharp. My anxiety was fleeting, as the magic of the realm soothed that.

"Is this the underworld?" I asked curiously, meeting his gaze. I had a feeling, despite his wolfish grin, that this meeting wasn't for pleasure. No, if he had called me *here*, wherever 'here' was - it was for a reason.

His form shimmered with gold as his jackal head was replaced by that of a handsome man in his forties with graying temples. "Unfortunately not, Nova. Although I would love for you to come visit us there someday... This is simply an in-between for communication. Far safer than pulling you from realm to realm."

"So I'm not dead?" I smirked slightly.

"No," he chuckled and motioned for me to follow him. I stepped forward as a hot wind ran over my skin, drawing attention to the black linen dress I now donned. Blue and green jewels glinted off my fingers, and my hair felt heavy with gold beads. Fascinating. I let out a small surprised sound as the wind blew harder, revealing black marble floors and high columns around us, seemingly appearing out of nowhere.

"Anubis," I asked quietly, "why am I here?"

He sighed and motioned for me to follow him, walls growing and appearing as they replaced the desert, welcoming us further into the temple-like structure. My skin shivered as my death magic floated around me in a smoky black form that seemed to match the surrounding space. Any other magic I possessed was silent.

"Osiris," he finally spoke, shaking his head, "wishes to meet his long-lost niece. He's growing soft with old age."

"You know," I noted my thought from before, "I am starting to feel pretty damn special. I didn't think being a descendant of a god was that important, considering it seems there are so many."

"It isn't," he looked at me curiously. "Usually."

Before I could respond, he continued, "In fact, if it was any other god besides Set, we probably wouldn't give a damn. As it stands, you are only his second descendant. Damn near as important as a *pure god* descendant. Probably the closest a demi-goddess could get, actually."

"What's the difference?" I arched a brow, never having heard the term.

Anubis's eyes brightened as if he was thrilled to answer the question at hand. Why? I had absolutely no idea. "Well, a few thousand years ago, we had a bit of an incident within the God realm. A nasty fight had broken out between the Greek, Roman, and Egyptian sectors. A completely unneeded fight, if you ask me, but gods are petty and the need to claim more sectors for themselves grew to be unbearable, apparently. They were also probably fucking bored. I wouldn't know. I was entertaining myself with other ventures..." I arched a brow but didn't question his amused chuckle.

"Anyway, after slaughtering a good amount of demi-gods, the Egyptians won and they decided that *pure god* descendants, those who resulted from the mating of two true gods, were no longer allowed. Apparently, there were far too many powerful beings on the Greek and Roman side. Therefore, as victors, they decided that within the three ancient realms there would be no longer any mixing of the pure bloodlines. Instead, only demi-god children could be born, as with your mother and Set."

Ah.

"So what happens if a true god mates with another?" I tilted my head, knowing it was rare that these gods listened to anyone or anything but their own desires. Who was I to burst that bubble, though?

He chuckled. "Breaking that pact would no doubt start a massive war. Gods, especially the older they become, are pesky and petulant. They would assume the parties involved were trying to amass power, and the child of such a union would be hunted mercilessly by the two other kingdoms. Not pretty at all."

"Shit," I wrinkled my nose. "That seems a bit absurd."

"Don't worry," he winked, making me nearly roll my eyes, "there are plenty of other options for you to choose from, if you are looking for a god to mate with."

"I am very well aware of my mating options, thank you very much." Really. Very. Very well aware and pleased with my choices. Although, let's be honest. How fucking weird was this whole 'mating' term? Like, I know 'fuck buddy' wasn't a great option either, but couldn't we go with a solid 'lover?' That seemed like a fairly good place to be, in my humble opinion.

"Yes," he hummed as we neared a pair of massive onyx doors flanked by statues of sentinels with the heads of jackals. "Your harem is fascinating, Daughter of Magic. Very interesting selection of men, with even more interesting tastes. How did you come to acquire them?"

I had so many sarcastic comments on the tip of my tongue, but luckily in that moment, the doors opened slowly and the scent of damp earth and death filled my senses. I closed my eyes as my power surged out from me, exploring the space I was realizing was very much a throne room.

My eyes widened in realization that I was facing another god. The third god I'd met to date, in fact. First Isis. Then Anubis. Now Osiris? I was really stacking these connections up. Like Pokemon cards or some shit.

"Daughter of Chaos!" Osiris greeted me. I blinked, wondering why this wasn't weird, but then chalked it up to me being slightly crazy.

The man in front of me appeared to be the epitome of health. His strong, chiseled face flashed with an emerald metallic sheen that highlighted his otherwise golden skin. He looked far more human than god, even with his long dark hair and plethora of jewelry. It may have helped that he was wearing a suit, but I had a feeling this form was more for me than anyone else. I mean, to be fair, the man was far over seven feet, and that was my guess from where he was sitting on the throne, so what were the chances he didn't have some god-like armor lying around?

"Osiris," I bowed my head slightly as Anubis let out a yawn and went to go lounge on a chaise nearby. A glass of wine appeared in my hand as he offered me a 'cheers' motion that had me smiling. I had to admit, despite being weird, I was coming to actually rather like my cousin.

The Lord of the Underworld - aka Anubis's father-slash-boss and Set's brother - motioned me forward as I walked up the large marble steps that seemed to be radiating heat. I took the dark onyx-colored chair that appeared on a step lower than his own, assuming naturally that it was mine. I sighed a bit because how the hell was stone this goddamn comfort-able? I was calling magic bullshit on this. Just saying.

"I never expected to see the day where Set would have his own child that wasn't from some fucked-up incident," he stated bluntly, making my lip twitch. "You seem to have turned out rather normal. That's a pleasant surprise."

I grinned at my uncle. "Normal? Not so much. But I would have to guess you are rather surprised and maybe a bit disappointed I exist in the first place? I mean, as much as I appreciate this, I wouldn't blame you for not liking me. You hate Set, right? I heard he pulled some really shitty stuff on you."

"Shitty stuff indeed," he sighed and then tilted his head in amusement. "Although I suspect you know the human version, would you like to hear the real one? Because as much as I hate to admit it, your father isn't at fault alone."

No shit.

"I would," I nodded, my curiosity winning out. Oh, like you wouldn't say yes! This was the Lord of the Underworld offering me horrific bed time stories, your fucking loss if you don't see the value in that shit.

"As you know, us gods have a penchant for..."

"Violence? Adultery? Fucking with mortals?" I questioned as Anubis barked out a laugh.

"Yes," the god grinned, "that and far more. As it stood, a few years back, maybe around the time that Earth was going into one of its many wars, I found myself in bed with Nephthys, our sister and Set's consort. He wasn't pleased with that, and as a result sought my death. Of course, he knew I would return and probably take vengeance, but he cut up my body and scattered the pieces across Egypt to make Isis furious. My loving wife took the time to find all of those pieces and restore me. You can bet that I found Set, and this pattern between us went back and forth. Violence against brother, although I am happy to say that neither of us slept with each other's consorts again. Small steps, right?"

"That's because Isis fucking hates Set," Anubis pointed out, smirking.

"Which was why I found it odd that she had taken such a liking to you, Daughter of Chaos, but now I am seeing you are far different from your father. In fact, you are much like my wife."

I nodded slowly, trying to ignore the very obvious mention of incest in his life because - what the fuck? Instead, I tried to keep things light.

"Well, I have to admit, the gods appearing in my backyard and dreams really freaked me out at first, but this is truly really cool," I shrugged.

Osiris looked over me before tilting his head at Anubis. "She's very funny. Far funnier and charming than Set."

"Right?" Anubis chuckled. "I was very disappointed to learn that she has no interest in taking a mate of her own kind."

And the gods wonder why they all turn out so fucked up. Gross.

"The god part is not the problem, *cousin*," I pointed out as he smirked knowingly. "I just don't do the down and dirty with my fam bam. You get me?"

Osiris sighed. "I have noticed that modern-day culture frowns upon sexual interaction with family."

Was this a real fucking conversation I was having? Like what the actual hell?

"Honestly? It's pretty gross," I pointed out, not feeling bad in the least.

The air shifted, vibrating, and my eyes fluttered, making me feel almost unstable. I gripped the arm rests of the chair, and the ringing in my ears had me forgetting what we were talking about before. "What the hell is that?"

"A son of Ramsey the Not-So-Great, I believe," Osiris grinned as Anubis chuckled at his father's joke. "Is he the one that beat you out of a place in her life? It's a bit amusing son, I can't lie."

I raised a hand, knowing they'd ignore me. "I would just like to state that he was never in the running--"

The Lord of the Underworld snapped his fingers as gold mist surrounded me and a grunt sounded in the room. My head snapped towards the sound and eyes widened, finding Nour standing in the center of the goddamn room looking very fucking confused. He was wearing his dark costume from the party, but as I watched him, it shifted into a suit much like my uncle and cousin's. I must have made a small sound because immediately his eyes snapped up to mine.

"Moonbeam?" he demanded as I offered him a small smile, a surge of insecurity from before hitting me like a goddamn truck. I did find it interesting that he was so focused on me that he didn't seem to even care about the other gods in the room.

"Hey," I stood awkwardly. "I didn't realize you could enter into--"

"I didn't." he frowned, looking at Osiris and Anubis in realization. "I'd come home and tried to wake you up. You seemed to have fallen asleep crying next to my brother and--"

"It's fine," I stepped down the stairs wanting to shut him up. *Come on dude!* Don't tell the badass gods I was crying, even if I couldn't remember *why* I'd been crying for the life of me.

I knew it was important, too. I just couldn't put my finger on it.

"Do you feel the weird tension?" Anubis voiced in a loud whisper. I scowled as my uncle chuckled, causing Nour to freeze, the reality of everything hitting him.

"Holy shit," he bit out. "Osiris, I didn't realize you were seeing anyone. I assumed like Isis--"

"Yes, yes, we are on vacation," he drawled and then smiled, "but family is family, isn't that so, Nova?"

"He's not wrong," I commented, finally reaching Nour. Instantly, his arms were around me and he tugged me against him, hard. All my insecurity from before floated away as I breathed out a sigh of relief. Thank fuck.

"Nova," Nour's voice grew deeper and quieter as I looked up at him, ignoring the quiet talking in the background. "Moonbeam, fuck, I am so sorry. I shouldn't have run out like that. I was so goddamn overwhelmed by how much I felt for you and I was worried that if I stayed in your presence a minute longer I was going to send you running by blurting out everything--"

"Nour," I grasped his face, going up on my toes slightly before speaking softly, "nothing you could say would scare me. I promise you."

I meant that. I think we all knew how I felt about Nour, and to say it was a bit of a crush was a goddamn lie. If anything, tonight had shown me just how stupidly crazy I was about him. Despite feeling insecure, those feelings weren't going anywhere, even if it would have been easier. A neater affair.

"Nova." He looked pained and my heart tightened as I decided to take another risk. It was dangerous, and frankly it could backfire like last time, but Nour wasn't a liar, and seeing him here and now? Looking into his silver eyes? I knew how he felt.

"No, I'm serious," I whispered. "The truth is, Nour... I had no idea what to say or do when you first returned. I was terrified because I couldn't hold on to my anger about you leaving once I realized why. I was terrified because in the absence of anger is something a lot bigger and a fuck ton more delicate. This summer meant so much to me, and I should have told you that before you left. I should have told you how much I cared about you, how much I'd come to... love you."

Ah shit.

I inhaled sharply. "I know that probably seems so fucking random and I am probably fucking this up. I mean, shit, we just had our first kiss and now I am telling you I love you. You must think I am a goddamn lunatic. It's true, though. You made me feel cared about this summer, and you are literally the only friend I've ever had. You make me laugh, and you always put me first, even when I was trying to keep my distance from you because I was scared. I mean, fuck, how could I not love you, Nour?"

His eyes were black as he watched me, his hands tightening on me, the air suspended with my words as he clarified, "You love me?"

"Yes," I confirmed softly, feeling like I was going to pass out because of how fucking nervous I was. *Yes, Nova. Good job. Add to your shit show by possibly being rejected by the only friend you've ever had. No big deal.*

"Nova," Nour's voice was soft and almost dangerous as he clasped my jaw. I closed my eyes slightly, bracing for all the very possible bad results this could yield. But then he spoke.

"I have loved you possibly from the first goddamn day I met you, when you walked right into your father's office like you owned the place. Ever since then I have been completely captivated by you. I don't call you moonbeam because of your eyes, although it's fitting. I call you moonbeam because for the first time in my dark, sad life, I felt hope being around you. I felt loved and like someone actually wanted to be around me--"

I seared my lips to his as relief washed over me at his sweet words. I couldn't help myself. Tears filled my eyes as I felt all reservation between us fade away. Fucking hell. This man loved me.

It was a different type of love than I felt for Everett. Not less intense or strong, but it had a different burn. A wildfire that had slowly burned its way up into my heart until I realized that all of my being was devastated by him, and I had no way to put out the flame of emotion. I had felt decimated when he left, and now in his arms? I felt at home. I felt like this man was fueling me, keeping the vulnerable part of my heart protected and safe.

"I love you," he whispered, his eyes nearly black with emotion. "I love you so damn much, Nova."

"You feel like home," I admitted, feeling embarrassed at how soft I was. I couldn't even feel bad though. I gave him a watery smile. "You totally owe me a trip to Bora Bora, though."

He flashed a sweet smile as I watched his eyes flash with a million different fascinating emotions. "I think we can arrange that… But Nova, you have to know, I wouldn't have been able to stay away for long. I need you to know that. When my brother sent for me, I was already in the goddamn state. I never fully left. I couldn't."

A voice rang out as Nour kissed me once again, deep and searing as I melted against his ridiculously large muscular body. I think I'd known that. I think I'd known he would never fully leave me.

"Well, now I feel like we did something good, son. I didn't even mean for that to fucking happen."

"See? I told you that you're getting soft," Anubis pointed out with a chuckle.

I swung around as Nour caught me against him with a possessive arm. "I am so sorry, I didn't mean to totally hijack our time--"

"No worries." Osiris grinned and then stretched his arms above his head with a groan. "Like I said, I'm on vacation. Plus, I see the love you two have for each other, and I can't help but appreciate it."

"It's an honor to meet you Osiris," Nour stated softly.

The god stood up, and I realized he was more like fucking eight feet or nine feet tall. "Well, I do think it's time to be getting back. Daughter of Chaos, Son of Ramsey the Great, I do hope to see you again. Remember, while my brother may be a bastard, you are always welcome in our home."

"Thank you," I said honestly, not knowing how the hell to feel.

Anubis winked at me as I rolled my eyes, the doors opening behind us. I turned and Nour grasped my hand, a black portal that seemingly led to the stars opening up. Inhaling sharply, I kissed him, and he offered me a boyish grin before we dove right back into our reality.

My body jolted as I was deposited back in the land of the living, so to speak. My emotions and memories connected in an overwhelming cocktail of mourning, fury, and love. I know. My brain and emotions were very much in disagreement with one another. To say I felt fucked up over what had occurred throughout the night was the understatement of the century.

I remembered it all.

No longer was I missing pieces of the memory that had plagued me like a blank slate within Osiris's oasis. No. Now every detail was standing out in technicolor, and I'd yet to even open my eyes. I absorbed the familiar scents of Ramsey and River. I clutched the hard muscular chest under my tear-soaked face as I tried to open my eyes, wincing in pain.

My entire body felt absolutely ravaged by the magic I'd used earlier. You know, when I slaughtered the witches that attacked Rowan and I? We all remembered my mass murder, right? I felt like over a dozen could count as 'mass'... but that was just my opinion.

I inhaled a gasp at the pain that radiated through my center. It felt as if my rib cage had been pulled open and filled with the memories of my mother's torture.

Throughout all of it though, from the surge of memories

and painful reality to my meeting with the Lord of the Under-world... one thing stood out like a beacon of light. Nour's sweet words.

He loved me. Nour fucking loved me.

"Moonbeam?" Nour's voice was rough and raspy as I blinked, not able to see clearly. My entire body trembled, as I felt dizzy from the change in where the fuck I was. You know, after being ripped from the god shit to back here. Add in the bile coming up my throat and the tears, and you've got a Nova shit show extravaganza.

My body suddenly decided it was going to say 'fuck me,' and I found myself sprinting towards the bathroom. I gasped as I dropped to my knees in front of the toilet and dry-heaved over the porcelain throne. Tears welled in my eyes as bile came up from my throat in an acidic, wine-tasting, toxic fountain.

Literally. Fuck. Me.

"Shit," someone said roughly as large hands pulled back my hair. I felt a sob break from my throat as everything hit me like a bulldozer. I wasn't even crying because I was upset. This shit hurt like hell, and on top of it I was fucking furious. I was going to destroy my father… no, Earnest. I was going to destroy Earnest. That fucker definitely did not deserve the title of 'father.'

I was going to slice him open and stuff him with maggot-filled dirt...

"I feel like a murderous rant while throwing up is not a good sign," Fox's voice echoed as I tried to not laugh, leaning over the toilet but no longer feeling sick. Holy hell. Tonight was just not my night, ladies and gents.

"Alright, boys," I coughed with my head still bent over after a rough breath. "I know we need to talk because holy shit, I can't even start to tell you... you know what, stories later. I need a toothbrush and a shower. Cool? Cool."

River, who I realized was behind me holding my hair, began barking out orders. Everett crouched down to my side as I looked at him, concern for me flooding his green eyes. His long fingers pushed back a stray curl as I closed my eyes, taking a deep breath.

"Come on, butterfly," River said softly, lifting me as Everett flushed down my throw up. What a man, am I right?

Running a hand over my face, I took the toothbrush August offered as I began to clean out my mouth in some-what of a daze. I scrubbed every inch of it - literally, I felt like my gums were bleeding - before I gargled mouthwash, spitting out the minty liquid and sighing in relief. Without checking to see who the hell was in the room, I let my slip from before fall to the ground as I stepped into the already hot water. I thought I heard a strangled groan, but I didn't check before pulling the fogged glass shut.

Honestly, more power to them if they still found me sexy after puking.

Inhaling the mist of heated water, I placed my head against the shower wall and just stood under the heated water. I wish I could tell you I was surprised when someone pressed up behind me and brushed their fingers through my thick hair. I wasn't though. I could, however, say I was surprised by who it was.

"Auggy?" I asked curiously, tilting my head back.

His eyes were nearly black as he offered me a small, tight smile, his entire body wracked with tension as he poured shampoo into his hand. I could see how upset he was, and I realized it must have been a goddamn nightmare finding Rowan and I in the state we'd been in.

I leaned back against his chest as his hands massaged my

scalp. Unfortunately, he was still in his boxers, so I couldn't feel all of him against me, but it was the type of comfort I needed right now. Even if I was turned on by the simple action.

"You two scared the shit out of me," he mumbled softly as I turned into him, tilting my head back to allow the hot water to wash away the shampoo.

"I'm sorry," I said as he offered me a sad smile and pressed a kiss to my nose.

He looked like he wanted to say more, but instead he smoothed the conditioner into my hair, allowing me to lean against him for full stability. Which was good, because I was essentially useless right now, if we were being truthful.

I had no idea how long we were in there before he finally turned off the shower and wrapped me in a massive fluffy robe that I knew wasn't mine but smelled wonderful. My eyes widened only slightly to find Ever still in the room sitting on the counter.

"Hey baby," he said softly, his brow furrowed. Auggy walked past me, and I couldn't help but feel concern penetrate my already exhausted emotions.

I wrapped my arms around Ever and kissed him gently before pulling away. I made my way into the bedroom, and my eyes immediately locked onto Rowan and then Nour. I couldn't help but smile a bit when I saw Nour. I walked towards Rowan, his passed out form still on the couch. His life force seemed worn out but okay. I felt bad for him because I could tell that my magic must have indirectly hit him, and I was going to guess that it hurt like a bitch. I kissed his forehead lightly before walking up to Nour, his body slightly tense but his eyes filled with warmth.

"Moonbeam," he swallowed and tugged me against him.

"Nour," I sighed happily, breathing in his scent.

"About what happened," he mumbled nervously.

I tilted my head up and placed a hand on his cheek. "Do you want to go on a walk later? You know, to talk about stuff and things..."

I blushed as he flashed a grin, nodding. "Yeah, I would love that, moonbeam." I could hear the *I love you* in his words, and I felt security and confidence run through me.

As I turned to go sit on the bed, Ramsey's chest appeared in front of me, causing me to look up. "Hey, big guy."

"Are you okay?" he demanded softly, his gold eyes filled with far more emotion than I expected.

I nodded and licked my lips. "But um, I may or may not have had a meeting with Osiris."

He blinked at me before his rough demand sounded. "What?! You went to the fucking Underworld?!"

Okay. So, putting a pause on how his rough demands had started turning me on… how adorable was this guy? I mean, shit, literally so freakin' cute. He would hate if he knew I thought that, which of course, made it so much better.

"Not exactly," I tilted my head and walked past him, "but I am in the process of sorting through all this and compart-mentalizing so we can talk. Give me a minute and I'll answer everything."

Fox watched me from where he sat next to Cassian on the bed. Instead of saying anything, I wiggled my way between them and sighed happily, facing the rest of the room. Now how did I even start to explain this utter and complete shit show?

"Okay," I nodded, clasping my fingers. "So, one... what the hell happened with the witches? Like, obviously I slaugh-tered them, but how were they able to get that close to our wards and how did they use their magic within them?"

"Rowan usually puts the wards in place," River offered

from where he was brooding against the wall, "but I have a feeling that it had nothing to do with the wards. Did your coven ever work with anyone from the Demonic realm?"

"Uh, not that I know of, why?"

Cassian grunted. "We found traces of unusual magic for witches."

"It was mixed with demon magic that probably enhanced theirs," Fox explained softly.

I blinked and nodded. *Good. Demons. That was what we needed to add to the mix.*

Nour snorted as I realized I'd said that out loud. Wonderful. I blew out a breath. "Alright, well, they are dead, and the wards we assume are secure right now?"

"Yeah," August nodded. "But we are going to take some of the magic signatures in the soil when we go to see King Desmond. Figure he may be able to tell us where it is from, specifically."

"Has he called?" I asked curiously as Auggy's fingers began to braid my hair from behind. Cute. Very cute.

"Contacted us while you were passed out, actually," Fox noted.

"We were going to try to leave tomorrow, but with everything that happened--"

"We should go," I stated softly. "After what happened tonight, we may want some space from their bullshit in Seattle."

Everett examined my face and my response to River's words before he grunted, "Only if you're sure, baby."

"Positive." I flashed a tired smile. "Family vacation after our first holiday together."

"Hey," Cassian smiled slightly, nudging my shoulder. "It *was* our first holiday together."

I couldn't help but hold his gaze for a moment, my ears

heating as I examined his happy expression. I wouldn't have taken Cassian as one to love holidays, but I found that somehow absolutely perfect. I squeezed his hand before focusing back on the room.

"Can we talk about you going to the Underworld?!" Ramsey demanded as I smirked slightly at his impatience.

"You are cute when grumpy," I pointed out as his ears heated, but he kept his grumpy face in place.

"Yes, well, after passing out, I woke up in a desert," I said flippantly. "Anubis showed up, and he said Osiris wanted to meet his long-lost niece. Apparently, because I am Set's only 'real' child, I am pretty freakin' important. So we had a bit of family bonding time and then... Nour got pulled in."

"I'd come back from my absence," he cleared his throat as Everett growled.

"Hey," I chided at my psycho, "We kissed and made up. We are good, I promise."

Everett grumbled as Nour flashed me a thankful smile and continued. "I tried to wake her up because she was crying, or had been, but I passed out, like I'd been hit over the fucking head... only to find myself in an in-between realm with Anubis and Osiris hanging out with Nova. Very odd. But yeah, nothing seemed off. They literally seemed to want to hang out."

"This is fucking unreal," Ramsey grunted. "Nova, sunshine, you of course are really damn special, but you have to understand how unusual this is."

"I know," I assured him before tilting my head and adding, "Which leads us to something I'd forgotten at the time but remembered in startling detail once I'd woken up."

Ramsey winced as I closed my eyes and breathed out, "Ramsey helped me realize, when he interacted with me in my dream, that the details of my nightmares were in fact memory. Every. Single. One."

The room seemed to be in paused shock.

"He fucking--"

"Yes," I nodded, inhaling sharply. "He tortured her. A lot. But that wasn't the important part. I mean obviously it was... but when he was fucking her up, she said something that I had forgotten until now."

Ramsey crouched down in front of me so that I had to look him in the face. Instead of giving him the words he wanted to ensure I was okay, I ran my hand through his thick hair and continued to speak. The guy totally leaned into my hand, and I realized how happy I was that he liked my touch. "She said '*I will never tell you, Earnest. I will never tell you, and one day, when they came for us, you will be slaughtered.*'"

The room seemed frozen as I nodded. "Yeah, so it's safe to assume that my mother and I were here for a reason and that she knew something that Earnest was pretty fucking eager to know. Maybe it was that Set was my father and he wanted to know where the inheritance had come from? But you said the inheritance would be from my mom's side... and who is 'they' coming from us? Was she talking about the Scarabs? I just have no idea what she meant, and it's going to drive me crazy until we find out."

"I know this is far-fetched," Auggy offered quietly, "but have you tried asking Isis what she knows?"

"I haven't," I frowned in realization. "But maybe you're right, maybe I should."

Shaking myself, I continued, "I think that about catches us up. Right? If so, I am going to probably go get ready for the day. What time do we want to leave? Also, did you ever let go of those high school guys? The assholes?"

Fox's eyes widened, cursing sharply as he jogged towards the door, making me laugh. Everett was in front of me, frowning. "You should try to get some sleep."

"I promise I've slept enough. I am ready to go get some answers from this Desmond guy, though. I think it's well established that Earnest is a bastard. I want to figure out why the power drains are happening, and more importantly, what Desmond knows about the Demonic realm doing it."

My psycho nodded and brushed my lips with his before everyone seemed to spring into action. Nour walked over and wrapped his arms around me. "Want to meet me outside in twenty to talk?"

"Yes please," I nodded as he brushed my nose with his because I was a fucking sap.

As he left, I looked at Rowan and grabbed a blanket, draping it over him and brushing his hair back. My head snapped up as Ramsey's gaze met mine from where he sat on the bed. Other than Rowan, the room was empty as I made my way towards him. Immediately, I stepped between his legs, and he wrapped his large hands around my waist.

"Thank you," I said honestly regarding the dream. "I needed that more than you probably realized."

He searched my face and nodded. "I have no idea how you shut down your emotions like that."

I offered a sad smile. "I'd say it's conditioning because of how I grew up. It's more than that, though. I'd known that those nightmares were real, but when I woke up the memories were foggy, and having clarity took away the fear and mystery from it. I was scared of how I would react, but if anything, I'm just more furious. More fucking ready to kill Earnest."

He smiled slightly before breathing out my name. "Nova, you still surprise me."

"In a good way?" I winked as he chuckled softly before tilting his head.

"My brother and you?" he offered.

My ears heated as I shrugged. "I'm not so mad at him anymore."

"I see. Is that all that happened?" His eyes were sparkling with that question.

"Yeah," I swallowed. "You know, I had to be civil and stuff--"

"Cute," he brushed his lips against mine, "but I know my twin, and he's on cloud nine right now, so whatever you said to him was a hell of a lot more than forgiveness."

I shrugged and ran a hand through my hair with a small smile. "I mean, maybe he just really wanted my forgiveness."

"Nova!" Fox called and my head snapped.

"Yes?"

"Come see the donut locations I've mapped out," he chuckled, making me jump into action. I tossed a kiss on Ram's cheek before leaving the room, his laugh following me out.

See? I was totally fine. And if I wasn't? Well, I always had donuts to solve any possible issues.

NOUR

How many times had we been in this exact position? It felt like hundreds despite it being only a dozen. Yet this time it felt so vastly different. Mostly because unlike the other times, when she'd fallen asleep against my chest under the moonlight in the shelter of the forest, I was no longer hiding how I felt about her. Well, that, and we were far closer to the house, essentially in the back yard because of those fucking witches. Better safe than sorry.

I could feel eyes on us, and I knew that the others were watching and keeping tabs on the wards. I didn't blame them. Nova, upon coming outside, had instantly curled up against my side, and while she didn't seem to be fully sleepy, I could feel that her magic had relaxed. I didn't feel the need to fill the silence; I was just happy to hold her how I'd always wanted. My hands tightened on her body just as a reminder that she was, in fact, here.

I shook my head, thinking back to the summer. Thinking back to how I'd nearly lost her. At the time, I hadn't known how she felt, and honestly, I would have never hoped for her to feel as strongly as I did. It was obvious that we had been both hiding a ton, and now? Well, now I felt more secure about my place in Nova's life than ever before.

Nova loved me.

I had lived most of my life trying to earn the love of those around me. Well, not love, per se, but respect or affection. Mainly, my absent father's attention. So to have Nova just admit it? Just to tell me bluntly that she loved me? It fucked with my head in the best way possible. It was something I'd needed without me even realizing that was the case.

Closing my eyes, I thought back to when I'd come back from my walk. The walk where I had convinced myself that I needed to just be honest with Nova, no matter how she felt. After coming to that conclusion, I'd almost immediately turned around. However, when I came to the estate, I felt fear sink into my bones realizing the party had been cleared out.

I wasn't positive what had happened at first, but when I came upstairs, Everett had instantly filled me in. Much to his pleasure, no doubt, because as he probably assumed, guilt hit me hard when I realized she'd gone on that walk with Rowan because of me. I'd sat on the edge of the bed running my fingers through her hair, resisting the urge to wake her or my brother up to ask why she was crying.

The moment that thought had crossed my mind, though, I was blacking out. Waking up within a realm that I didn't recognize, I had instantly noticed Nova and hadn't paid any fucking attention to Osiris himself sitting on a throne.

If we were being frank, even if I hadn't been in an odd new place, I probably would have only been able to pay attention to her. She had looked absolutely unreal sitting there surrounded by black marble, her form swarmed by dark linen and jewels that highlighted her gorgeous figure.

If I hadn't been sure of her heritage before, I would have been after seeing her in God realm apparel. It had fit her so perfectly, and while I hadn't mentioned it to anyone, I was starting to think that we were missing something. Something much larger than any of the mages or Nova had considered. Something that was potentially dangerous and seemingly unbelievable.

Then again, I didn't put anything past these gods.

Specifically, Anubis and Isis. Don't ask me why, but the attention they paid Nova seemed very odd to me. I thought it had been me just acting protective, but the concept of Osiris wanting to meet her hadn't given me nearly the same feeling. No, there was something bigger here that had my magic going haywire. I didn't like the way Anubis looked at Nova, and I didn't think it was even a sexual thing. He looked at her like he was thrilled about some secret none of us knew.

My visions had gotten progressively darker and more abstract as the days passed. I was seeing shit that terrified me, because most of it revolved around Nova getting hurt. I'd say it was my subconscious, but I would be dumb to discount the messages my magic was trying to send me. I closed my eyes, thinking through the vision I'd had last night.

Breathing in the scents of oils and candles, my eyes opened to find myself standing on a slab of marble over-looking a massive expanse of temple fitted with an altar at the front. It reminded me of the Egyptian sector in the God realm, but something was different. Something wasn't right here.

Gods from everywhere, Greek to Eastern European, seemed to gather, their eyes ahead where a woman stood in a cloak that shadowed her features. Behind her stood a larger woman that was very visible. Isis. A low chant began as my eyes narrowed on the small figure. I was unsurprised when the cloak dropped to reveal Nova.

In the darkness of the temple, it was very obvious that my moonbeam was naked because of her iridescent fucking skin.

I would have claimed this was some fucked up sex dream, because I was easily getting a hard on from just my imagination of what she looked like naked, but I knew it was more than that.

My eyes widened as the slab I stood on began to shift, rumbling as I hung onto it. Somewhere above me, the voices from what sounded like a modern day Bible story blurred in my ear, blocking out the words presumably Isis was saying behind Nova.

I tried to get off the slab as I watched my little witch kneel on top of the altar, her head angled up and mouth moving in silent prayer. I grunted as I was thrown back, fury raging through me at being unable to stop what I knew would be a goddamn bloody affair.

"Nova," I snarled as I watched her pick up a jagged dagger.

I let out a roar as she stabbed herself right in the chest, her eyes fluttering shut as blood began to pour out, her movement sharp as she opened her chest. Voices cheered around her as the sound of battle broke out underneath me.

Nova's small hands reached inside her chest, yanking her still beating heart out. I called her name and her eyes reached mine. My stomach dropped as she squeezed her heart enough that the blood poured around her, breaking apart the organ that kept her alive. I knew she was supposed to be immortal, but right now? In this dream? It sure as fuck didn't feel that way.

I could see her eyes flutter shut and her body collapse as the words 'sacrificial lamb' echoed in a booming chuckle.

That was when I'd woken up.

"Nour?" Nova's soft voice asked as she looked at me in alarm. I frowned, looking down at her, and loosened my grip, realizing I was probably hurting her a bit.

"Sorry, moonbeam," I grunted, trying to still my beating heart. "I'm fine, just remembering a vision I had."

Searching my face, her fingers ran along my chin and neck in thought. "How bad are they?"

"Bad," I answered hesitantly, wincing.

"And they are about me?" she whispered, her face paling.

"Most of them," I sighed. "But they are growing harder to understand, more abstract and a fuck ton darker."

"You don't think it's like a bad dream, right? I don't know your magic and how it works, but maybe because of how you feel about me--"

"I wish it was, just because of how much I love you, Nova." I kissed her gently. "But don't worry too much, moonbeam. There are some positive ones as well. I know we are going to end up in the God realm for sure, but past that it gets a bit hazy."

With some women, I would have considered sugar coating the issue at hand, but I knew Nova wouldn't appreciate that. The woman was fearless, and she wouldn't want to be babied. If she asked a question, I would answer honestly.

"You do love me, don't you?" she teased, removing the tension from the situation.

"Understatement, moonbeam." I grasped her jaw and kissed her deeply. She let out a breathy sound, making me nearly groan.

I didn't trust myself fully when it came to my control regarding Nova. I'd gotten so used to not touching or attacking her that I was worried about what would happen when that control snapped. I didn't want to rush what this was between us. I wanted to savor it because I didn't plan on ever fucking ending it. She was mine, and I would never love another woman like I loved her. That wasn't in question.

"I love you, Nour," she whispered softly, her eyes filling with emotion.

I tugged her against me and buried my head against her neck, lifting her off the ground so that I could breathe in her stormy scent. I felt my skin prickle as she wrapped her arms around my neck, her fingers playing against my skin. Gods, I fucking loved her touch. So goddamn much.

"We need to get ready to leave," Ramsey said, his voice breaking through our moment. I didn't mind though, mostly because I knew my brother well enough to know that he was falling down the same rabbit hole as myself.

Nova wiggled down, and I chuckled as she passed my brother, offering him a wink and making him grunt. I wouldn't even deny I watched her perfect, perky ass walking away. The woman was so fucking hot it was unfair to every one of us.

"You good?" my brother curiously asked, his eyes skeptical, probably at our change in relationship. I didn't very often tell him about my visions, but one like last night? I would have normally told him, considering the extreme of it. But with it being about Nova, I didn't want to risk that. Who knew what the hell he would do. Probably never let her hold a knife again or even go to the God realm, even though we all knew it was essential.

Ramsey hadn't been joking about us not being able to return without her. We'd gotten the order directly from Set himself, and you didn't fuck with that. Well, Nova did, but that was different. The woman did whatever the hell she wanted.

"Yeah. Actually," I sighed and then flashed a smile, "she said she loved me."

Ramsey's eyes widened as he demanded, "What the hell?"

"Yeah," I nodded and smiled. "I was going to say it anyway, but she said it first. So yeah, we aren't fighting anymore, to say the least." I was totally downplaying this, for the record.

Mostly because it would work up Ram, and that was funny as fuck.

"How the fuck did you go from her saying she was mad at you about seashells to saying 'I love you?'" he growled in confusion.

I chuckled as I passed him. "Ram you are thinking about all this way too much. Just go with how you feel. I love her, it's that simple."

"Have you lost your mind?" he asked. "They are crazy enough--"

"It's Nova," I admitted. "You either go along with the chaos or you don't. You know that, brother. There isn't a schedule or rationale when it comes to Nova."

It never seemed more clear than when I said it out loud.

"I'm going on a walk," Ramsey grunted. As my brother walked off, I was tempted to roll my eyes. He needed to chill the fuck out.

Nova quite literally embodied the opposite of how he lived his entire life. It was good for him. She was good for all of us. I'd known it from the first moment I'd met her.

Now I needed to go find the woman I loved so I could tell her again. You know, just in case she forgot or some shit...

EVERETT

W e hadn't taken off yet, and I was already feeling frustrated about being in the air. I wasn't a huge fan of flying to begin with, but even more so right now when my magic had been acting so fucking difficult. I felt far better when I was connected to some source of death. As in, where bodies were buried underneath my feet. And trust me, there were far more of them than people realized underneath their feet every single damn day.

"Ever," Nova's amused voice sounded as I looked to where my girl was sitting. Her hair was in a messy updo, showing off her gorgeous face and delicate features as she flipped through some magazines she'd gotten at the gas station before the drive over. She called it 'trash news.' I had no idea what it was, but it along with the donuts we'd gotten seemed to make her happy.

I was still pissed because of what the fuck she was wearing, but apparently it was in fact hot in Arizona, so I had to 'deal with it.' Narrowing my eyes at her tiny high-waisted black shorts, I considered how much effort it would take to tear them off her smooth skin. Probably not much, considering they were cut in several places to show off her legs and ass. I mean, don't get me wrong. With the dark boots she wore and tight lace-up top, the woman looked fucking hot. But too hot, if that made sense. Like I wanted to take her to the floor of our private jet and fuck her hard enough that her sassy mouth could only moan my name.

If I was thinking about that, it meant other people outside of our team were as well. I didn't like that shit at all. *At. Fucking. All.*

"Everett," she said again as I snapped from my thoughts, muttering a curse. I walked towards her and threw myself into the leather seat across from where she sat.

Cassian offered me a smirk before going back to showing Fox what he was working on. I wanted to punch the smug bastard. It had been far too long since I was last inside Nova, and I had the possessive urge to mark her body up. My magic didn't like that someone else had been in her last. It was stupid as hell, but it still didn't stop the urge. My eyes flickered to Fox's bite on her neck that had yet to go away.

I wanted to mark her permanently.

I also had the urge to taste her blood. Mostly because I wanted to consume everything that was Nova, but I wasn't positive how she would feel about that. I mean, really. I wanted to fuck her from behind and bite down on her neck hard enough that she actually bled on my lips so I could drink down her essence. But I knew a bite mark wouldn't last forever...

Maybe I would tattoo my name onto her ass or something. I smirked at how much she'd fucking kill me if I ever pulled that shit. I would wake up with her name on my forehead, and you know what? I would wear it proudly. That was how fucked I was over this woman. Could you blame me though?

"The flight is only a little over two hours," Nour announced, walking from the cockpit where our pilots were.

I had no idea what the hell happened to the two of them last night, but Nova's interaction with this Osiris asshole had worked my magic up a lot. Through the bond between the two of us that continued to grow tighter and tighter, I could also feel the soft affection and love she felt for Nour. I was glad they'd worked it out, because I was pretty much over him being so goddamn evasive. I was well aware how all of this ended, and there was no point in fighting it.

Then again, I'd never really fought any aspect of my nature. Not like River, who was openly staring at Nova from where he sat next to Ramsey. I wasn't positive what they were talking about, but my bet was our little witch. Usually was.

I suppose it would be good for me to consider what exactly it meant to have an intertwined life force with Nova. I mean, that shit could kill me, right? If she pulled too much on my life force? Yet I could say with complete honesty that it didn't bother me in the least. If she killed me, then she did. It would be most likely because she was somehow keeping herself alive, so in my eyes, completely worth it. I used to live for my family, but I was well fucking aware of what I lived for now.

Or who *I lived for now.*

"Fuck," Rowan grumbled from where he was reclined next to Nova. "Is it just me, or is it way too sunny in here?"

"It's because of me," Nova preened with a prim little sexy smile. "Right, Ramsey?"

"What?" Rowan asked, looking exhausted.

"He calls me 'sunshine,'" she pointed out and smirked as Ramsey grunted.

River chuckled as Nova's eyes sharpened. "Yeah, sprinkles? Is that funny to you?"

"You're going to get it," River warned, narrowing his eyes.

I shook my head. I think all of us on the team had been very well aware of the side River was stuffing down and holding hostage. I had no idea why he was bothering with that, but to each his own. My smile grew thinking of how Nova was pulling it out of him, whether he wanted her to or not. Honestly, her ability to do that was fucking hot. Then again, I still believed insanity was a positive attribute rather than a negative.

Closing my eyes, I tried to focus on what we would be handling going forward. I wasn't positive this trip would yield anything, but I was willing to give it a go. King Desmond was actually fairly reasonable compared to others that we could have been working with.

He was also one of the more liked kings within the Demonic realm, although there were fairly slim pickings to start with.

The Demonic realm was separated into several smaller realms. Desmond, often referred to as the King of Smoke, was the king of the Dukhan realm. *The Smoke realm.* The entire place was filled with jinn. Honestly, they were some of the easier demons to deal with. I hadn't had a ton of experience with the Demonic realm overall, but my experiences with jinn had always been productive.

I'd heard a rumor that he was Earth-bound and had been for a bit. I had also heard a rumor that it was for a very specific reason, or should I say specific *woman.* But I suppose we would find out soon, wouldn't we?

The part I was not looking forward to? Seeing the fucking Reid brothers. It was nothing against lion shifters. By all definitions we should get along, considering their sadistic streak, but call it intuition that having us all in the same area wouldn't go well.

Opening my eyes, I raised a brow, finding that Nova was now very comfortable on my lap. I chuckled, realizing she'd eaten five donuts and presumably had crashed from a sugar rush. Had she eaten anything else today?

My brow furrowed at that thought, glad that River was attempting to keep track of shit like that. August looked over Nova before shaking his head and going back to what he was reading. I could see the happiness radiating off him, which was a relief when compared to last night. I think August had been genuinely terrified, the concept of losing both Rowan and Nova topping his 'worst nightmare' list, no doubt.

For the longest, I'd considered our team happy. Then I realized we had been simply 'okay.' With Nova, though? With Nova we were fucking happy despite the shit going on. I knew River was worried we'd lose her, but that implied we didn't have control over the situation. I promise you, getting Nova away from me would take a lot more than some goddamn gods.

"We will be landing soon," Nour noted before looking back down at his laptop. I ran a hand through my hair and leaned down to press a kiss to Nova's ear.

"Baby," I bit her ear lightly. "You need to wake up."

Smiling sleepily, she turned on her back so that she was looking up at me. I felt a surge of thankfulness that she was okay, healthy and alive after yesterday's events. I wouldn't even try to fucking minimize the fear I felt finding her passed the fuck out in the forest with death magic surrounding her. If she hadn't slaughtered those assholes, I would have done so with pleasure. In fact, I would love right now to kill several people, including Earnest, but none of my options were available so I would just have to deal with it until an opportunity presented itself.

"No." She stretched like a cat with a yawn.

"Yes." I rubbed a thumb over the strip of skin between her shorts and top. I nearly groaned, my cock hardening fully, as a shiver broke across her skin. My magic and hers were doing their usual shit, their co-dependent nature growing more and more fucking noticeable as time went on.

Her face turned thoughtful, as if she didn't notice how fucking hard I was, and she ran a finger over my lips. "Ever?"

"Yeah, baby?" I asked curiously.

"What is your family like?"

I saw Cassian tense, knowing that I didn't often talk about my past before the team for good reason, but I didn't mind her question. I had decided long ago that whatever the fuck they'd done to me and the effect they had was already established in my head, and all I could do was move on. Now, did I still have fucking triggers? Yeah, I was a bit fucked up, to say the least, but I could answer her question. That I could do.

"I was found on the border of the Horde," I admitted quietly, my thumb brushing her plump bottom lip. "I was adopted by a couple that found me."

She blinked, sadness filtering through her gaze despite trying to hide it, so I continued. "Apparently, although I'm not positive I believe it fully, I'd already had my blood ink tattoo on me. It's the one on my back."

"The skull?" she asked softly as I nodded. I wasn't particularly surprised she had noticed it, but it still made my magic fucking thrilled that she was paying that much attention to us. I know, it was a helpless cause at this point. I was screwed.

"The people that found me were fucking bastards," I admitted easily, almost in a memorized way. "They had me fight in a local circuit, and if I didn't fight I'd get beat. I tried to never use my magic because it was illegal to have a blood ink tattoo at my age. Hell, it is still looked down upon to be a necro, but it's better now. They knew that it was fucking torture killing people without my magic, though. Being in a life and death situation and not letting my magic take over was damn near impossible."

"Are they still alive?" she asked quietly, her eyes filled with anger. Was she angry for me? I couldn't help but smile at Nova's perfection. My baby was the fucking sweetest.

"No," I smirked. "No, they are very dead. I made sure of that."

I hadn't just killed them, either. I'd tortured them before burying them alive and still breathing, enjoying a bottle of scotch on top of their makeshift graves until I felt their life forces extinguish permanently.

"Good." Her eyes sparkled with malice. "So how did you end up in the Red Masques?"

"When I was a bit older, I was contacted by Byron and Edwin, who had heard about me through someone that had seen me at the fighting ring... and yeah, that was that. I joined the Red Masques. Although until about a year or so ago, we kept my magic ability a secret. But once Edwin found another necromancer, and one that had a relationship to the new Queen through her sister, he thought it was safer to admit to it."

Her eyes flickered over to River in thought, and I nearly laughed at that. Nova was damn persistent, and I knew she was going to get the story out of River. The one that he had yet to even tell me. Whether that was a good or bad thing really didn't fucking matter. It could release all hell, but with Nova, she demanded one hundred percent, and I would give it to her. It was never in question how much of me she had. I just wished my brother would get the fuck on board.

Also, that he would stop being an asshole, because when he was upset with her that one night? I hadn't been joking about burying him alive. I mean... I probably wouldn't have killed him, but a bit of time underground changed a person. Just saying.

My thoughts turned to when I realized Nova was gone that first time. When I realized just how important she'd become to me.

"Everett."

I looked up to meet River's gaze from where I sat against the living room wall, a bottle of scotch sitting next to me as I poured my fifth drink or something. It didn't really matter, did it? Or maybe it did. Maybe if I got wasted enough, she would appear.

"Who does she think she is?" I demanded of River, his eyes dark and concerned.

"What do you mean?" he asked with a sigh, sitting against the wall next to me. It was late and almost everyone was sleeping, or trying to. Mostly licking their wounds. Fox had yet to talk since this afternoon. This little witch was fucking everything up.

I wanted her to fuck everything up... next to me. Not wherever the fuck she was.

"I mean," I took a drink, "she just fucking left, River. She just fucking disappeared, as if she--" I just stopped, unable to finish my sentence.

"I know," he grunted. "We are going to find her, man. We are starting fresh in the morning. None of the airlines had record--"

"I don't care about any of that," I muttered. "I just want her here."

River looked at the bottle next to me and took a sip as I tried to shake myself from how fucking drunk I was, but that shit wasn't going anywhere. He grimaced. Yeah, it wasn't my favorite either. Then again, after combing the local area for her power signature and finding nothing, it didn't really matter to me what I was drinking. As long as it was alcoholic.

"We are going to find her," River said again.

"She's never leaving again after we do," I promised, feeling like I was repeating myself. I'd been promising the same shit to myself these past few hours. A promise I may not be able to keep.

My brother put his head down and voiced my worst fear in a soft tone. "What if she doesn't want to come back, man?"

"That's not an option," I growled sharply, not willing to consider that. "We know why she left, and her not coming back isn't a fucking option. She's just confused."

River grunted and took another drink. I frowned, realizing just how much she fucking meant to me. Realizing again how much I needed her to come back. The anger, hurt, and a fuck ton of other irrational emotions I felt towards her absence overwhelmed me. For the first time in my life, I didn't know what the hell to do.

What I did know? She was fucking coming back. Nova was ours, and she was going to realize that real damn soon.

"I love you," I stated softly as her head snapped back to me and a smile lit up her face. Our plane came to a landing, bumping slightly, as I tugged her more solidly against me.

"Hey, I love you too, bud," she teased, bopping my nose before sitting up and taking off her seatbelt.

Instantly, Nova was bouncing with energy, and I watched as she looked outside, my own eyes tracking the almost alien-like landscape. Palm trees were about the only green I could see. Everything else was in browns and tans, with a blue sky that was lacking any storms. I smirked, wondering if Arizona was about to see their first thunderstorm in some time.

"Is anyone meeting us?" I asked Fox as he looked up from his laptop.

"They are sending a car," he noted. As the plane opened up and we began to disembark, I couldn't help but smile at the excitement rolling through Nova. The woman was an honest-to-god Energizer bunny sometimes.

"Let's go meet our new friends!" Nova sang, trying to pep up Ramsey. I nearly rolled my eyes at the bastard's attempt to not play along with her but decided to intervene for my own selfish reasons.

"Come on, baby." I scooped her up and in a quick movement transferred her to my back so she was hanging on me like a monkey. I heard Ramsey growl slightly, making me feel all that more antagonistic. His loss.

"Ever," she giggled at my move as I made our way towards a large black SUV waiting for us.

"What is King Desmond like?" Nova asked more seriously after a moment.

"Interesting. You'll see," I offered, not really knowing how else to describe him.

Nova didn't ask anything else and I was glad. I honestly felt like the Reid brothers and Desmond were just the type of fucking people you had to meet yourself.

NOVA

"Holy shit," I mumbled as we pulled through a pair of massive gates.

Now, I'd never been to Arizona before, but this shifter compound outside of Phoenix? Well, I felt like it embodied all things 'desert-y.'

The blazing sun was beating down through pure blue skies, which I found amusing, because *let's see how long that lasts, right?* Palm trees stood proud amongst a beautiful tan landscape with rocks and cacti. Bright houses with Spanish tile roofs littered every street we went down after passing the heavily armed gate. A gate that had been guarded by massive men I realized were shifters as I continued to assemble a small list inside of my head of magic signatures and who they correlated to. Or what type of creature they correlated to. I didn't like the idea of not understanding the world around me fully.

There was a charge to the air I didn't understand, and I found myself absorbing every element of my surroundings. As we turned a corner, our driver silent, I couldn't help but find myself impressed by the massive glass and stone mansion we pulled up towards. I mean, it wasn't really my thing, but I could nevertheless appreciate the aesthetic of it.

"This isn't the Reid residence," River pointed out to the driver.

He *would* know what their house looked like ahead of time. Freakin' over-controlling nut job. As if hearing my thoughts, he narrowed his eyes suspiciously. I offered him a wink, unable to control goading him a bit. What? Worst case scenario, I would get fucked, right? As if that was the worst case in anyone's book! It was my hope right now, if we were being honest.

"Alpha Reid is currently at the Louvre residence."

Louvre. Louvre. Why the hell did that sound so familiar?

As I stepped out of the car, the front door opened. It was a concrete slab that swung outwards. Instantly my eyebrows went up, because *holy crap* - can we say shifter power? Like woah. I thought Maya and her mates had a lot, and they did, but this was far more savage and feral feeling. It filled the air with something else I didn't understand fully. It felt like it was radiating from the building behind the man walking down the steps towards us. I couldn't help but smile a bit as clouds began to gather.

My magic was such a goddamn show-off, do you see this shit? She was such an attention whore. I couldn't blame her, though. We couldn't exactly let anyone be scarier than us, could we?

"Hello," I chirped positively as I felt River's arm wrap around my waist.

"I'm assuming you are not Everett? Desmond said someone named 'Everett' had to come into our house with his team," the man rumbled, sounding very upset about the concept. I had to admit, the guy was handsome, very tall and with long hair tied back. His power told me I should be scared of him, but honestly, nothing much scared me anymore. At least not other supernatural creatures, I should say.

"No." I couldn't help but grin and nodded towards the man next to me, who was now vibrating with power. "This would be Ever."

"Dean Reid?" Everett offered as the two of them shook hands briefly before disengaging, their magic very, very different and completely at odds.

"That's me," he nearly growled. "Come inside so we can get this done as fast as fucking possible."

"Grumpy," I mumbled as an observation, making Fox chuckle. I saw Dean tense, but for whatever reason he didn't respond as he led us into the house.

It was because I was scary, wasn't it? That made the most sense to me.

The minute we crossed the threshold, my magic snarled, expanding out possessively and completely covering my men. All of them shifted but didn't fucking question it, which was good because I could not fucking explain why she was behaving this way. My eyes widened as we reached the kitchen, my magic narrowing her precision and wrapping even tighter, but calming down somewhat now that she had apparently found the source of the 'issue.'

"Oh!" I tilted my head. "*Louvre*. Now I know why I recognized that name."

August chuckled at my outburst, but I was too busy cate-gorizing the room in a span of maybe a second or so, my magic on high alert as if guarding my men from something. I had no idea what, considering they seemed so damn relaxed.

The massive concrete foyer we stood in had two-story ceilings and a glass and metal decor style that felt hard and masculine. A kitchen, not seemingly made for much use, was where the group of seven stood.

Lorcan Louvre.

Fashion model. Hot mess. Apparently, if I was taking a guess here, *supernatural?* I couldn't tell for the life of me what she was though. Besides beautiful. Because let's face it, that was just the honest-to-god truth.

She had to be a few inches, maybe two, taller than myself, and her multi-colored blonde and blue-green hair had me smiling. The woman was tan as fuck and essentially my exact opposite, down to how she was dressed. A small light blue tank top and boyfriend jeans hung off her thin frame. Her seafoam green eyes met mine curiously as I tried to determine her magic, but there was a massive wall between us and I couldn't tell you why. Honestly, I was hella jealous of her vibe right now.

Outside, the sky rumbled as the very grumpy shifter wrapped his arm around her. Ah, that made sense. He probably didn't want people in his home because he was feeling protective over her. I understood much better now.

"I'm Nova," I added awkwardly after wrapping up my observation of her.

"Lorcan," she offered with a small smile. "But seems you knew that."

"Girl," I laughed, "if you don't want people to know who you are, you may be going about it the wrong way."

"Everett, right?" a man interrupted, making me scowl and evoking a small laugh from Lorcan's mouth. I turned to watch a handsome man with bright blue and green eyes cross the floor to shake hands. I stepped back slightly as introductions were made, just watching each one of them, trying to decide if we liked them or not. Well, more specifically, my magic was deciding if we liked them or not.

I learned that the man who had stepped forward was apparently King Desmond. I could feel the magic rolling off of him, and color me impressed, but he was crazy powerful. Not that I could explain his magic exactly, but my eyes tracked almost invisible blue and green wisps of fog that seemed to cling to him. I had a feeling this man could disappear right into thin air if necessary.

As my magic rolled over each of the individuals, their actual introductions meaning little to me, I did take a moment to appreciate that they were a very good-looking group of people. Like *model* good looks.

Apparently the grumpy shifter was named Dean Reid, and he was alpha to the local pride, whose compound we were currently in. Something that made far too much sense. As I said, he had a lot of power rolling off him, and it was rather unique in how untamable it seemed. The man truly seemed more animal than human. Then again, so did his apparent brothers. The more heavily tattooed one was named Rhett, and the other was Cash. Both contained less power and dominance than Dean but seemed equally as vicious.

Would they feel awkward if they knew how much I was dissecting them right now?

Next we were introduced to Draven, who appeared as what I imagined the devil mythos was derived from. You know the type. I truly had no idea what his magic was, but I could tell that he was old. Like really fucking old. My magic narrowed her eyes at him, not trusting him in comparison to the others because he wasn't identifiable.

Adriel was far more easy to determine because the man had pointed ears and looked like some elf warrior from *Lord of the Rings*. I was tempted to ask him if he knew how similar he looked to the character, but I didn't really want to have to explain my Tolken obsession if he wasn't aware of the Earth realm story. Besides, I could see shadows gathering around him, and call me crazy but I was almost damn positive the guy wasn't someone you wanted to fuck with. Apparently, he and Draven were kings or something, but that title meant very little to me currently.

"... and I'm Nova!" I pointed out once again as the circuit of introductions finished on me. I had completed my thorough examination of each of the possible threats in the room and found them to be dangerous but fairly neutralized. "Now, if we are done with pleasantries, I would love to know what exactly you are, Lorcan?"

What? I literally never claimed I was patient. Or tactful.

The room seemed to freeze. Well, everyone outside of my boys did. They just looked at me curiously. Before you ask, my magic was still curling around them, and I think they could tell because half of them had that cocky look they got whenever I got possessive. Sorry not sorry. My boys almost killed some humans for saying some crass words to me while drunk, they could deal with it.

"I'm sorry, what?" Lorcan asked, frowning. Her energy vibrated.

"What *are* you?" I tilted my head. "The energy poking at the magic I have surrounding myself and my boys. What is it? I know what the others are, besides Draven, but what are you?"

An odd look came over her. "That's not really important to you."

I arched a brow. "Is this a *Star Wars* thing, like '*These are not the droids you are looking for*?'"

Lorcan snorted and shook her head. "What the hell are *you*?"

"I think you should answer first," I grumbled, but then

said flippantly, "Demi-goddess. I'm a demi-goddess, and these are my monsters."

"Monsters?" the Rhett dude asked.

"The term 'mages' wouldn't be very inclusive to Ramsey and Nour," I pointed out.

Lorcan smirked and looked at her boys, specifically Adriel. "Is it possible she's immune?"

"Demi-gods shouldn't be…" he frowned. "Besides angels and full gods, that shouldn't be possible. Even with some full gods, unless they are extremely powerful, they can be affected. I've heard of top tier gods being able to..."

"Oh my god," I groaned, interrupting him. "Woman. What are you?"

Dean growled, but Lorcan patted his chest. "I'm a siren, and why you nine are not affected is beyond me."

"I know nothing about sirens." I turned toward my men, who mostly seemed just as clueless as me.

Ramsey spoke, shrugging. "I just thought they were extinct."

"We were supposed to be," Lorcan sighed. "Alright, I am going to try this once because I can't get a read on any of your desires."

"Oh, this is fun!" I exclaimed.

I felt her magic expand out as she narrowed her eyes. "Go back outside and get in the car."

I raised my brows in curiosity as my boys looked around, all of us expecting something. Or maybe I just was. Either way, I was disappointed when nothing happened, even if it was supposedly a good thing.

"Well I'll be damned," Desmond chuckled. "That's insane. I wonder why the others are included in that though?"

"My magic is possessive as hell," I noted. "Now Lorcan,

while they talk about demonic soil and magic draining, let's go outside and talk about fun stuff."

"Lorcan," Dean grumbled.

"I'm fine." She kissed him lightly as he huffed, and I nearly skipped past, landing myself next to the statuesque woman.

I'd spent most of my life in Washington. I'd traveled a bit with my father, but even then I'd stayed fairly insulated. So to say that Arizona was a different world? That was a very large understatement.

Everything around us was picture perfect. I could see mountains, the tan and green-spotted desert landscape, and massive palm trees that reminded me of an oasis. Her backyard pool was large with massive, comfortable furniture surrounding it, a pool house far to the right of the yard. I threw myself down on a large plush chair as the skies rumbled, making her brow dip as she looked at me.

"I'm a descendant of Set, god of Chaos, hence the stormy weather and stuff. Don't worry, if it starts raining I'll make sure we keep dry," I promised as she nodded, seeming to accept that before sitting down on her own lounge chair looking pensive.

Maybe pensive wasn't the right word for Lorcan. I actually wasn't positive how to describe her. She had a haunted edge to her and seemed to be surrounded by vibrating magic that was on the verge of exploding out of her, seemingly only repressed by her own desire to do so. I was going to bet, despite not knowing a lot about sirens, that if the woman let loose, she could really fuck some shit up.

Lorcan shook her head, saying, "I didn't expect any of this when Desmond mentioned he had to meet with a Red Masques team."

"It was a bit last minute," I explained. "We only received

our contact information to reach out to Desmond a few days ago. Plus, I've got to be honest, I am only half sure why we are here. Well, that and the donuts. Totally here for the donuts."

It wasn't completely honest, because I was well aware why we were here. But when people felt out of the loop, they usually didn't like to feel alone in that sense. So as far as Lorcan knew, I didn't have a clue what was going on. Maybe it would be easier for her to talk about what happened in the Demonic realm instead of feeling interrogated.

My question? How the hell did I casually bring that up?

"I don't even remember the last time I had a donut," Lorcan arched a brow as if the thought surprised her.

"Lorcan!" I offered a horrified look. "You have to. We could even go right now. Honestly, I should have brought the half box I had from the jet. This place near our house that we get them from? Pure heaven, I swear to the gods."

Thunder rolled as her eyes widened, making me smile. Alright, so that was a very neat little coincidence there. Or it was possible the gods were listening to me, nosy bastards.

After a moment, without bringing up the donuts, much to my disappointment, she asked, "What is the need for the meeting? We've been a bit busy today... so I didn't get to ask."

Searching her face, I decided to offer a bit of truth. I'd always been terrible with secrets. "So long story short, we found out my 'father' has been draining people for magic. Cool, right? Well, apparently it's a bit of a thing, because in the Horde they had the same issue. The Queen and her men had heard a rumor of something similar happening in the Demonic realm. Did you experience -- Lorcan?"

Well, hell, I was going to ask her what she'd experienced, but her eyes had turned black and her skin chalk white. If I wasn't as observant as I am, I may have not noticed. Upon hearing her name, she swallowed and moved her gaze away.

"You don't have to," I shook my head, feeling awkward. "I had just heard you'd been down there, but I get it if you don't--"

"It's not that." She inhaled and looked back at me. "You said this has become a problem?"

"That's what we are gathering," I shrugged. "I know the guys wanted to ask Desmond about some other stuff as well, but yeah, that is the main reason we are here."

Lorcan looked thoughtful for a moment before speaking softly. "Something very similar did happen. Sorry, it initially caught me off guard, but you're not wrong. The demon who owned Broken House, the place I'd been imprisoned in during my time down there, was draining power from those he kept hostage in his 'hotel of horrors.' I thought it had been more of a feeling or just some bullshit, but if what you are saying is true than that would mean he is killing them for--" Her voice broke off as I saw her eyes fill with something dark and sad before she tried to smooth it over. Damn, this woman was fantastic at blanking out her emotions.

"We don't have to talk about the rest of it," I offered. "Honestly, just to know it was happening is enough to justify us looking into it."

"I just don't know if I can handle fully talking about it," she admitted softly, almost looking disappointed in herself, which was totally unneeded. I understood not being able to talk about some shit more than most.

"You don't need to explain any more." I reached over and squeezed her hand. "I am literally horrible when it comes to dealing with emotions, specifically mine, so I totally under-stand not wanting to delve into whatever it was you went through. Plus, I am more than likely to suggest revenge or some violent act instead of talking through it."

Lorcan flashed a dark smile. "I like that. The violence part."

"It's what I do," I chimed as she took out a cigarette and lit it. "Well, actually it's what my boys do, and then I decided I liked the way they handled shit. Violence is way more effective than I originally realized."

She laughed and then shook her head. "Honestly, it's refreshing. Everything is so damn intense lately. You're cool, Nova. I'm glad that we met... especially, well, since we seem to both have harems. Should we talk about that? I feel like we sort of have to--"

"Right!?" I sat up with excitement. "I thought it was only me. Then I found out the Queen from the Horde has like five husbands and Vegas is with like ten different men. Apparently it's a thing! Which is good, because I couldn't slow the boat with those psychos in there, even if I wanted to."

Lorcan leaned forward with a small smile. "Are yours crazy also?"

"I can't even begin to explain half of it," I sighed as if it bothered me. "We had a Halloween party yesterday, right? And some asshole made some jerk comment and three of my guys had him and his friends upstairs for the rest of the night doing god knows what. All I know is that they came back with blood on them. Then this other time, one of them almost killed my father for me - trust me, he deserved it, but shit, I had not expected that."

"You don't even have to explain," she nodded. "Certain members of my little group are actually psychotic. One of them tortured a demon and remembered that I had threatened to cut off the bastard's balls... and well, did it."

"That's love," I nodded and then smiled. "Is it wrong that I love it?"

"No, it's hot as hell," Lorcan concluded.

Before I could say anything back, Rhett walked out from inside, his eyes immediately finding Lorcan's and shading with relief. Cute.

"Bunny," he said softly and crouched down, "they are going to be heading down to the Demonic realm--"

"Glad they are making decisions without me," I grumbled, feeling frustrated.

Lorcan shook her head. "I don't think that's a very good idea, Rhett."

"They want to observe the power drain on their own."

Lorcan's jaw tightened. "I really think that's a bad idea."

I squeezed her shoulder gently, standing up. "Lorcan. We are totally fine, trust me. Although I would have appreciated being asked for my input!" I yelled the last part, garnering chuckles from inside.

Ramsey appeared in the door and curled his finger, calling me forward as I left my new friend and sauntered towards my demi-god. I ran a teasing finger up his chest and neck before he caught it and offered me a scowl, but he couldn't hide the heat in his gaze.

What? He was bossy and it was hot.

"Hey you," I winked but then scowled and narrowed my eyes. "Nevermind, I'm actually mad at you. You made plans without even asking me."

Ramsey let out a low rumble as Fox's voice called out, "Gorgeous, we want to go down to the Demonic realm and see what we can find, you game?"

"See!" I grinned as the sky cracked with thunder as I twirled into the room. "That's how you ask. But yes, of course, I'm one hundred percent on board. You don't even need to ask."

August barked out a laugh as River narrowed his eyes. "Nova."

"Yes, sprinkles?"

Everett shook his head. "Baby, you are going to get it if you're not careful."

"Maybe," I shrugged, "but I bet you're too eager to go down to the Demonic realm to give a hell about that. I know you are all using this as a possible excuse to kill shit."

"Never," Fox offered a look of mock horror.

"Baby girl," Cassian's voice was nearly a purr as he offered me a cocky smile, "we don't kill things."

"You're making us look bad in front of new people," Rowan grinned antagonistically. "Doesn't get you many popularity points."

"Row-baby," I teased, "pretty sure I proved my popularity with that party..."

"She's really not off-base when it comes to killing shit," August admitted.

"We are very, very much looking forward to killing things," Everett announced and then sighed. "Although my current list is impossible to finish at the moment."

"Everett," River warned.

"What? I can't lie to my girl."

"Plus, he has a list, River. You should appreciate that level of organization, even if it's because he's a serial killer," I smirked.

"Don't worry, moonbeam," Nour wrapped his arms around me, causing my heart to accelerate. I mean, come on, the man had told me he loved me, how the fuck else was I supposed to react? "I won't kill anything."

"Hey, now," I looked up at him. "I never said it was a bad thing."

Ramsey growled, "Nova, I swear to the Maker--"

A laugh sounded as Lorcan sat down, seemingly entertained as they all stared at us with confusion.

Dean blinked. "How? How the hell are you all not exhausted all of the time? The group of you are goddamn hyperactive--"

"Dean!" Lorcan scolded.

"It's true," Rowan pointed out. "We run on chaos and violence."

"We should package that into an energy drink!" I announced.

"You are also insane," Adriel muttered.

"Pretty sure we are all insane here," I said primly. "No need to rate. You are just probably better at hiding it. Or not. I couldn't tell you, because I was thinking about my monsters' violent streak and all the fun we are going to have down there."

"A drink," Cash groaned and stood. "I need a fucking drink."

"So when are we going to the Demonic realm?" I asked, leaning my head against Nour.

"Desmond is going to open a portal for us once we grab some stuff from the Reid estate," River explained.

I blinked and turned to Lorcan. "Do you have a badass outfit I could borrow?"

"I think I still have some stuff here," I thought I heard her mumble. Did they not live here? That would be some shit my boys would pull just to make sure no one would come into our actual home.

"Nova can't do anything without a costume change," Rowan pointed out.

I happily followed my new friend toward the stairs, and I heard Ramsey make a frustrated noise. "Nova, if you come down here with less goddamn clothes on than now--"

"You will what?" I arched a brow as River chuckled. "What will you do, Ram?"

Ramsey inhaled, looking like he was about to lose it and hopefully bend me over, as I winked and followed Lorcan into a room.

What?! I was curious to know what the hell he'd do!

Lorcan's room was stunning, although it did seem fairly empty, making me wonder where she actually lived. My eyes traced what seemed to be fairly new drywall near the door of the bathroom and the closet, the paint not matching exactly.

I stepped into the closet as my eyebrows shot up. "This is amazing."

"I have a lot of designers sending me shit," she exhaled and then shook her head. "Take whatever you want. Seriously. The stuff I wear isn't even in here, if we are being honest."

"I would love it if designers sent me stuff," I pointed out.

Lorcan looked at my outfit. "You dress like that a lot?"

"Now I do," I nodded.

"Send your address to me and I'll send you anything that seems to fit the bill," she shrugged.

"Are we the same size?" I cocked a brow.

"You're shorter," she pointed out, "but it should be fine."

I had been more talking about my ass... What? It was pretty fantastic and perky from running. Made it hard to wear jeans sometimes, though. Just saying.

"You know, until a month ago I had to wear a tan dress almost every day. Isn't that sad?" I offered, grabbing a few promising items. I sort of understood what she meant about this not being the clothes she wore. Half of it didn't seem her style.

"Yes, actually," Lorcan admitted.

Not giving a fuck about modesty - and also because Lorcan was sitting and flipping through a magazine she'd clearly left here - I wiggled off my shorts and pulled on long black, almost military-style pants that worked with the top I already had on. I pulled the top half of my hair into two mini buns and left the rest of it down. Adjusting my boobs in the corset top, I laced my boots back up and smirked.

This was like *Nova the Badass: Tomb Raider Edition.*

"You need to be careful down there," she noted softly. "They play by very different rules."

"Like what?" I asked as a seriousness ran over me. I inhaled, noticing that it had yet to rain, and instead of moisture in the air, something else seemed to be growing. Fuck. My magic needed to chill out, but she was clearly worked up about the concept of us going down there.

An alert buzzed Lorcan's phone as she arched a brow. "Dust storm."

Ah, fuck.

"Butterfly!" River's masculine voice echoed through the large space downstairs.

Immediately I crossed the room into the elevated hallway and looked over the glass railing. "I know! I know! I just figured it would be a fucking thunderstorm. A dust storm? That's a new one, even for me."

August prodded, "Any way that you can pull it back, sunflower? My magic is acting up in response." I could see the truth in his words, his shoulders tense and his eyes darkening.

I inhaled, closing my eyes and trying to pull back my power, but the bitch just offered me a narrow-eyed glance before going back to standing in front of our men. I opened my eyes and grunted, "Yeah, no. That isn't going to happen. She won't move. Very protective today."

"Probably my fault," Lorcan admitted. "Since they are immune, it is probably because of your magic, and so it won't chill out until they are away from me."

"Well, we're leaving soon," I waved my hand, not wanting to worry her. "What's a little sand storm, right? It seems very sunny here, maybe a bit of stormy weather will do some good."

I took out my phone and opened the messaging app before she could respond. "Here, message your phone so we have each other's numbers."

She nodded and did it quickly before handing it back. "Also, didn't mean to pry, but you have a message."

"Oh?" Who in the hell was messaging me?

"Who is it, gorgeous?" Fox asked, sounding jealous.

"If it's a dude, I'm going to lose my shit," I heard Rowan mumble as one of Lorcan's men laughed.

I smirked but instead of teasing him just said, "Maya."

Maya: Nova! I was serious about dying my hair fully. Will you come with me if I do?

That would be a fuck yes.

Me: Absolutely! When I get back into town?

Looking up at Lorcan I spoke, "You should meet her, she's absolutely wonderful. We ran into each other at the costume store."

Lorcan frowned slightly. "Maya? Why the hell does that name sound so familiar?"

"Brown hair? Massive gold eyes? Adorable? Like, ridiculously so?" I provided.

Something shaded Lorcan's eyes as if a sad memory had

come to her. "Oh yeah, shit, I think I met her at Vogue back in September."

"Oh, cool!" I put away my phone. "What I'm hearing is that we need to all hang out together?"

"Sure," Lorcan nodded despite looking a bit sad.

"We good to go, baby?" Ever called. I hugged Lorcan quickly and bounded down the steps eagerly.

"Alright! I am officially ready. Off to the Demonic realm we go, my monsters!"

I smirked as they grumbled, and I couldn't help but love their reaction. I wasn't lying, they were my monsters.

CASSIAN

"Cassian," she growled quietly, the sound reminding me of a kitten. I smirked, wrapping my arm around her hot, sexy little body.

Luckily, her magic had relaxed now that we were at the Reid estate and the only person around was King Desmond. Not that I had minded her magic rolling over my skin. It wasn't any worse than what mine did to hers. I did, however, get off at the fucking idea of her being possessive. Never jealous, because the woman never needed to question how I felt about her. But possessive? That was hot as hell.

I nipped her shoulder as she let out a soft sound, my hand skimming over her toned stomach. I had been playing with her hair, but as she squirmed against me, ignoring Desmond's conversation with the others, I wrapped the silky locks around my hand and tilted her neck to the side.

"Baby girl," I chided, "you aren't listening. What if you miss something important?"

She let out a small amused sound. "I don't need anyone to tell me how to be a badass."

That was *very* accurate.

M. SINCLAIR

"Want to look at weapons instead?" I grinned as she perked up. What? I was a fucking metal mage, and that shit was far more interesting than whatever River was concerned over. Plus, I was very eager for some alone time with Nova after last night. You know, when I cut her Halloween outfit from her body and fucked her against the tree? Yeah. That.

"We are going to look at the weapons," Nova announced, tugging my hand as Fox scowled, feeling left out. I couldn't help but smile as she led the way towards an open door to our left. Apparently she'd been listening to Desmond enough to know where the dangerous shit was.

"I need a cool sword or gun," she announced as she turned and walked backward, her smile dangerous.

"Daggers are far more useful at close range," I pointed out as my eyes flickered over her outfit. Useful for cutting the clothes off my baby girl. I nearly groaned at the memory of the metal blade I had against her soft skin. I had no excuse for how much that shit turned me on.

I think part of it was the trust aspect. Like she trusted me to have a weapon that close to her. Trusted me that I would never do anything to hurt her. More than that though, my magic was so hard and unyielding, and Nova was the opposite of that. She was chaotic and wild. On a metaphorical level, my magic wanted to restrict and tie her up, keeping her contained by our sharp edges in a possessive way. On a physical level, the concept of the sharp edges of my magic against her soft vulnerable skin made me hard as hell. So yeah, it was essentially an 'all in' type of deal.

"What type of dagger?" she asked as she stood in front of a display case of knives. I stepped up behind her, my hands smoothing over her hips before she leaned back against me, tilting her head up so that I was staring into her stunning eyes.

"For you or for me?" I smirked.

She hummed, "For you."

I lifted a hand to grab a dark obsidian-handled blade, spinning it in my right hand before presenting it to her. Her lips pulled into a smile.

"That's bigger than the one you used the other night," she purred.

My cock jumped against her ass as she grinned further. "Did you like doing that, Cassian? Using a knife on me?"

I narrowed my eyes, trying to not portray my amusement. I pressed the dagger against her elegant throat, on its side and flat. She froze, her eyes heating instead of filling with concern. My baby girl was kinky as hell, and I was fucking loving it.

"That's not in question," I admitted softly. "What about you, Nova? Do you like it?"

"Yes," she breathed as I flicked the knife up, the sharp edge biting into her skin just slightly as she moaned. I couldn't help but lean down and kiss her as I pulled the knife away, not wanting to actually hurt her... but instead leave a mark. A thin cut. I would have loved if she also had my cum on her, but I couldn't always get what I fucking wanted. Unfortunately.

I brought the knife up to my lips and licked the blood off of it after pulling away, her eyes going hooded as she turned towards me. I dropped the knife as she seared her lips to mine, making me groan in relief. Fucking hell.

Without a second thought, I had her against the wall, my tongue brushing against her soft lips as she let me in. Her entire body melded into mine, and she became completely open to my kiss, her hands tightening in my hair.

"Cass," she whimpered as I pulled back, breathing roughly. My eyes flashed down to her lips that were slightly blood stained.

"Goddamnit," my brother's voice echoed.

Nova let out a soft giggle, turning her head as my eyes moved down to the mark I'd left on her neck. I dipped my head and sucked on the cut, her small moan making me fucking thrilled, before I pulled back to look at the bruised skin. Perfect.

"This is going to be a long day," Fox mumbled.

"Please don't fuck in here," Desmond sighed as the others joined us. Nova blushed as I pulled her back against me, wrapping my arms around her protectively and narrowing my eyes at the demon.

"I am going to glamour your magic so that it registers as demonic while you are down there. But if you use active magic it will be pretty fucking obvious what you are hiding, and depending on how much you use, it may even break the glamour," Desmond explained as I felt his magic expand to surround us.

Nova wiggled uncomfortably, but I simply bit her shoulder slightly and she relaxed against me fully. I felt her magic tighten around her, and I nearly rolled my eyes at the way mine snarled at Desmond's magic trying to glamour us. I knew it was necessary, but did I want him that fucking close to my girl? No.

Desmond's magic was off the fucking charts, especially compared to most demons I knew, and it clashed so directly with my fae mage magic that I felt almost twitchy at the feel of it.

"When I portal you," he continued, "you're going to be placed directly outside the 'Alam realm in my kingdom. I can't portal you directly inside, so you will have to cross yourself."

"Once you are inside the realm, you need to go directly to Broken House. It looks like an Art Deco hotel. *Do not* go

anywhere else, because getting trapped is completely possible. As it stands, Broken House is really only safe during
the day. If they ask you if you are a guest, say no and tell
them you are just going to the show. All audience members
attending the show have a safety clause to protect them
from being caught in there. You would have something
similar as a guest... but then you would be expected to
hunt."

"Hunt?" Nova arched a brow.

"Broken House is a hotel where Mr. Black, the demon
you will want to keep an eye on, treats his guests to hunting
exotic supernatural creatures. It was where Lorcan and her
brother were brought when they were kidnapped, which is
why they have such extensive knowledge." Desmond grit out
the last part, something super dark flashing in his gaze before
he managed to hide it. Yeah. I wasn't buying that shit.

"Oh wow," Nova mumbled before shaking herself.

"I should warn you, this show is focused on torture as the
main source of entertainment. You should be able to get a
good grasp on the power drain problem from it, but past that
I'm not sure what else you will be able to tell," Desmond
sighed.

"If we are close to the power drain asshole I will probably
be able to get a better grasp of the issue," Nova admitted. "So
let me just make sure I've got this straight. Enter the Pain
realm, go to torture show, and watch power drain asshole Mr.
Black put on his performance? And then while we are there
we should be able to figure out how extreme it is and maybe
who suggested it to him if we can get behind stage or some
shit--"

"I wouldn't do that," Desmond grunted.

"Does that check out to everyone?" my girl asked the
boys, ignoring the demon king, much to his frustration.

"She heard the torture part right?" the guy asked looking at me, which I found amusing.

Nova laughed and spoke bluntly, making me look at her like a goddamn lovesick fool.

"Desmond, let me be straight with you. In the past month, I not only found out that the man I thought was my father is a serial killer but that he has killed far over two hundred people - supernatural mostly, but not always - before draining their magic. He's also a necrophiliac. I'm not joking, he fucks dead bodies. I've seen a woman ripped open with a wig on her head that matches the shade of my dead mother, who he beat senseless and killed every night, only for her to come back so he could do it again. I have seen pictures of my asshole ex-fiance filming my father doing this disgusting shit while bodies hung on hooks bleeding out in the background. Let me be clear. A torture show will not phase me. Will it infuriate me? Absolutely. But surprise me? Gross me out? The time for that is far gone. And don't worry about these guys, they will be just fine. I do appreciate the warning and concern, though."

The room was silent before Fox broke out laughing, and I shook my head, pressing my forehead to her delicate shoulder. Her blunt nature didn't surprise any of us, but Desmond just stared at her before muttering something under his breath and stepping away from us.

Probably wanting us out of his hair, he snapped and began to open up a portal. As everyone grabbed what they were bringing, Nova stepped away from me, picking up the dagger from before and winking.

"Sunshine," Ramsey spoke as River offered me a dry look at the cut across her throat.

"Yeah, big guy?" she chirped happily.

"Be fucking careful."

I expected her to tease him, but instead she walked up to him and kissed his cheek. "Don't worry, Ram. We've got this."

We did. I wasn't very concerned.

"That wasn't a 'yes.'" he growled slightly, making Nova laugh.

"Alright, let's get this shit done," River called. Nova nodded and bounced towards Everett as I grabbed a few more daggers and other shit, rolled my shoulders back, cracked my neck, and smiled at the prospect of violence.

Without another word, Nova tugged Everett with her into the void of space.

NOVA

Portaling was always a very odd experience to me. I mean, I suppose not odd as much as unsettling. My head buzzed as I dove into the void Desmond opened for us, and unlike the Horde portal, which had felt like a slow-moving river, this felt sharp and dangerous. This felt more like white water rafting during a goddamn thunderstorm and flooding.

So, yeah. That's fun.

I was jolted out of the interdimensional realm portal and before I knew it. A groan came out of my mouth as I landed on my ass, pain radiating through me as I managed to roll over on my stomach after laying down in pain. Everett landed next to me a bit more smoothly, crouching in near perfect balance before standing up fully and running a hand through his hair.

"Those suck," I mumbled as he tugged me off the ground, both of us looking around. Although, whenever I was this close to any of my boys, it was difficult to focus.

However, the legitimate beauty of the space around me sure as hell was tugging at my attention, making me look around in wonder. Well, hell. I guess I just had low expectations for the Demonic realm, because where we had landed? Absolutely stunning, like a goddamn Mediterranean paradise.

A massive brownstone gate covered in ivy and orange blossoms stood in front of us, somehow softening the effect of the solid closed door and ridiculously high walls. I turned and spun away from Ever as I examined the rest of the land. My eyes widened as I mentally gave props to King Desmond for having such a beautiful kingdom. I mean, I couldn't see a ton of it, but from what I could see? I was impressed.

I guess when I thought of the Demonic realm... I'd thought of hell? I mean, call me stupid, but I felt like that was a reasonable fucking assumption. I of course had no idea what was on the other side of the gate, but on this side the skies were a bright blue with white fluffy clouds and richly colored vegetation.

In the distance, as I narrowed my eyes and used my magic just a bit, I could make out a massive castle that looked Spanish in style. Trees ran in long, vertical paths that led towards the kingdom, lush and heavy with fresh fruit. I had the urge to explore the path and Demonic realm overall, but I guessed I'd have to wait until I figured out the rest of my shit, because I didn't have time for a vacation.

Alright, let's be real. The first order of business was actually going to be Bora Bora, but this may be second on my list.

"So how the hell do we get through this gate?" I asked curiously as I turned to face my men. I smirked as Fox's eyes drew up from where he'd been staring at my ass. Dirty bastard. Ramsey stood next to me, tense and worried, but I ignored him, refusing to give him more ammunition. Everything was going to be fine. He was just stressed and worried. That was all this was.

"Just walk in, I assume," Rowan offered as I followed

him towards the gate, slipping out of the grasp of Mr. Grumpy as River saddled up next to me. My eyes flickered up to him as something dark flashed in his gaze, a hand wrapping around the back of my neck in a possessive, tight hold. I sighed into it, feeling more relaxed as he looked over my expression before cursing, a rumble escaping his chest.

I wasn't afraid to admit that I loved River's dominance of me in bed. It was hot as hell. Now, was he afraid of that? Yeah. Yeah he was. That was fine, though. I could be fucking fearless for the both of us.

August walked next to me, and as we neared the gate, the material shimmered, a gold square appearing with the indentation of a hand. I nearly groaned, knowing what the hell this was. Well, at least I had a good assumption.

"We need to do a blood sacrifice," Fox confirmed. "Well, at least I can assume that, considering the scent of the hand indent."

"Everything in goddamn magic requires blood," I muttered, taking out my dagger.

"Nova--" River rumbled as I sliced down my hand, tucked the dagger away, and turned to look at him while pressing my hand into the indent.

"Goddamnit, Nova," Ramsey growled.

"Hey," Nour voiced, making me smile. "Someone had to do it. Both of you stop giving her shit."

"Agreed," Ever voiced.

"Are we ganging up on River and Ramsey?" Fox tilted his head. "That's fun."

"They are pretty similar, so it wouldn't be hard," Cassian drawled.

Rowan stretched his arms above his head before flashing me a smile, the door swinging open. "Thanks, wildcat."

My eyes narrowed in on his bare, stretched abs as I realized my tattoo was still there. My mouth popped open, realizing he had written 'wildcat' in it and kept it. He winked as I blushed, August chuckling and ushering me through the very clear wards. I shivered against my alchemy mage as he ran his nose along my neck. All of us paused as we entered into the new demonic sector.

Holy hell.

"Well, this is trippy," I admitted.

When I was told we were going to the sector of the Demonic realm called the 'Pain' realm, I didn't exactly think of 1960s California. But that was literally the only way I could describe it besides saying it seemed to be the inspiration for the song *Hotel California.*

In front of us spanned something I could only describe as the L.A. strip, or what you would imagine it to look like forty years or so ago. Neon signs flashed along palm-lined streets, and a dusky red sky gave everything an eerie glow and permanent feeling of sunset. Beautiful people crowded the strip, drinking and laughing in designer clothes, the sound of waves from a massive purple ocean expanding off the docks to our right filling our ears. It was beautiful. No joke, absolutely stunning.

Too bad this was the Pain realm, or else I'd consider this a solid vacation option, as well. Could you tell that I wanted to travel? Was my wanderlust obvious?

"Shit," Fox inhaled sharply. "I don't know who is bleeding, but there is a goddamn ton of blood being shed around here."

River inhaled uncomfortably. "Yeah, this is fucked up."

I frowned, my magic already annoyed at the possibility of innocent creatures being hurt. "I really am going to hate this, aren't I?

"I can't even describe it as death magic, the bullshit going on around here." Everett's admission made me more concerned, because if the necromancer is worried... just saying.

"Alright." I inhaled and started walking. "Where are we headed?"

"Up ahead," August warned as my eyes focused on our target.

A massive retro hotel with large windows and bright blue and pink awnings stood proudly with a flashing sign. *Broken House*. It should have been charming, yet despite its pristine condition, I could feel the chills rolling over my skin. I narrowed my gaze on a different entrance than the main one because, call me cautious, but I was going to avoid walking into the damn place as much as I could.

Before we could get there, I stumbled, a chest very purposefully appearing in front of me. My eyes narrowed as I looked up at a handsome man that was staring at me intently. I stepped back as he tilted his head in a predatory move, his eyes flashing silver as he looked me over.

"Yeah, fuck no," Everett snarled, grabbing me and putting me behind him. I almost smiled at the man's frustrated expression.

"How much?" His clear english accent had me almost laughing.

"I'm sorry?" Rowan chuckled softly as Fox ran a hand up and down my spine. I think it was in an attempt to calm himself.

"How much to buy her for a night?" he demanded.

Nour shook his head as I rose on my toes and fixed him with a look. "Did you just call me a goddamn hooker?"

The man arched a brow and looked back at Everett. The mage was vibrating with tension, and I was thankful for River as he stepped up. He'd deal with this diplomatically so we could continue on our way. Well, I had guessed he would be level headed, but a small laugh came from my throat as he hit the man. Like fucking punched him. A solid hit that had no magic behind it at all and sent the man to the ground, hitting his head on the concrete and knocking him out.

I blinked and squeezed River's hand. "Thanks for defending my honor, sweetie."

River grunted as I stepped over the man, kicking him slightly before proceeding towards our destination. Call me a fucking hooker and you get hit by my hot boyfriend. Well, one of them. Maybe more. Like who the hell did he think he was? Was this a thing here? That was fucked up. I scowled, wanting to go back and hurt him for disrespecting me. Bastard.

I passed in front of the main front door and followed the massive line that was growing in front of another pair of massive black doors with 'Broken' on one side and 'House' on the other. My men and I got into the back of line, and I found myself relaxing a bit, finding familiarity in the talking around me.

Mind you, they were demons talking about killing people and torture, but still it was calming me. I leaned back against Cassian, who massaged the back of my head as the boys talked casually, more than likely trying to not stick out by looking tense or uncomfortable.

After all, since we were seeing the show, it was assumed that we were into this stuff.

As we neared the front of the line, I estimated that maybe a half an hour had passed. Music, a mix between the broken keys of a piano and techno - I know, it's very odd - began to blast, and its disjointed tune had me frowning uncomfortably. Everett closed his eyes, exhaling before seeming to shake something.

Oh. Shit. It was the music. Damn, I always forgot how sensitive he was to noise.

Nerves began to penetrate my system, so I tried to act excited, plastering a smile on and bouncing slightly. Yet as we got closer to the entrance, I realized we probably didn't need to sit through a show to find proof of the pull.

I could fucking feel it.

Every inch of my skin crawled, and my magic shifted uncomfortably, clearly pissed at how we were being restrained by this glamour while being attacked by another's power. Breathing through it, I tried to convince myself it was nothing, but I could feel the drain slowly seeping and pulling on me. If this was what I felt as an audience member, I couldn't imagine what it was like for those trapped here.

I swallowed as we stood behind a couple that was much larger, it seemed, than normal, maybe around eight feet in height. The man standing at the door instructed them to do something, and the scent of blood permeated the air before they entered.

As they walked in, my eyes widened slightly on the man looking at us with a calculated, predatory interest. He had to be around 6'7" or so, and half of him was actually rather handsome, like a Mr. Clean-type vibe, on his right side. On his left side, it seemed his face had been melted. Legitimately melted. His single black eye, void of any white, flickered over me before he flashed a rather scary smile.

"Ticket please." He pointed towards a large obsidian case that was covered in blood. I arched a brow as he handed me a sharp blade. I narrowed my eyes on it because… I had no idea where that had been.

Ramsey growled. Stepping forward, I flashed him a look, but I could see all the men looking upset. The man saw their reaction, though, so I distracted him by pulling my blade out and slowly dragging it across my palm, reopening the cut I'd made to get us through the gate. I winced just slightly, but the man's eyes were on the blood spilling.

"Fox?" I offered my dagger as the blood mage stepped forward.

The guard shook his head. "I don't want his blood."

"So what do you propose for a ticket?" I grit out.

"More of yours. A cut for each."

A snarl broke as several of my men disagreed, but I just stared at the man and then looked at them. "It's nothing. Come on, let's just get this over with."

I could see arguments everywhere, but at this point if we didn't do it, this guy was going to be suspicious as hell. I had a feeling bloodshed was an everyday, common thing here.

"Gorgeous," Fox growled as I offered him the same hand.

"Other one. Unmarked places," the guard added. Fucking asshole.

I offered my opposite hand, and Fox's obsidian gaze melted silver as he slowly drew the blade across my palm. I let the blood drip as he muttered a curse, passing me. Rowan stepped up next and offered me a look as if I had lost my goddamn mind.

"Trust me," I spoke softly as I offered the soft part of my forearm. He pressed the knife in a thin line, but enough that it swelled with blood and dripped down my fingers into the container.

When August stepped up I tried to convey that he needed to relax, but his magic wasn't fucking having it. He cut the soft skin of my palm under my thumb. I tensed, breathing through my nose as I started to feel a bit dizzy. To be fair, I felt like I'd bled a lot in the past twenty-four hours.

Nour was in front of me then, and he leaned in, surprising me with a kiss while drawing a sharp knife cut on my other forearm. My body focused more on the pleasure than the pain, and I let out a soft small, frustrated sound as he stepped away with a wink.

"Baby girl," Cassian offered me a blank expression, but his eyes were filled with anger at the situation. I stepped into him as he kissed my pulse lightly before drawing a knife across it gently, the other cuts healing as this one opened and began to bleed rather heavily. I almost let out a moan as he kissed it again, blood on his lips as he stepped away.

I told you Cassian was fucking insane.

"River," I purred as he stepped up and fixed me with a look.

"This is fucking ridiculous," he stated softly, stepping into me as I looked at his lips.

"I don't mind it," I smirked as I ran my bloody hand up his chest and winked. "It's sort of like all of you marking me."

Because I was fucking insane.

Also because I knew I had to act like it wasn't bothering me or he wouldn't fucking do it. His eyes darkened as the monster under his skin flared to life. I shivered as he dipped his lips down to kiss me and cut across my shoulder, a bit deeper, enough to make me let out a sound. It should have been one of pain, but instead I moaned. He groaned, looking all sorts of fucked up with the situation and stepped back with a sharp nip to my lip.

"Baby," Ever inhaled looking over me. You know, because I was soaked in blood now. "This shouldn't be hot, but it is."

"I'll make sure to keep it on," I smirked knowingly.

Without a second of hesitation, because Ever didn't fuck around, he cut down my bicep. The blood dripped and dripped, my pulse finally healing. He stepped back with a wink and I looked towards Ramsey.

Ah, fuck.

"Ram," I stated softly as he offered me a hard look.

"No, Nova," he said, his jaw clenched so tight I was worried he'd break it. I knew that the issue lied in the fact that he had been traincd to protect me, and well, cutting me open wasn't exactly that.

I grabbed his shirt and pulled him towards me as I kept his gaze. "I need you in there. Please."

"Fucking hell, woman," he growled before I felt the blade press to the top of my hand as he stormed away.

I looked at the entrance guard, who looked over me with heated eyes. Or eye, I should say. I flipped him off and followed the boys in. Fuck him.

We were in the show. The hardest part was done… or so I thought.

NOVA

Our seats were actually fairly nice. You know, because seating was important while watching a horror show. I sat down and looked at all the cuts I had, which were healing impressively fast. I swallowed, still feeling a bit dizzy, but instead focused on the room.

It looked a bit like a circus tent. I'm not joking. It had these massive walls with a tent-like ceiling, and the seats were set up in a large crescent moon shape. In the center of it all was a space that seemed to be filled with torture devices, from flame throwers to hammers to places to tie people up. It was all very demented, and if it wasn't for what happened here I would probably be able to appreciate it.

"That should have never happened," Ram growled.

I looked at him from where I sat on his lap, because where the fuck else would I be? I didn't have a choice, if you were wondering. I know, I was so sad. Instead of letting him complain, I dipped my lips down to brush his, making him relax just slightly. Soft bastard. Well, emotionally. Physically? He was hard as fuck underneath me.

Looking around, I kept my eyes open, wondering if there

was any way we could try to see this Mr. Black beforehand, or if the fucker had an office of some kind. I just had a feeling once the show started we wouldn't have the opportunity to sneak around. Right now though? Everyone was busy and moving about. If we got caught we could blame it on being confused.

"Fox, come with me. I wanna take a walk."

"Nova," River warned.

"Anyone else want to come?' I asked innocently.

River stood, and Ram seemed to relax a bit. Really dude? You trust the man that likes inflicting sexy pain on me to keep me safe? I mean, he would, but I felt like Ram didn't trust my abilities. Smiling happily, the two of them followed me out of the rows and I decided to take a left, seeing less people that way.

They talked casually, not saying anything of importance as we got to the end of the seats, and I noticed a section of the wall that was actually set back to create a hallway for people to enter and exit during the show. I let out a soft hum and casually walked into it, the boys growing quiet as they followed me. My magic was coiled, but as the sounds of the audience went away, the silence seemed to darken everything.

I narrowed my eyes up ahead, trying to not look down at the cages lining the walls. Not the time. You have a mission. You can't save everyone. Plus, from what I'd gathered, they couldn't leave even if I let them out. Not that I was positive if there were people or animals in there, which was exactly why I was keeping my sights ahead.

River's hand warmed my back as I stopped, hearing voices trailing the place. I backed us up against the wall, inhaling the scent of blood and something that reminded me of melted skin. I shook myself.

"Mr. Black, everything is prepared," a voice said softly.

The man didn't respond, but I was able to see his form receding as I winced. Holy fuck. The man looked like a spider. Super tall and skinny, with legs and arms that seemed to be everywhere at once. I couldn't see what he was wearing, but tufts of hair stuck out everywhere as the scent of sulfur filtered through the air, making me scrunch my nose.

Then I felt his magic.

Well, holy hell, they hadn't been lying. He had a fuck ton of magic, and absolutely none of it was good. I shook myself as he disappeared, and I nodded towards the hallway. The boys followed, River taking back as I looked into empty doorway after empty doorway. I finally found a black, solid wood door and pressed my ear against it, not hearing anything.

"Do you sense anyone in there?" I asked River, knowing he couldn't use his healing magic much without breaking the glamour. When he shook his head, I jostled the handle and it opened, allowing us to step into an unexpected bedroom.

Holy hell, it was a goddamn mess in here.

Not like you'd expect, either. It wasn't clothes that were scattered across the floor. No, it was bodies, and I tried to not focus on that too much for the sake of my fucking sanity. Fox let out a small curse as I narrowed my eyes to look for a desk, a drawer, anything… there it was.

I played fucking hop scotch over the corpses as the others stayed where they were. You know, this bastard should meet Earnest. I bet they would have a lot to fucking talk about. Shaking my head, I reached a desk with two drawers attached to it. I had a feeling this bastard may be just insane enough to leave shit in reach.

For a moment I felt dizzy, everything shaking in my vision, making me press my hand to the desk, feeling unstable. I had no idea what it was about this place, but it was really fucking with my magic. She looked at me with frustration from where she was trapped in the glamour, her body slumped and tired looking. Same girl. Same.

I knew why this place didn't suit us. If I embodied the chaos of the living, this was death. The purest, darkest form of death and sadness, ensconced in one location. It was fucked up, and that was coming from me.

Refocusing on the task at hand, I began opening drawers and was disappointed to find nothing. I looked around as I moved towards a closet, opening it and jumping slightly when I found bloody tools and an assortment of torture devices hanging on the walls. Goddamnit. Didn't this man keep work and personal life separate at all?

I mean, I guess when you do what you love, you never work a day in your life, right? Even when that love consisted of brutally torturing people in private and public life.

I felt River and Fox enter the closet, the dim light from the bedroom windows making it clear that there was no systematic filing cabinet like dear old dad had provided for us. I should have assumed it wouldn't have been that easy, but it was still frustrating as hell.

"What? No 'this is why I am performing a massive power drain on everyone here' folder?" I mumbled, making Fox chuckle softly.

Speaking of the power drain, I could literally feel myself weakening every moment we spent here, the blood loss from earlier really not helping. I blinked, trying to refocus. I must have swayed slightly, because River touched my back in a stabilizing way. He offered me a worried look, getting ready to ask if I was okay, no doubt - before we heard them.

Them being whoever was outside the main door of the bedroom. I jumped out of his arms and closed the closet door securely before stepping back, putting a finger to my mouth as both men froze in realization. I inhaled sharply, feeling that surge of sickly power and really hoping that we were glamoured enough that he'd assume our magic was from all the dead fucking demons hanging around and piling up on his floor.

"Mr. Black, I don't understand," a nasally voice spoke.

"Are you dumb?" a sharp voice asked before turning sad. "I said to find me more people for tonight. Ever since we lost my little *star*, it hasn't been the same. They grew used to those levels of entertainment."

"But you are going to get her back soon, right sir?" the other asked.

The man chuckled while opening up a drawer and grabbing something, "Of course I am, you idiot. But for now we need more performers. More death. Go find me some."

River wrapped an arm around my waist securely, clearly realizing I was losing my stability, my vision turning spotty. It didn't help that in the darkness of this closet, with my blood mage and him, I could feel the electric energy between us, turning me on and making me soaked way too fucking fast to be normal. Fox nearly let out a low, throaty sound despite us being in the dark.

"Yes," the male voice said outside, sounding upset. "Yes, I know. I'm sorry--"

Did he have a phone?

Fox moved closer to the door, trying to listen as I closed my eyes, a wave of heat rolling over my body. My magic offered me a frustrated look, because fuck if I didn't understand. I squirmed against River slightly, his cock rock hard against my ass, as a rumble nearly broke from his throat. A small, frustrated sound came from my lips as his hand wrapped around my mouth, keeping me silent as my body broke out into a flush.

What the hell was going on with me?

My nipples tightened underneath my corset top as River's fingers smoothed the skin between my pants and corset, clearly trying to soothe me. Instead, I arched back into him, needing his touch or Fox's to cool me off because I was pretty damn close to losing it.

When I heard a door close, I felt his magic leave and I relaxed just slightly, hoping Fox caught anything important he said… because I couldn't care less right now. There was only thing I cared about, and it was why River's hands weren't on me more. Okay, two, because why wasn't Fox touching me either? A whine broke from my throat as River pressed his head to my shoulder, muttering a curse.

"Gorgeous," Fox chided, sounding strained. His voice was lower than normal, which was a feat. "You almost got us caught."

River bit down on my shoulder, hard, and a moan slipped out. I could feel my magic trying to act out, and I realized that if she wasn't going to lash out traditionally, she sure as fuck was going to get it out a different way. My knees felt weak, and I let out a small whimper as Fox wrapped his hands around my waist, trapping me between the two of them. Like a goddamn sex sandwich.

"Please," I whispered, hoping they would get with the program. Fox let out a growl as his lips met mine, making me arch back and rub against River, his fingers toying with the snap of my pants. When he popped it open, I easily stepped out of my boots and the pants, willing and excited to get this fucking show on the road. Literally. Fucking show.

"Risking our lives like that," River tsk-ed as he stood up fully behind me, his hands running up my nearly bare legs as Fox pulled on my bottom lip with his teeth, making me tremble.

"Shit," I whispered as Fox pulled down my top, my breasts spilling free as he groaned. Every sound, every touch, was intensified by how dark it was in here. His name left my lips as he bit down gently on the tightened skin of my breasts while grazing my nipple. My clit pulsed as I tried to not cry out, River's fingers finding their way under my lace panties as he began to play with me in light, teasing touches that felt like torture.

"Please," I begged, not afraid to admit how goddamn needy I was.

"Please what?" Fox demanded as I felt his fingers begin to rub my clit, River's working in and out of me, the sound of how wet I was echoing through the room. I moaned their names as River wrapped my hair around his hand and pulled my head to the side, exposing my neck to his lips and teeth.

"He asked you a question, Nova," River demanded sharply.

Like I could even fucking focus right now.

A wave of even more dangerous lust slammed into me, turning my body molten as I felt the glamour crack slightly. It was overwhelming, and I knew if they didn't fuck this frustration out of me soon, I was going to lose it. This couldn't be normal. My breathing and pulse roared and sped like a race car, and I felt like I was going into goddamn heat.

"Fuck," Fox groaned. "Your magic is going crazy, gorgeous. What do you need?"

"She needs to be fucked, is what she needs," River determined as I whimpered, nodding enthusiastically.

"Yes," I gasped as Fox's mouth trailed across my neck, licking at the blood still there before nicking a spot and causing more blood to seep down my exposed breasts. "I need you."

"Just him?" River entertained, sounding way too fucking amused.

"Both of you," I determined as Fox smiled against my skin. Shit, had I really just said that?

"I don't know if you can handle that," Fox said as his magic broke out a bit, wrapping around me. River's was already very dangerously crawling against my skin like a goddamn poisonous plant.

"I can," I promised and then jumped as River's cock, hot and hard, pressed right against my opening. Oh shit. Fox chuckled, holding my jaw in a possessive grip as I let out a cry when River slammed into me. Fox groaned, meeting my lips while his fingers began to move faster and faster on my clit. River held himself deep inside of me, clearly trying to restrain himself as I clenched around him, crying out my first orgasm as Fox caught it in a kiss.

"Holy fuck," I whispered, but before I could finish, River was slamming into me again. I found myself on the closet floor getting rammed doggy style by River as Fox knelt in front of me, gripping my hair in a firm, hard hold that had my eyes tearing up.

"Goddamnit," Fox hissed, "watching you get fucked is beautiful."

"River!" I whimpered as he increased his speed and brought a hand across my ass, my hand gripping Fox's belt. "Fox, I want you too. Please."

His chuckle was soft and dark. "Yeah, gorgeous? Do you want me in your mouth or River fucking your ass? It's the only way Nova, your pick. Which one do you fucking want?" I could hear how worked up he was, and River let out a snarl at the concept of being in my ass, which I was loving.

"The second!" I whined as River groaned, slowing his pace slightly. I let out a frustrated sound as River pulled out and Fox unbuckled his jeans, pushing them down before pulling me forward so that I was straddling him, his cool piercing brushing my hot, wet heat.

River pushed open the door as he let out a growl. "Yeah, I gotta fucking see this."

Oh man, why did I feel like I was in way over my head here?

"Fox," I dug my nails into the man below me as I slid down on him, his cock stretching me in a different but equally as fucking perfect way as River. I moaned his name as he forced me to take the last few inches, slamming me down by pulling my hips, making me come right on him almost immediately.

River cursed, and I shivered as I felt his fingers right against my tight ass, making me arch like a goddamn animal in heat. Fox gripped my waist, holding me down as he stared into my face with an intensity and possession that nearly had me coming again right there and then.

"Holy shit," Fox groaned, "you are so fucking tight. River, dude, you didn't tell me how goddamn tight she was."

"Fucking heaven," River determined as his familiar length pressed against my ass, a bit of fear and a fuck ton of excitement coursing through me. "I can't wait to see how tight this ass is, butterfly. You ever have anyone in your ass?"

I almost didn't hear this question, caught up on how deep Fox felt inside of me, my hips rolling as River squeezed my ass, making me moan. I whimpered as he rubbed my clit, making me relax into Fox as I stopped thinking about how fucking large he was. How in the hell was he going to fit in my ass? I moaned as he ran his fingers along my wet heat and spread it across my tight ass, his finger pressing into me. I whimpered at the pressure and wondered how the fuck it would feel when his massive length was buried inside of me.

"Nova," River hissed slightly, his teeth nipping my ear and making me tremble. "Answer the question."

"You know I haven't-- Sweet Christ!" I screamed as he slid right into me, making tears well in my eyes as I nearly passed out. My body felt more full than it had ever been, and I whimpered, needing some type of movement, my body feeling achy and needy. Believe me, I got what I was asking for.

The two of them started moving in unison, and for the first time, I remembered just how goddamn large these men were. I mean, holy shit they were huge, and being fucked in between them was an experience, to say the least.

Fox's face was twisted in pleasure as his fingers bit into my waist with a bruising strength, his length pulsating inside of me as I rolled my hips. River's large hands gripped my ass as he continued to fight in and out of me, his almost feral grunts making my body shake with pleasure. I could feel both of them trying to temper their control, and while I appreciated it, that wasn't going to do.

Letting out a moan, my power seeped out through the crack in my glamour, instantly attracting and ramping up theirs.

"Nova," River demanded sharply.

"Stop controlling yourselves," I demanded as Fox inhaled sharply.

"No complaint from me," Fox growled as he began to rut into me, my body pressed between the two of theirs as River took a deep, punishing pace to Fox's feral and animalistic movements. I cried out, my voice going hoarse as I felt my center tightening, my magic ramping up. I had no idea if anyone could hear us, but I didn't really give a fuck right now. They could kill us later.

"Holy hell," River snarled, pulling my hair back again.

Fox instantly latched onto my neck and pierced my skin, making me climax all over him. My body would have practically sagged if it wasn't for their hard grip on me.

I felt time itself suspend as they pounded into me, my mind becoming dizzy with pleasure and my limbs almost prickling with numbness. I could feel River's monster skimming right along the surface, not fully coming out to play, but still punishing me in a way that was relieving him. His groans had me pushing back into him as Fox tugged me forward. Fox's wild, lethal energy surrounded me completely, and he pounded into me with wild abandon. I felt myself completely give into them and my eyes nearly rolled back as another climax rolled over me.

"I'm going to fucking cum," Fox warned, and I felt him slam inside of me before emptying himself, River keeping his punishing pace for a few more strokes before burying himself as well.

Both of them came inside of me as I melted within the River and Fox panini of smexiness I'd made. My eyes closed as everything around me went black.

Good. I loved passing out in a demonic realm where we were in potential danger.

Peachy.

"Nova," River's voice was soft and pleading, "come on, we've got to get back to the show. I promise you, we will get out of here as soon as we can."

I frowned, rolling over as the scent of blood filled the space. "We haven't found the important stuff. We need to do that."

Right? We hadn't, had we? I already was feeling far

stronger, my magic looking way less stressed. I think it had been the glamour making her freaked out, and the frustration we just took out on my guys? Yeah, you could say that fucking helped.

"Actually," Fox whispered, "we may have what we need."

"What?" River asked quietly.

"I didn't really understand it at the time, but when Black was talking to whoever the hell was on the phone, he specifically said that he was getting enough power. He also said something about someone named Titania."

I frowned, trying to recall the name. "Like the Fae Queen?" I questioned. "She's essentially a god in fae culture." I finally sat up, sighing as the world around me went spinny.

"Maybe?" Fox arched a brow.

"Fuck," I mumbled. "I feel like we don't know any more than we did before."

"We've confirmed that the power drain exists and that there's a connection to Titania. Now we know for sure that we are headed in the right fucking direction. I think we need to give Titania a visit in the God realm," River mumbled, running a hand through my hair. "Nova, butterfly, are you okay?"

I squinted my eyes at him and then Fox. "You two just double teamed me, and Fox drank my blood after I'd been cut open several times to get into this stupid place. Okay isn't the word. Sexually satisfied? Oh fuck yes. But do I need a shower, some donuts, and cuddles? One hundred percent demanding it."

"The descendant has spoken," Fox winked.

As they helped me out I tried to not look around the room we left, slipping back into the hallway. I could hear Black's voice over some type of speaker system, starting the show, and as we walked behind the bleachers, I sighed in relief, knowing that we were in the clear.

But fucking hell, my body was sore.

We climbed towards our seats, no one giving us much mind. Ramsey's eyes widened as I walked towards them, the guys chuckling as I slumped between Everett and Ram.

"What the fuck did you guys do to her?" Ram accused.

"Fucking everything," I mumbled happily, tucking my nose against Everett's neck.

I could hear the others talking as Fox tried to use coded words to relay the plan moving forward. I shook myself, trying to wake up, but hell, I was just not feeling this bullshit anymore.

"We don't have to stay," I murmured in realization.

"Let's get out of here then," August suggested before looking over me and smirking with affection in his gaze. "I heard you need donuts and cuddles."

"Auggy, those words are fucking orgasmic," I sighed.

"I know something else that is--" I put my hand over Fox's mouth as Cassian chuckled. Goddamn bastards.

As we stood up to exit, I looked back, and my eyes narrowed at this stupid fucking place. I knew I couldn't destroy it, but someone needed to. Maybe I would give them a goddamn start.

"Can't stomach it?" door man goaded.

I ignored him as the guys followed me out. That was about when I pushed the glamour off me, my magic flooding the space as the sky rumbled. It was a short walk to the gate, so I walked backwards, facing my boys and winking.

The lightning bolt that hit the Broken House, specifically the show area, had the power shorting and a fire starting. Oops. People rushed out, and I watched happily.

"What was that?" Everett asked, laughing as we reached

the gate. Before anyone could complain, I slit my hand again and stuck it on there.

"That was my 'fuck you,'" I explained primly before swaying on my feet. Once we crossed the gate, I felt the power drain lifting off me as all the men groaned, not having realized the effect it'd been having. The gates closed with a deafening sound as I nodded, looking at all of them.

I smiled and let out a small giggle.

"What?" Nour asked.

"I guess the show *won't* go on," I winked as they all groaned at my bad joke.

Yeah, I was funny as fuck.

EPILOGUE

Nova

"Is she okay?" a soft voice murmured as I blinked open my eyes into a brilliant array of lights, mainly sun bouncing off glass, filling the space we were in.

It took a few solid seconds for me to remember where the hell I was or what the hell had happened. My thoughts trailed from King Desmond reappearing after our departure from the Pain realm to arriving back on Earth when we… hopped on the jet? Had that happened? My memory was foggy, and even now I could feel myself falling back asleep.

Where were we?

I tried to sit up, knowing Everett and Cassian were on either side of me.

"Baby?" Everett asked softly.

I inhaled and looked around at him and then Cassian, trying to piece together where the hell I was. My body was so sore and weak. I knew we weren't in Seattle, because the earth didn't feel the same outside of this room. The skies outside were clear, although to their credit, the clouds grew thicker the longer I stared at them.

Then I felt it.

A dry heat rolled over my skin as I ran my fingers across the white linen I was sleeping on. A balcony covered in white curtains was in front of me, and I narrowed my eyes, trying to focus on the view outside instead of being distracted by the men near me.

"What is going on?" I frowned and looked down at myself. I think I had taken a shower on the jet... possibly. I remembered the sight of blood draining down the tile floor of the shower. Now I was in a pair of silk sleep shorts and a tiny little tank top. I ran my fingers through my hair, trying to sort through my magic. My magic, who blinked her eyes open and rolled over, surrounded by all of my men's magic. Understandable.

"Baby girl?" Cassian asked softly as I frowned.

"Fuck," I mumbled, "this is like a hangover times ten. Fucking stupid Demonic realm power drain..."

Ever said something to someone at the door as I ran my fingers over my face, wincing as I took a deep breath, pain radiating through my body. Shit. I had never felt this shitty. Ever. Not even when I pulled a goddamn bullet out of my stomach.

"Nova," Cass touched my hand, "how about you go back to sleep?"

"She's already slept four days," Rowan said from the end of the bed, looking concerned. I reached out and touched his hand as he intertwined our fingers and bent down to gently kiss the back of my hand.

"Four days?" I arched my brow, my eyes closing again.

"Maybe she's sick," August said softly, his hand finding its way to the back of my neck. "Or maybe it was the blood loss."

"She's not sick," River stated firmly. "But the power drain

really fucked with her magic, and the glamour didn't allow for her to deal with it properly."

"It affected our god magic way more than you guys," Nour confirmed. "I still feel like shit." Oh no. I didn't like that. I didn't want them to be hurt at all.

I let out a small yawn and stretched my arms above my head before someone placed a hot mug in my hands. I looked up at Fox as he offered me a tense smile in an attempt to look like he wasn't worried. Finally, after a few sips and feeling comforted by their normal talking, I stood. Ramsey's chest was right in front as I patted it and moved past him, walking towards the balcony.

"Someone should tell her," Everett pointed out with amusement in his voice.

"Tell me what?" I asked, pushing away the curtains.

My mouth dropped open as a small laugh broke through my lips. Ah, yes, I was remembering where the hell we were now.

"It's the portal spot for the God realm," Nour explained softly, wrapping an arm around my waist.

I nodded. It sure as fuck was.... Well, shit. Nothing like waking up halfway across the world. This was happening. This was real.

We were in Egypt and finally going to the God realm.

PUBLISHED WORK

M. Sinclair has crafted different universes with unique plotlines, character cameos, and shared universe events. As a reader, this means that you may see your favorite character or characters… appear in multiple books besides their own storyline.

Universe 1
Established in 2019
Vengeance Series
Book 1 - Savages
Book 2 - Lunatics
Book 3 - Monsters
Book 4 - Psychos
Complete Series

The Red Masques Series
Book 1 - Raven Blood
Book 2 - Ashes & Bones
Book 3 - Shadow Glass
Book 4 - Fire & Smoke

Book 5 - Dark King
Complete Series
Tears of the Siren Series
Book 1 - Horror of Your Heart
Book 2 - Broken House
Book 3 - Neon Drops

The Dead and Not So Dead Trilogy
Book 1 - Queen of the Dead
Book 2 - Team Time with the Dead
Book 3 - Dying the Dead
Descendant Series
Book 1 - Descendant of Chaos
Book 2 - Descendant of Blood
Book 3 - Descendant of Sin

Reborn Series
Book 1 - Reborn In Flames
Book 2 - Soaring in Flames
The Wronged Trilogy
Book 1 - Wicked Blaze Correctional

Lost in Fae
Book 1 - Finding Fae

Universe 2
Established in 2020
Court of Rella
Book 1 - Fae Fiefdom

Standalones

Peridot (Jewels Cafe Series)

Time Sensibility (Women of Time)

Willowdale Village Collection
A stand-alone collection about the women of Willowdale Village.

Voiceless
Fearless

Collaborations

Rebel Hearts Heists Duet *(M. Sinclair & Melissa Adams)*
Book 1 - Steal Me
Book 2 - Keep Me

Forbidden Fairytales *(The Grim Sisters - M. Sinclair & CY Jones)*
Book 1 - Stolen Hood
Book 2 - Knights of Sin
Book 3 - Deadly Games

ABOUT THE AUTHOR

International Best Seller

M. Sinclair is a Chicago native, parent to 3 cats, and can be found writing almost every moment of the day. Despite being new to publishing, M. Sinclair has been writing for nearly 10 years now. Currently, in love with the Reverse Harem genre, she plans to publish an array of works that are considered romance, suspense, and horror within the year. M. Sinclair lives by the notion that there is enough room for all types of heroines in this world and being saved is as important as saving others. If you love fantasy romance, obsessive possessive alpha males, and tough FMCs, then M. Sinclair is for you!

Just remember to love cats... that's not negotiable.

STALK ME... REALLY, I'M INTO IT.

Instagram: msinclairwrites
Facebook: Sinclair's Ravens (New content announced!)
Twitter: @writes_sinclair
Newsletter: Link
Amazon: M. Sinclair
Goodreads: M. Sinclair
Bookbub: M. Sinclair
Website: Official M. Sinclair Website

Printed in Great Britain
by Amazon